Three Steps to the
Making of an Assassin

Jack Cashman

PAGE PUBLISHING, INC.
New York, NY

First originally published by Page Publishing, Inc. 2019

ISBN 978-1-64584-528-7 (Paperback)
ISBN 978-1-64584-529-4 (Digital)

Printed in the United States of America

Author's Page

THE 1960s WERE A VERY turbulent time in America. Political turmoil, racial unrest, and the Vietnam War combined to shape the lives of Americans growing up in that time. This book tells the story of two friends whose lives were changed and sent in different directions by the events of the 1960s. Like any work of historical fiction, a fair amount of research has to be done to blend historical events into the story.

I want to thank two friends whose lives were actually disrupted by the war. Two Vietnam veterans, who helped in writing this book by relaying to me their own experiences in that war. I want to thank them both for their help and for their service.

I also want to thank another friend, Gerry Conley, a practicing attorney in Portland, Maine, for his help in writing the sections that involve legal matters. The assistance of these three good friends was invaluable.

I also want to thank Barbara Tucker, who has helped me with the layout of the manuscript and corrected my many spelling errors.

Lastly, I want to thank my family for all their support over many years.

Chapter I

July 18, 1967

JACK ROACH SAT ON A leather bench outside the juvenile courtroom in the Penobscot County Courthouse, trying to figure out how a seventeen-year-old boy can get charged with being a habitual offender. His best friend, Bruce King, was in the juvenile courts judge's chambers with his mother, answering to that exact charge. He had now been in there for over an hour, a length of time that Jack could only conclude was not good news. The two friends had come to Bangor from Old Orchard Beach where they had been staying for the week, for Bruce's court appearance. They hated to leave Old Orchard Beach, where they had been enjoying a good deal of wine, women, and song. They thought they would be back before the day was over. Immediately upon arrival, Bruce was ushered into the judge's chambers for a closed-door session with the judge, two police officers from their home town of Old Town, a lawyer from the district attorney's office and his mother. This left Jack to sit outside and dwell on his friend's predicament while he thought about how things got this far. Neither of the two were angels, but "habitual offender"? At seventeen, it seemed a bit over the top. The two of them had always found it difficult to take anything seriously. This might end up being serious. He was thinking that he would like to be a fly on the wall to hear what was being said. He and Bruce went back a ways so he could imagine the events that were being discussed.

Jack and Bruce first met playing fifth-grade basketball at the local YMCA. They both came from large families—Jack had four sisters and a brother; Bruce had four brothers and two sisters. Both grew up in, or close to, poverty. Jack's family was better off financially than Bruce's, but neither was awash in wealth. Bruce's father had died at forty-six, leaving his widow to raise seven children. The first time they met, Jack and Bruce got into a fight, which was broken up by one of the supervisors at the YMCA before any blood was spilled. Fighting was not uncommon in the mill town they called home, and both had learned to fight early, and they both considered themselves tough guys. It was a tough town filled with hardworking people. There were three shoe shops, a woolen mill, a pie plate factory, two canoe companies, and a paper mill, as well as several smaller operations that made up the employment opportunities in Old Town, Maine. The area also included a Native American reservation on which Jack and Bruce had spent a good deal of their youth. Altogether, it added up to a small mill town with a tough reputation. They both felt some obligation to enhance that tough reputation. At seventeen, Bruce stood five feet, nine inches tall with broad shoulders and a rugged build overall. Jack was taller at six feet and had a wirier build. Both were good-looking young men, and both were ready to fight at the drop of a hat. Jack would later admit as he grew older that neither of them were as tough as they thought they were, but Bruce was probably the tougher of the two.

They became good friends after the initial fight. Jack's family owned a small restaurant that was open twenty-four hours a day, serving shift workers and travelers as well as local shoppers. Jack's father had lost his job in 1960 and opened the restaurant on 100% borrowed money. The first six or seven years of operation were spent just trying to dig his way out of the debt he incurred to open that place. All six of the Roach family children worked in the restaurant along with their parents. On weekends, the place would fill up with hungry drinkers after the eight downtown bars closed. Jack started working there at thirteen and got his friend Bruce a job there less than a year later. The crowds that came in after the bars closed usually included some very drunk patrons, and it was not unusual for fights to break out. Jack, his first couple of nights working around these drunk patrons, was scared to death, but he made sure none of them knew it. Jack's father, Jack Sr., would have the unpleasant task of stepping between two drunken brawlers in order to keep from having his restaurant broken up. Jack Sr., while not a big man, handled himself well in these situations. One night, while waiting on tables at fifteen years old, Jack Junior took a punch in the face from a drunken man, for no reason other than he was taking his order. His father and good friend Bruce came to his rescue before he was hit again. The restaurant could be a rough-and-tumble place on the weekends. Working in that environment at such young ages only served to make the two teenagers all the tougher.

The two friends were what Jack's mother referred to "as thick as thieves." They ran together socially, worked together, and shortly after going to work in the restaurant, Bruce moved into the Roach's home. Jack's problems were Bruce's problems and vice versa. If you fought one, you fought them both. On one occasion, after school at the junior high school, Bruce heard about two good-sized fellow students saying they planned to get Jack Roach and "beat the shit out of him." Bruce confronted the pair and told them they would have to get through him to get to Jack. The pair decided to drop the whole idea rather than fight both Bruce and Jack.

Getting back to the late-night drunken patrons at the restaurant, on many nights at closing, Jack and Bruce would team up to take money from the last group of bar hoppers to leave the restaurant. Bruce would suggest that he and Jack flip with one of the patrons; odd man wins the three quarters. This exercise was particularly popular with two French Canadian woodcutters who were in every weekend.

The three would flip their coins then land them on the back of their left hand covered by their right hand. Bruce would hold his coin on its edge so he could flip it either way. Jack and the woodcutter would show their coins first, then Bruce would flip his to whichever side made Jack or Bruce the winner. The Canadians, in their inebriated state, would fall for it every weekend. This would land the two friends an easy three or four dollars to supplement their pay. Four dollars in the 1960s could buy two six-packs of Budweiser, which is where their money usually went.

Given the environment they grew up in, fighting and drinking became the recreation for the two friends. A bit later, they added cannabis to their lifestyle. These activities alone, while illegal for a pair of teenagers, were not the sole reasons for Bruce's predicament on this day. Not the sole reason but contributing factors. Other factors included tying a dead bear to the rear bumper of a car and dragging it through the downtown or leaving two cases of empty beer bottles on the police chief's front steps, or a late-night defecation on the mayor of Bangor's desk. The story in the following day's police beat identified the culprit as the "phantom defecator." All these could have been factors, but they were not caught doing them. As Jack waited on the bench, he chronicled in his mind the real events that brought things to this point.

* * * * *

May 12, 1966

Bruce borrowed a car from a friend so he could take his driver's test to get his driver's license. In Maine at the time, a sixteen-year-old could take a written test to get his permit and then a driver's test to get his license. Bruce had his permit and was scheduled for his test. He took it with the friend's car and passed it. To celebrate, he and Jack got hold of enough beer to get drunk on and cruised around drinking it in the friend's car so Bruce could show off his newly acquired license. As the day turned into night, a rather inebriated Bruce King took a corner way too wide in the college town of Orono and drove straight into a barbershop. Police cars and tow trucks pulled the two youths and the car out of the shop. The next day's headlines in the local paper's police beat said, "Old Town Boy Has a Close Shave." They laughed about this byline for years.

The two friends escaped unharmed but the car and barbershop were not so lucky. For this escapade Bruce, as the driver of the car, got probation.

* * * * *

September 20, 1966

Jack and Bruce, along with a third friend and a twenty-five-year-old Woolworth management trainee (who hailed from Lewiston and was nicknamed Lewiston Man), supplied some of the alcohol and pot for a garage party in nearby Bangor. The party was raided by the Bangor Police. Bruce and the older man who had purchased the alcohol got out the back door. Jack and the third friend were not so lucky. They were both placed under arrest and were being marched to a squad car by one of Bangor's finest. Jack broke away from the officer's grip and ran. The officer hollered for him to stop but did not give chase. Jack ran through a field and tripped over something, going ass over teakettle. When he looked back to see what he tripped over, he saw it was Bruce, who was lying in the tall grass with the Woolworth management trainee who had purchased the alcohol. After a good laugh, they decided to go back and get their friend who was in the back seat of one of the police cars. The two of them, Jack and Bruce crawled on their bellies in the ditch to get up to the squad car. The back doors of these cars can't be opened from the inside, so Jack opened the door and let their friend out. All four of them made their escape back to Old Town. As was his trademark, Jack left a slip of paper on which he had drawn a perfect picture of a hand, giving the middle finger in the back seat for the officer to view when he returned to find his prisoner gone.

Other party attendees were not so fortunate. They identified Jack and Bruce as well as their older companion as providing a good amount of alcohol and pot. The following Monday, state liquor inspectors had the Old Town Police bring the two friends up to the Old Town Police Station for questioning. They put them in two separate rooms. Inspector Doyle from the Maine State Liquor Authority questioned Bruce first then came in to question Jack. His first remark upon entering the room was, "Well, you may as well tell me everything. Your pal, Bruce, spilled his guts."

Jack laughed out loud at this, actually bending over and slapping his leg.

"You find this funny, Mr. Roach?"

"I find it funny that you want me to believe Bruce told you anything because I know he didn't. I'm going to tell you even less, so don't waste your breath and my time."

Doyle stood stone-faced, looking at the laughing teenager. Finally, he shook his head and walked out.

Thus was the end of the questioning. The two got away from this event with no charges against them. Their older friend was not as lucky as he was convicted of supplying alcohol to minors, without the testimony of Jack and Bruce. The third friend whom Jack and Bruce saved from the squad car told Inspector Doyle everything. So Lewiston Man ended up paying a large fine and losing his job, something they both always felt bad about.

In a related story, a scant three weeks after the questioning from Inspector Doyle, the two friends were drinking in a Bangor tavern where they were routinely served, even though they were five years under the legal drinking age. Bruce actually looked older, but why they served Jack, who barely looked sixteen, was a mystery. As they sat drinking at the bar, the door opened, and in walked the very same Inspector Doyle. Jack nudged Bruce and pointed to the new entrant while grabbing his beer and heading for the men's room. Bruce, always cool under pressure, stayed at the bar sipping his beer.

After hiding in the men's room for five or ten minutes, Jack opened the door a crack, looking out to see if Doyle had left. He had not left. He was sitting in Jack's vacated seat, carrying on a conversation with Bruce as if they were old friends. He apparently did not recognize him as the minor he had recently questioned, and after a few minutes of friendly chatter, he up and left, giving Bruce a friendly slap on the back as he moved out. Jack came out to regain his seat asking Bruce what they had talked about. Apparently, Doyle was a sports fan and he talked about the success of the University of Maine's football team. Go figure!

These events, plus a couple of arrests for illegal possession of alcohol set the stage, but one incident put it over the top. One incident put Bruce in the position he sat in on this day.

* * * * *

June 10, 1967

After spending the afternoon drinking, Jack and Bruce headed for a dance at a local school auditorium. There were dances every Friday night, and Bruce and Jack usually showed up at them with a good buzz on. Upon their arrival, they saw that an Old Town City cop had cornered one of their friends who was also drunk. Bruce took it upon himself to interfere by pushing their friend away from the cop, through the door into the dance area. Officer Graggen, objecting to the interference, grabbed Bruce by the shoulder. This proved to be a bad move as all hell broke out.

Bruce wheeled around and landed a right hook to Graggen's jaw. The two went into full combat with Bruce gaining the upper hand. A second attending officer came in behind Bruce and began choking him by placing his night stick under Bruce's chin and pulling back on it. Seeing his friend choking badly, Jack jumped in, grabbed the second cop, Office Carrier, and put him in a headlock. The scuffle went on until reinforcements arrived, breaking everything up. Jack and Bruce were both put in the Old Town city jail and charged with assaulting a police officer. Before the charges were filed, the police decided to go after their real target, Bruce King. So the two assault charges were set aside in favor of the "habitual offender living a life of vice" charge that brought things to today. Jack's charges were never refiled, so he never appeared in court to answer to them. The locals had the guy they wanted, Bruce King. They could wait to deal with Jack.

As Jack sat running these events through his mind, his concentration was broken by the entrance of an army recruiter. As he watched the recruiter walk into the courtroom his best friend was in, his thought was that this is not good. There was no possible way that the addition of this fellow to the mix was going to make things better for Bruce. It was the height of the Vietnam War and the armed forces were hungry for new recruits. Unruly youths from poor families were prime candidates for the war effort.

A half hour later, Bruce, the recruiter, and Bruce's mother walked out together. Behind them the two Old Town cops had wide smiles on their faces, yet another sign that things were not going good for Bruce. Jack got up to greet his friend. "So what happened?"

"Well, they gave me two choices, I can either go to jail or I can go with this guy," Bruce said, pointing at the recruiter who stood ten feet away, talking to an obviously distraught mother.

"So what are you going to do?"

"I'm going with him," he answered while pointing to the recruiter.

"You are joining the army?" Jack was stunned by the suddenness of all this. They had come in that day expecting probation, then a return to Old Orchard Beach.

"What fucking choice do I have? I'm not going to jail."

Jack noticed Bruce's mother was crying. "What is the time frame? I mean how much time do you have?"

"I'm going with him right now. I guess I'll see you after boot camp."

With that, Bruce walked out of the building with an army recruiter, leaving Jack staring after the two of them, still stunned by the swift sentencing of his friend. An amazing turn of events. Jack had been expecting that the worst outcome would be a short stay in the South Portland reform school. Certainly he did not expect this outcome. A hitch in the army during war time. In his heart, at that moment, Jack knew their friendship would never be the same. He also knew that the carefree days of taking nothing serious were over. A song was running through his mind, the Bobby Fuller Four hit record, "I Fought the Law and the Law Won."

Chapter II

IN THE FALL OF 1967, Jack began his senior year of high school, while his friend Bruce was going through boot camp. The previous three years of what the two of them always considered harmless fun had resulted in Bruce's new involuntary career. To Jack, it did not seem entirely fair that they had both had illegal possession court appearances. They both had the "assaulting an officer" indictments, yet Bruce was in the army while he was making plans for college. It would become even more clear to him later that the reasons centered more around economics than actual acts against the law. The poorest kids had always served as cannon fodder during wartime. This knowledge would prove to be a strong part of the basis of his future anti-war sentiment. The idea that wars benefitted the wealthy financially while they were fought by the poor would always stick in his craw.

For now, he went about the same lifestyle without the companionship of his longtime friend. He continued his partying with different friends, introducing them to the suppliers of alcohol and pot that he and Bruce had cultivated over the years. Bruce had given them all nicknames: the Joker, Teddy Bear, Fat Man, Houdini, and Eggplant. The last nickname can only be explained by visual observation. These were the men who aided the misspent youth of the two of them. He got his second and final juvenile court appearance the week before Bruce came home on leave after boot camp. Pinched for the second time for illegal possession of alcohol.

Police stopped him for going fifty-five in a thirty-five-mile per hour zone, and he did a lousy job of hiding a half-full pint of whiskey under his seat. Thankful that they did not make him empty his pockets because they would have also found a half-smoked joint. He had given the arresting officer a good deal of verbal abuse so at his court appearance the judge added ten dollars to his fine because, as the judge put it, "You have a big mouth." Jack couldn't argue with that statement.

Upon Bruce's return on leave, they got together and had a good laugh about Jack's latest brush with the long arm of the law. "How come they didn't march your stupid ass into court and sign you up for the army?" Bruce queried. "Hey, Uncle Sam took one look at me and said, 'Who the fuck wants you.'" The whole matter was discussed as they settled into a three-day drinking session at Eggplant's house that involved a dozen other close friends. It turned out to be one of their more memorable parties with booze, women, and song. Just one more fun-filled adventure for the two friends who took nothing seriously. They didn't get into any serious discussions until the day before Bruce was headed back to Fort Dix. They mostly spent their time picking up where they left off before the army came into play. Jack was curious about Bruce's new life, and they finally got into it when Jack asked, "Tell me about the army. How was boot camp?"

"It's tough. It's like eight straight weeks of football practice for twelve hours a day."

They had both played high school football, liking the game but hating the practice sessions.

"That's the physical part, but how about the discipline?" Jack asked, wondering how his free spirit pal had survived taking orders.

"You learn early to keep your mouth shut, speak when spoken to and never out of line."

The response was wildly out of character for Bruce. "That doesn't sound like my pal, Bruce," Jack observed.

"Different world, Jack. I don't think you would make it. You'd spend two or three weeks in the brig then get discharged." This line was delivered with a broad smile, but Bruce went on. "You have to follow orders or pay a price. I will be seeing action in a war zone eventually, and you follow orders or people die." Jack knew full well that the "war zone" meant Vietnam. He already had a number of his friends serving there. The war was on television news nightly. He wondered when he would first get the news that a friend of his had been killed in action. Now his best friend was headed over there.

For the first time in the week he had been home, Jack was struck with the fact that his friend had changed a lot. He was far more serious than the Bruce he remembered. "You think you will be sent to Vietnam?"

Bruce snickered at this question. Very few recruits escaped a tour of duty in Vietnam. He never expected he would be that lucky.

"Almost certainly, when I go back, I'm going into advanced infantry training and jump school. I will be sent to Vietnam shortly after that schooling is over. When I get to Nam, I will be seeing a lot of action."

While not a veteran, Jack knew very well what "jump school" meant. Bruce would most likely be part of a unit that was constantly in danger.

"Jesus, Bruce, did you pick this assignment, or was it picked for you?"

"I'm ready for it, Jack. What the fuck, if you're going to do this, you may as well do it right." Obviously, his friend was not looking to play it safe.

The adaptation to his new life and his willingness, even enthusiasm, to join the fight in this far-off land caught his friend a bit by surprise. Bruce had never shied away from a fight, but those fights weren't with guns, grenades, and missile launchers. The worse that could happen in those fights was lost teeth or a broken nose. This was far different. He was not only ready for combat but he also seemed to be looking forward to it. He had been forced into his situation, but he seemed to relish the opportunity. Jack thought of the song by Country Joe and the Fish "Don't Ask Me, I Don't Give a Damn, Next Stop Is Vietnam."

* * * * *

As Bruce left to go for advanced training, Jack continued school and filled out college applications. They got together again over Christmas. Bruce was home on leave, having finished his advanced training. Again, it was like old times as they partied together and joined other friends. Bruce displayed his old lack of seriousness. At a New Year's Eve party the two attended, Bruce got himself hooked up with an old flame. He timed things so that he ended up in bed with her shortly after eleven thirty. The next morning, he bragged to Jack, sporting a big grin, "Hey, I had sex from 1967 to 1968." However, in spite of occasional lapses into the old Bruce, it seemed to Jack that Bruce changed more every time he saw him. He seemed to be developing an "all business, less fun" attitude and a far more serious side. Jack wrote it off to the fact that he would soon be headed in harm's way so he had to change his focus in life. Jack did not like the changes. His hope was that when the army hitch was over, he would revert to the old Bruce. What he did not see in himself was that he was also maturing. His own life was changing, and he too was becoming more serious, more committed to his future place in life. Jack found out in February of 1968 that he had been accepted at the University of Maine. At the same time, Bruce had been sent to Vietnam. He arrived in the war zone a week before his eighteenth birthday. Their lives could not have taken more diverse paths. As Jack thought about his friend in Vietnam, he wondered if he would ever see him again.

Chapter III

Vietnam

BRUCE ARRIVED IN VIETNAM EARLY in 1968 stationed at Phan Rang as a member of the 101st airborne first brigade. Phan Rang was a training facility for the 101st soldiers, and he went right into proficiency training. Every arriving soldier had to do an additional two weeks of in-country training, mines, booby traps, maps, and terrain. All things you should know about fighting specific to Vietnam. There's nothing like training on the actual terrain you will be fighting in to get you acclimated. He anticipated seeing action in the long-range reconnaissance patrol or LURP. This involved being dropped behind enemy lines, working your way back while gathering information on enemy positions—dangerous assignments, but exactly what Bruce wanted. He had a couple of friends from back home, brothers who lived on the Penobscot Reservation who were LURPs, and he wanted to join them in that dangerous business. That had been his thought when he joined the 101st.

As this initial two weeks of training ended, another opportunity presented itself that took his attention away from potential LURP training. Word came down through the chain of command that they were looking for volunteers to enter into sniper training. Having always considered himself an excellent shot with a rifle, this was another potential assignment that held his interest. He went to see his company commander, Captain Reynolds, to discuss the possibility. "Sir, I'm interested in volunteering to become a sniper and would like to know what's involved." Reynolds did not respond immediately, preferring to mull over the request while examining the soldier doing the asking.

"What makes you think you can qualify as a sniper, soldier?"

"I have handled guns all my life in Maine, and if I do say so myself, I'm a crack shot, sir. In Maine, we do a lot of hunting. I have three older brothers, and they, plus my father, taught me how to hunt and handle a gun at a young age. I was the best shot in my family when I was only ten."

Captain Reynolds looked over this young recruit who seemed to be so anxious to serve in all aspects of combat. Reynolds was a hard-nosed lifer who had seen a lot of recruits come and go. The young ones were more eager. Sometimes too eager, thinking they were ready for any task the army gave out. Whether they had the necessary skills was another matter.

"I don't know how familiar you are with the role Marine snipers play in this war, but the volunteers we are looking for will not be playing the same role. This will be designed for our needs, you won't receive full sniper's training like the Marine snipers. This is for a specific need, more counter offensive than offense. So if you think this is some opportunity for a glamourous job or that you can be the next Carlos Hathcock, you're wrong. Even after you go through the training, you will still be just another soldier."

Reynolds was referring to the famous marine sniper who set the standard for all other snipers.

"Sir, I just want to know what's involved in the training and what the job entails. I'm not looking for glamour. Being just another soldier is fine with me."

Reynolds nodded as he continued to look the young recruit over. The answer that he heard from him was the answer he was looking to hear.

"You will be trained here at the base by Marines. They are the best snipers in the world and they will train you and other volunteers on the use of the Marine's weapon of choice, the Winchester Model 70, 30–6 with the Unert Scope. The training will take a couple of weeks. It's only a fraction of the training Marine snipers go through because it will only be a fraction of your duties. I say again so you will understand, you will not be a full-time sniper."

"I understand, sir." Bruce was not sure he did understand, but he knew better than to argue with the captain.

"Good. The reason we need snipers is to take out entrenched enemy positions that are pinning down platoons we are trying to move or we may need a sniper to open an exchange with a forward position to help us assess the strength of the enemy. These are examples of the kind of work you will be asked to do. It's a function you can perform if you're good enough, along with your other duties. You would not have full sniper training or be a full-time sniper like the Marines. You will be assigned other duties and be ordered to perform sniper duties only when the situation calls for it. Do you understand that, soldier?"

"Yes, sir."

"Then I will put you in the program, and we will see if you are the crack shot you claim to be or if your claims are pure bullshit."

With that, Bruce began sniper training. He was not the only army recruit taking the training, but he soon established himself as the best shot among the group. His remarks to his company commander were not bullshit. He had handled rifles for years and was indeed a crack shot. After the third day he was being told by a marine instructor that he was in the wrong branch of the service. His marksmanship was phenomenal, clearly the best shooter in the class.

"You shoot well enough to be a Marine, but you're in the army. What's the matter, are you not tough enough to be a Marine?" He stood five feet away, grinning at Bruce as he delivered the insult.

Bruce was smart enough not to take offense or get his back up because of the remark. It would not be smart to open an argument with his marine instructor if he intended to be recommended for sniper duty.

"No, sir. Toughness is not a problem. I was not given a choice as to which branch I would serve in, but I'm proud to be in the army." Bruce filled him in on how he ended up in the army by court order. The marine listened to the story, smiling a bit at the idea of this young teenager being a habitual anything. He didn't look old enough to have caused that much trouble. "The army may have gotten a good deal," was the response from the marine trainer as he walked away.

* * * * *

In Maine

In the spring of 1968, as he prepared to graduate from high school, Jack, like the rest of the world, was shocked by the assassinations of Martin Luther King and Robert Kennedy. He had lived through the assassination of President Kennedy, but this was different. He was very young when the president was shot. Now he was eighteen years old, and in spite of his devil-may-care social life, he was well aware of the social unrest in his country. He had also begun to have a very keen interest in politics. Nineteen sixty-eight would be the first presidential election in which he was mature enough to hold an interest and he was a Bobby Kennedy supporter. He feared what turmoil these deaths would foster. He wondered where his country was headed. His youthful innocence had been shattered by these terrible acts. He saw nobody left in the field of candidates for president that could match Kennedy. He was very disillusioned. Still, his main focus was preparing for college. He got a job that summer working as a carpenter's assistant. He worked eight hours a day Monday through Friday at that job then cooked in the family restaurant on Friday night and Saturday. He banked his pay from the carpenter's assistant job to pay for his first year in college. It was a time when tuition at a state university was affordable enough that summer employment plus a school year job could pay much of the cost.

In September, he started classes at the university, and he was glad to give up the day job. The hard work at various jobs every summer convinced him to stay in school and get his college degree.

College life was far different from his days in high school. The attitude of his professors was that you were there to learn. It was your responsibility to take advantage of the opportunity. If you didn't want to, there were plenty of people ready to take your seat. College deferments could still keep you out of the service and out of Vietnam. So competition to get into college was keen. The studies were far more difficult, and Jack couldn't just slide through without putting in the study time as he had done in high school. The workload was far more intense, and the subject matter was far more complicated.

Still, being a party animal, he was exploring the social opportunities. He went through rush week, pledging to Phi Eta Kappa fraternity. He found the initiation to be quite juvenile, but the fraternity parties, and the female students they attracted made it all worthwhile.

Jack could not afford to live on campus, but his home was only three miles away, so he stayed living there and commuted to the school, hitch hiking in on most days. His membership in Phi Eta was as a nonresident. His family's restaurant was no longer open twenty-four hours a day, but he still worked there on Friday nights and Saturdays. It gave him spending money during the school year. He would always have to earn the money for his tuition and books, working for a construction company in the summer months. While he came to enjoy college, none of it, the cost or the studies, came easy. He had to work hard to take care of both. He did excel at his studies, making the Dean's List in six of his eight semesters. There was another element of college life that was beginning to capture his interest as much as fraternity parties and coeds. That was the antiwar movement that was prevalent on almost every college campus. Bruce had arrived in Vietnam just in time for the TET offensive. Jack had arrived in college just in time for the intensified antiwar protesting that was brought to a head by that military offensive. The TET offensive was a coordinated attack on nearly one hundred cities and outposts by eighty-five thousand North Vietnamese soldiers. It was a major departure from the North Vietnamese army, who had relied on guerilla warfare preceding the offensive. The attacks were held off by the South Vietnamese and Americans. However, it was the turning point in the war that showed the American public that victory was not "just around the corner."

Sentiment against the war had started in the early sixties, mostly just among academics. It gained strength in 1965 as the bombing campaigns picked up. On October 21, 1967, one hundred thousand protestors marched on Washington. Jack was vaguely aware of that event but paid it little mind until he was assigned to read Norman Mailer's "Armies of the Night" in his freshman English literature class. That book, describing in detail the October 1967 march, brought Jack's awareness of how unjust the whole war was to a new level. It also established Mailer as one of his favorite writers. Then the TET offensive made it clear this was not going to end soon, nor would it end well. Again, antiwar protests intensified, and Jack began participating in them.

Chapter IV

In Vietnam
April 18, 1968

BRUCE KING IS PART OF a squad moving through Kon Tum Province in the central highlands of Vietnam. Incoming fire from a forward position has temporarily halted their progress. Word is sent from the squad leader that they need a sniper to take up a position to eliminate the enemy fire.

PFC King was sent out through the bush with a spotter to find a position from which to identify where the enemy fire was originating. Bruce was extremely excited about the assignment and determined to show what he could do as a sniper. Staying low, working their way through bamboo thickets to a higher ground, the two soldiers settled into a position that both gave them cover as well as a good view of the forward area. They lay on their stomachs in thick brush with only their heads sticking out. Patiently watching the area, King's spotter, PFC Tony Fignoni, saw a puff of smoke far ahead as a shot was fired from the right of their position. He pointed it out to Bruce. Concentrating on the area that he saw the smoke, he saw slight movement in the bushes and what looked like the top of an enemy's head. The shooters were well concealed but not well enough.

Fignoni gave Bruce what he estimated as the distance. "About three hundred yards ahead of the squad and one hundred and fifty yards from us at three o'clock."

Bruce nodded as he concentrated on the same area. He said, "I saw the smoke and there's been two more shots fired with more smoke. It seems like there are two or three of them. Two or three Viet Cong who are going to regret coming to work today."

"I agree with that. Can you get them from here?" Fignoni asked.

Bruce looked at his spotter with an expression that said he had asked a stupid question.

"I believe I can. It's not the distance that is the problem. I can barely see the top of two heads. They are pretty well entrenched, but don't you worry, their time has come."

Bruce continued to study the position of his targets. Finally, he winked at Fignoni and said, "Showtime."

With that, he sighted in his Winchester. Taking his time peering through the scope, he took a deep breath, relaxed, and closed and opened his eyes. He aimed for the very top of the distant shooter's head and squeezed off a shot. Through the scope, he saw the head of the Viet Cong explode. A second enemy soldier next to the first target instinctively rose and turned in King's direction, trying to judge where the shooter was positioned. King fired quickly, killing the second man with another head shot. As he continued to view the area through his scope, he saw bushes move as a third shooter hurried away. He waited for a clear shot at number 3, but he never got a look at an actual person, just the bushes moving. He fired a third shot anyway, just to hurry the Viet Cong's escape. He had no idea if he hit the third man, but he knew he had at least scared him away. He and Fignoni waited a few minutes to make sure. Seeing no more movement and no more shooting from the position, they concluded their mission was accomplished.

Returning to his platoon, he informed the platoon commander that all was clear. It was his first effort at sniper fire, and his spotter made sure the platoon members were informed of his success. Upon their return, Fignoni told the rest of the troops what happened.

"It was at least one hundred and fifty yards, and he got two of the three. Both shots in the head. The boy can shoot."

The listening audience was suitably impressed, as was the squad leader, Lieutenant Lowell.

"Private King, you were able to take out both shooters. That's pretty fair marksmanship. How far away were you?"

"About a hundred and fifty yards, sir, by the estimate of my spotter. One shot, one kill, sir. But there appeared to be a third VC that I never got a shot at."

"Don't feel bad about that. You scared him off, and we are moving again. Mission accomplished."

It turned out that Bruce did not get enough chances to use his sniper skills. It was part of his soldiering that he took pride in doing. He was well aware that he was good at it, and he appreciated any opportunity to demonstrate his skills. He wanted to be the "best of the best." He wondered often if he would have been better off in the Marine Corps as a full-time sniper.

Still, even though the limited capacity in which he was being used as a sniper left him wanting more, he excelled at the position whenever he was called to duty. His reputation as a marksman grew among his fellow soldiers. On his fourth opportunity, his performance raised some eyebrows. Out on patrol as part of a squad, his commander had received word of a Viet Cong machine gun replacement in his immediate forward area. The word came from a LURP advance team. The commander was not going to lead his troops into a machine gun emplacement.

Bruce was once again called in for sniper duty, and he accepted the duty with enthusiasm.

"Private King, we are aware of a VC machine gun unit in this immediate area. I don't want to walk into a turkey shoot. Take a spotter and see if you can identify the enemy position, take them out if you can. If you can't, or if there is heavy backup for the machine gunners, report back to me what we are looking at taking on."

"Yes, sir." Bruce again was excited for another chance to show what he could do as a sniper.

Bruce and his spotter, Private Tony Fignoni, a recruit from New Jersey who had become a close friend of Bruce, headed off through the bush looking for the enemy position. They had gone forward a mile or more, seeking the highest vantage point to survey the area. At one point, they were stopped in their tracks by a rustling of the brush ahead of them. Thinking they may be walking straight into an approaching enemy unit, Bruce and his spotter both shouldered their weapons. Anxiously waiting to see what came out of the brush, the seconds went by like minutes. Finally, an animal emerged about forty feet in front of them. They both blew out a sigh of relief.

"Goddamn rock apes," Tony observed.

They moved on, eventually finding a vantage point that opened up a good view of the forward area. They surveyed the area and found readily visible a good four hundred yards ahead of them at eleven o'clock three machine gun emplacements. Three VC sat behind their emplacements with their bamboo tubes looking in three directions. Two other VC with field glasses around their necks stood behind them, viewing the surrounding area.

Bruce radioed back to his squad that he had finally found his target. He gave the position to the squad so that they could move into a position to flank the Viet Cong position. They discussed back and forth whether Bruce should try to take them out. He felt with the distance involved and the cover he had that he had the advantage. First his Winchester would be more accurate at a four-hundred-yard shot than the machine gun. Secondly, the VC would take a moment to figure out where the first one or even two shots came from. By the time they figured it out, two or even three of them would be dead. Of course, these calculations depended on Bruce making shots from four hundred yards or more away. His confidence level was high, and he was sure he could make the hit. He relayed his confidence to the squad commander. The commander had his doubts, but he was well aware of Bruce's reputation. After a few minutes of back-and-forth debate, Bruce was told to take the shot and report back.

He shouldered his weapon and took aim first at the machine gun operator whose tube was looking in his direction, which was also the gunner closest to him. Again, following the instructions of his marine trainer, he took a deep breath, closed and opened his eyes, and rechecked his scope. He squeezed off the first round and four hundred yards away, a soldier's chest blew apart and he fell dead. The other four VC were caught by surprise and tried to quickly determine where the shot came from, but before they could, a second shot blew up the head of the soldier behind the middle machine gun emplacement. Now the VC standing behind the gun emplacements pointed in Bruce's direction as he lifted the field glasses to his eyes for a better look. The second standing VC was trying to rip the dead body out from behind the machine gun closest to Bruce's position and the first one he had hit. His idea was to move in and take over the machine gun. He didn't make it. His third shot took out that soldier before he was able to accomplish his task, and he fell dead on top of the first machine gun operator Bruce had killed. He was piling up bodies in rapid succession. He was taking very little time between shots. The Viet Cong soldiers were left with very little time to react.

Bruce and his spotter were well concealed in their position so all the two remaining Viet Cong could determine, even with field glasses, was the general area in which they were hiding. The third machine gun had been swung around and aimed in Bruce's direction. A volley of fire was aimed in his direction, but it fell short by fifty or sixty yards hitting the ground in front of him three quarters of the way up the hill from which he was firing. Bruce fired his fourth shot at the machine gun operator firing at their position and hit him in the chest, ending the machine gun fire as he fell dead, lying across his machine gun. Four down, one to go.

The last remaining VC had managed to replace his dead comrade in the middle emplacement and fire his machine gun in Bruce's direction. His volley came closer, and he was gradually working the rounds up the embankment getting even closer. Bruce's fifth and final shot stopped the shooter in the nick of time as he had sprayed bullets within ten feet of Bruce's position. The bullet that took off the top his head ended his progress, and he fell over dead. All five Viet Cong lay dead after an amazing display of marksmanship.

"Wow." Bruce's spotter Private Tony Fignoni could not contain his enthusiasm. "That was fucking unbelievable. You took out the whole fucking group with just five shots from four hundred yards, incredible."

Bruce smiled. "All in a day's work, Tony, all in a day's work. Remember, one shot, one kill."

"Yeah, five shots, five kills."

They high-fived one another in a muted celebration of the accomplishment.

He radioed back that the machine gun emplacement was no longer an issue. His reputation as an extraordinary marksman was assured. Still, the way he was being used as a sniper limited his role in that capacity. For the most part, his twelve-month tour was spent as part of squad patrols not as a sniper. In that capacity, he took part in a number of firefights. He distinguished himself here as well. His entire combat experience was making Bruce an extraordinary soldier with a well-earned reputation amongst his fellow soldiers.

* * * * *

August 9, 1968

Bruce was sent out as part of a squad of twelve soldiers on a search-and-destroy mission. Information had been received of a small Viet Cong unit in the area laying booby traps. The mission was to seek this unit out and take them out. After two hours of hiking through thick brush, as they approached a small stream, the VC unit they were seeking stepped out of the thick brush on the other side of the stream almost directly across from them. Both units were surprised by the other. An immediate fire fight broke out, both sides firing away even as they sought cover, surprised soldiers firing somewhat wildly in their panic.

The VC unit was made up of ten heavily armed soldiers. They took cover as they fired on the US squad, who did the same. Both sides took immediate hits, with two US soldiers being wounded and at least that many VC going down. As cover was taken, it became more difficult to score hits. As the firefight continued, the danger for the Americans was that they did not know if there may be a larger VC unit within striking distance that this small squad could call in for reinforcements. They did not want to suddenly find themselves drastically outnumbered and pinned down.

Five minutes into the fighting, Bruce approached his commander and suggested he could take two men downstream, flank the VC position, and drive them out or kill them with grenades. Given the danger of the VC calling in reinforcements, the mission was quickly approved so Bruce and two other soldiers headed downstream, staying low behind the cover of heavy bamboo thickets.

After moving quickly for nearly a half mile, they crossed the stream. When they reached the other side, Bruce held out his hand for his fellow soldiers to stop. He pointed to his ear, signaling for them to listen. When they did, they heard what Bruce had already heard. Someone or something was coming toward them from the direction of the VC unit. The three soldiers took cover and waited. As the sounds grew closer, it became obvious that they were hearing footsteps of soldiers headed their way.

After a short wait, two VC soldiers appeared out of the brush. They apparently had the same idea as the Americans and were moving to out flank the American position. Bruce put his finger to his lips motioning for quiet. Then he took out his knife, motioning for the others to do the same. He did not want to make any noise that would tip off the enemy that they were moving in behind them so using their firearms was not an option. When the two VC soldiers were close enough, the Americans jumped out and surprised them, grabbing them before they could use their rifles. A brief hand to hand struggle ensued in which the two VC were killed quietly by knife, Bruce taking out one of them. They pulled the bodies into the brush to hide them from view in case there may be more coming.

That being done, the three Americans continued on, eventually working their way behind the remaining six Viet Cong who continued shooting at the Americans across the stream. Once they were in position, they each readied a grenade. On Bruce's signal, three grenades were thrown into the heavy brush that had been protecting the six North Vietnamese soldiers. Three were killed instantly; the other three were hurt badly and had no choice but to surrender. Their weapons and explosives confiscated, they were forced to confess where they had already set booby traps before they were brought back to camp for interrogation as prisoners of war. The traps were defused, making the mission a complete success. Bruce King's quick thinking and the action he took had saved the lives of US soldiers.

* * * * *

October 23, 1968

Bruce was part of a platoon sent to provide backup for a squad that was protecting a small village and had come under fire from a VC unit. As they arrived on the scene, they found the US soldiers already on-site were under heavy fire, pinned down in the village they were protecting. A pair of US soldiers who had been wounded were pinned down in a very vulnerable place between the rest of their unit and the attacking Viet Cong. They lay wounded, hiding behind a Vietnamese hand plow and a dead water buffalo.

Bruce's platoon spread out and engaged the enemy. Bruce and Tony Fignoni, seeing the wounded soldiers that were in harm's way, Bruce called for covering fire and began low crawling to their position under the cover of the heavy fire being created by the backup platoon. As the two crawled to the location of the wounded men, Viet Cong fire was aimed at them, but miraculously, they reached the two wounded soldiers unharmed. While Bruce carried them to safety one at a time, Fignoni, along with the rest of the American troops, covered him with fire. The wounded soldiers were saved by their heroic actions. He and Fignoni risked their own lives to bring two wounded colleagues to safety. They were both awarded a bronze star for this action.

His heroics in the field did not go unnoticed. His proficiency as a sniper, along with his heroic actions in the field, had caught the attention of higher-ranking officials. As the war was wearing on, it became necessary for commanding officers to recruit seasoned soldiers for second tours of duty. Experienced combat soldiers who had proven their mettle under fire were a valuable commodity. Bruce King had distinguished himself as a valuable commodity.

In January 1969, his tour of duty in Vietnam coming to a close, Bruce received word to report to his company commander, Major Collins. Upon entering headquarters, he was received by the major and one other officer. Collins immediately turned the encounter over to the other officer.

"Private King, this is Colonel David Haywood, and he would like to talk with you."

Bruce had heard plenty about Colonel Haywood and was well aware of his reputation. He turned to Colonel Haywood. "Sir, I have heard a great deal about you. Your reputation precedes you and is very impressive."

Haywood responded, "Reputations are usually blown up with a lot of bullshit over time, but I appreciate the compliment. You are nearing the end of your tour here in Vietnam, and frankly, your own reputation is impressive, Private King."

Bruce looked at the colonel as he received the compliment. He wondered why this celebrated leader wanted to see him.

"Thank you, sir." Bruce did not know how else to respond to such high praise from a famous colonel.

"Take a seat, soldier, I want to speak to you about a second tour."

A second tour, the three words gave Bruce a jolt. He had not given any thought to such a possibility. He had been thinking of nothing recently except heading home.

All three took a seat, Major Collins behind his desk and Bruce and Haywood in folding chairs in front of the desk. Bruce was taken aback by Haywood's suggestion of a second tour. The thought of twelve more months in this hellhole was not what he had in mind. Rather, he had been thinking how great it would be to get back to Maine. Haywood saw the troubled look in Bruce's reaction and knew he had some convincing to do. So he went directly at it, no beating around the bush.

"I have created a very special squad called the Tiger Force. It's a platoon made up of paratroopers of First Brigade 1/327, 101st. Our purpose is to counter guerilla warfare tactics by using the same tactics employed by the VC. I would like you to consider a second tour of duty as part of this elite platoon. I fully understand the seriousness of this request, but you need to understand how important I feel it is that you consider it. Most soldiers feel after one tour that they have done their duty. They have done their duty and there is no obligation to do another tour. But soldiers like you are needed to finish this job."

It was obvious the colonel preferred the direct approach.

Bruce paused a bit to consider the proposal before he answered. He had heard of Tiger Force. The unit had been active for a few years, and the members saw heavy action. They were indeed considered to be an elite squad. The members were picked for the squad based on their performance in training sessions as well as in the field. To be considered was an honor in itself. Haywood did the picking as well as the recruiting himself. The fact that he had singled out Bruce was extremely flattering.

"Sir, I'm flattered you would consider me for your platoon. I know the reputation of Tiger Force, but I'm not that familiar with their MOs." Bruce was concerned about their missions and the type of duty he would be asked to perform.

"The platoon engages in long-range reconnaissance, counter insurgency, and guerilla tactics behind enemy lines. I know you have seen a lot of action in the last twelve months, but that will pale next to the work you will be doing on your second tour. It's heavy action, soldier, but it is also tremendously important action. You will be performing the utmost important duty for your country, the kind of duty that will help us win this war."

That statement made it clear that he was not only being asked to stay for another twelve months, but he was also being asked to accept a position in this platoon that would put him even more at risk, that would put him in even greater life threatening danger.

"With all due respect, sir, I feel fortunate to have lived through one tour over here. Signing up for a second tour, while increasing the danger level, does not seem to be a smart move."

"Son, you are a good soldier. Exactly the type of brave soldier I have recruited into this platoon. You have shown yourself over the past twelve months to be able to handle dangerous duty. You excel in that type of danger. I need a man like you in this platoon. Your country needs you in this platoon. If that were not the case, I would not be asking."

Again, Bruce paused to consider his response. He looked the colonel in the eye for a long moment. This was a man with an almost legendary aura about him. A soldier with a bigger than life reputation who was requesting his service. Service in a unit that was gaining its own bigger than life reputation.

After a lengthy pause, Bruce said, "I will have to give this some thought, sir. I have been looking forward to returning to the States. The thought of coming back here is the farthest thing from my mind."

"You have a little more than two weeks left in this tour. You will be going state side for a time no matter what your decision is on my offer. Take the next two weeks to think this over, and give me an answer before you leave. I trust a brave soldier like you will make the best decision for his country."

A statement that begged the question was what's best for the country also what was best for Bruce King.

"Thank you, sir."

With that, the meeting ended. Bruce spent the next two weeks thinking of nothing else than this decision. He had eighteen months left to serve in the army. He had no idea where they would be sending him, but of course, he knew if he accepted this challenge, two-thirds of his remaining time would be spent right here. He had accepted the danger. In fact, he knew Haywood was right that he had thrived on the danger. Coming back as a member of an elite platoon had to be weighed against finishing his tour of duty in far less dangerous circumstances. He had to be careful not to let Haywood's stroking of his ego bring him to a poor decision. His answer went back and forth daily for the entire two-week period. He discussed it with other soldiers, even with the unit's chaplain. He spent a lot of time talking it over with his new friend, Tony Fignoni. Fignoni told him point-blank he would not do it if he had been asked. Other friends in his unit were less negative. Many felt it was an honor to be picked for Tiger Force and that he should take on the challenge. In the end, it was his decision to make and his alone. After two weeks of wrestling with it, and before he left Vietnam, he gave his answer.

Chapter V

March 1969

Bruce returned to the States, landing in San Francisco and continuing on to Fort Deven's, where he reported. He had two weeks leave coming to him, so he headed for Maine to see his friends and family. His first stop after getting back to Old Town was the restaurant where he had worked for almost three years before joining the army. He was greeted warmly by the Roach family. Jack Sr. and Polly plus two of Jack's sisters were working that day and were happy to see him. The staff at the restaurant plus many of the regular customers welcomed him like the returning hero. Like many who returned from Vietnam, he was not warmly received everywhere, but he was at Jack's restaurant. His friend Jack was still at the university, so Bruce waited for him at the restaurant. While he waited, he worked the room just like a politician, greeting old friends and carrying on conversations. He was asked repeatedly about the war, which was only natural, but Bruce, like many other returning vets, was not that anxious to talk about it. He would always change the subject by asking whoever he was talking to a question about their family.

The two friends were reunited when Jack walked in on his return from classes. He was pleasantly surprised to see Bruce there. He had given no advance notice of his return. They retired to Jack's house to have a few drinks and catch up on things.

The Roach family home was a one-hundred-year-old colonial less than a block from the restaurant. They sat in the kitchen, opened a couple of cans of beer, and discussed his experience in Vietnam to the extent Bruce was willing to discuss his experience.

After touching on the war in general and what Jack had been up to while Bruce was away, Jack got into the heart of the matter.

"You survived the war, and you don't look any worse for wear," Jack said. Jack had a broad smile on his face happy to be talking with Bruce again. It had been a long time.

"Well, I haven't quite survived it yet," Bruce said as he took a long pull on his can of beer.

"What do you mean, are you all right?" Jack was afraid of some unseen injury like post-traumatic stress.

"Oh yeah, I'm fine, but I have signed up for a second tour of duty. I'm going back in two months."

Jack was absolutely shocked by this news. He could not believe anyone would want to go through fighting a war twice, especially his old friend, who never really seemed suited for the military in the first place.

"Holy shit, you have got to be fucking kidding me. Why the fuck would you do such a crazy-ass thing?"

Bruce took another long pull on his beer before answering, "Jack, you don't understand. I have a chance to be part of a unique and prized unit. I'm good at what they have assigned me to do, so good at it that I have been recruited to serve in a special unit, a unit that could decide the outcome of the war. It's like being picked to an all-star team. I could not say no. I didn't want to say no. It's an opportunity to prove myself."

Jack was stunned at this news. He just sat shaking his head and looking at a very changed best friend. He thought he knew Bruce, but this was not the same guy he had hung with over the past years. He understood and applauded the patriotic attitude, but what he was going to do was above and beyond the call of duty. One thing was for certain, when Bruce told Jack he didn't understand, he was 100 percent correct.

"I want to serve my country, Jack."

"This is not a popular war, Bruce. Many people have taken to protesting the entire conflict. I understand you want to serve your country, but is this the best decision?"

"I ran into some of these protesters in the San Francisco airport. Me and a couple of other returning soldiers had a bit of a confrontation with them. One of them spit on a marine who was on the same flight with me. So he and I and two other marines got into a fight with about a dozen protesters. Airport security had to break it up. I got some good shots in on the spitter. It was actually kind of fun, like the old days around here."

Jack did not want to tell his old friend that he had attended a protest or two himself. The University of Maine was considered a quiet campus. Still there were antiwar activists on campus, even on a quiet campus. Jack attended several rallies on the library steps in the spring of his freshman year. He spent a good deal of time reading about major protest rallies on campuses like Columbia and Stanford. He listened to a lot of Bob Dylan and read a lot of Abby Hoffman. By the spring semester of his freshman year, he was fully convinced that the war was being fought simply to feed the greed of the military industrial complex and that it had absolutely no strategic value in terms of the welfare of the United States or the world in general. Opinions that would be proven to be correct in later years. Seeing his best friend putting his life on the line for a second tour in this awful mistake of a conflict was perplexing.

What's more, the unfairness of the fact that people who could afford to go to college got a draft deferment and wealthy Americans in general didn't seem to be involved in the fighting. By and large, it was a war being fought only by the poor like his friend Bruce.

"I certainly don't condone anything like them spitting on you, but still, Bruce, it is a very unpopular war."

Bruce nodded his head but said nothing as he took another drink.

"Well, you have really thrown me for a loop. I never expected to hear this from you. Have you told your mother?"

"No, this is my first stop. I will see her tomorrow if it's all right if I stay here tonight?"

Bruce had moved in with the Roach family, living there for two years before he joined the army. It felt more like home to him than his own home. So on his return, he wanted to continue to live at the Roaches' house as long as he was in town.

"Of course, you can stay here. Let's have a few beers, call a few friends, and for tonight just act like this whole army thing never happened." As he said this, Jack was thinking that he truly wished the army thing had never happened. He wished the two of them were still working at the restaurant, raising hell on their free time, and laughing at life all the while.

That night they spent with the Roach family in conversation. While he seldom spoke about it, Jack Roach Senior was in the army in World War II. What's more, he had one brother killed in Sicily and another brother wounded in the Normandy D-Day invasion. He had served in the Pacific, ending his tour of duty with the occupying army in Japan. Bruce had taken his R&R in Japan, so they talked a lot about army life, war, and more pleasantly, Japan. Bruce had actually visited some of the same areas in Japan as Jack Sr. Some old pictures were brought out that were taken in the forties during the occupation and Bruce told Jack Sr. how some of the same places had changed. Jack Sr. seemed to enjoy the reminiscing.

They were joined off and on by Jack's mother, Pauline, and his younger brother, David. They talked through the evening with Jack and Bruce, enjoying a good bit of alcoholic beverages. Jack Sr. did not drink alcohol but always had a supply in the house. Bruce had often wondered how a man who didn't drink at all was able to tolerate a pack of drunks around him. But tolerate them he did, while even making sure there was plenty around to drink.

The following morning, Jack was heading off for his nine o'clock class while Bruce was going to see his mother, as well as the rest of his family. They were having coffee at the Roach family's kitchen table, along with Jack's mother, father, and two sisters.

"So, what's your plans for the week, Bruce my boy?" asked Jack Sr.

"Well, I think this weekend we should get some of the old crew together to have a get-together."

"Well, the two of you damn well better stay out of trouble," Jack's mother chimed in with a stern look from the stove as she prepared breakfast. Jack and Bruce just smiled at her, which she did not find amusing.

Jack Sr. said, "You two clowns better listen to her."

Bruce answered, "Not to worry. I have army discipline." This line was delivered with a smile.

Polly and Jack Sr. responded to this statement with a scornful look at both Bruce and young Jack. "When the two of you get together, discipline goes out the front door," was Polly's assessment.

"Is anyone else home on leave that you know about, Jack?"

"Yeah, I saw Adrian Francis a couple of days ago downtown. I think he told me he was here for the week." Adrian was a Native American from the Penobscot Indian Nation. He and his brother were both in the 173rd Airborne. Bruce knew that they were both doing dangerous work.

"Man, I would like to see him. We did run into each other in Nam, but not for a long enough time. He's doing what I thought I might be doing, he and his brother are both LURPs. They see a lot action."

"Okay, for us civilians, what is a LURP?" Jack asked.

"Long Range Reconnaissance Patrol. They drop him behind enemy lines from a helicopter using a sling. Then he works his way back to the base while gathering information on enemy troop positions. He and his brother are both doing that duty. It's dangerous work, and they are both decorated combat veterans."

"That's a very dangerous assignment," Jack Sr. noted. "Those two boys deserve a lot of credit for bravery. As you do, Bruce."

"Yeah, it sounds really dangerous," Jack said.

"It is, but there aren't many duties over there that aren't."

"That's why I can't understand you going back for a second tour."

"You're going back for a second tour, Bruce?" Polly said in a shocked tone of voice as she and the rest of the family had surprised looks, hearing this for the first time.

Bruce looked around the table at the surprised faces and said, "I don't expect anyone can understand. You would have to be over there to understand it. But I'm going back because I'm good at what I do over there, and the job is not finished."

Everyone around the table expressed heartfelt concern for Bruce going back. Jack Sr. summed it all up. "Bruce, we applaud your valor, but we all are concerned that you come back safely."

Bruce said he understood and appreciated everyone's concern. He had every intention of coming back safely, he told them.

With that, they finished their coffee, Jack heading off to class and Bruce heading to his mother's house. The King family home was a rundown two-story affair in desperate need of repair, three blocks from the Roach home and across the street from a canoe factory. His mother was also not pleased with the announcement that he would be going back. They had a bit of an argument. It was a tense encounter. His mother, Dorothy, had already lost her husband and later her oldest son to a hunting accident. "Bruce, I can't lose another son. My heart won't take it. You survived one tour. Why can't you call that good?"

Bruce explained his pride in being selected to this special unit. He explained his desire to continue to serve. In the end, his mother did not understand and Bruce did not expect that she would. As he left her, there were tears in her eyes and she wondered if she would see him again.

Following that visit, Bruce spent the rest of that Thursday looking up other old friends and planning activities for the weekend for himself and Jack. He was planning to party with Jack and as many mutual friends as he could find on the weekend, just like old times.

He was able to track down Adrian Francis, and the two of them shared a few beers and some Vietnam stories at Adrian's home on the Penobscot Indian Reservation. They planned to get together again on Friday night when Jack got out of work.

The weekend was spent with Bruce and Jack getting together with the friends they had hung with over the years. They shared a lot of memories, but noticeably absent from the flow of conversation was any stories from Bruce concerning his experience in Vietnam. He spoke about the war with Adrian Francis when the two were alone but did not offer any stories when in a group or when alone with Jack. If asked a question, he would give a short generic answer with little real insight offered. The same was true of Adrian. It was like they shared a secret that only Vietnam soldiers were let in on.

Bruce's time in Vietnam was not entirely spent fighting. There was downtime at the base in which he shared some relative relaxation with other soldiers. Bruce had struck up a friendship with a member of his unit who also served from time to time as his spotter.

Tony Fignoni was East Coast Italian with all the appropriate accents and slang terms. He had the classic Mediterranean look, dark skin and curly black hair. Bruce would often tell him his real father must be Dean Martin. He was tall at six feet, one inch, and handsome, a hit with the ladies.

Like Bruce, he enjoyed having a few drinks, smoking pot or hash, and basically looking for a good time. All these traits were qualities Bruce looked for in a friend, and he certainly found them with Tony.

They went on R&R together in Japan. They did do a good bit of sightseeing, but most of the time, they spent chasing Japanese women while drinking barrels of sake. Bruce had only relayed the sightseeing stories to Jack Sr., keeping his other exploits out of the conversation.

They came back to the States at the same time, so Bruce was planning to see him while they were both on leave.

So on Sunday evening as the two returned to Jack's home, Bruce surprised his friend with an announcement.

"I'm headed to New Jersey tomorrow to meet up with a guy I served with in Nam."

Jack spun around to look at Bruce as they were walking through the door at Jack's house. He was sorry to hear he was leaving so soon. He had thought Bruce would be in Old Town for four or five more days.

"Really, you've only been here a few days. When do you have to report back?"

Bruce knew the news would not be well received, which is why he held off delivering it. "I have to be back at Devens on Friday. But I want to spend a few days with Tony on my way back. You will be taking classes all week anyway." Jack was obviously disappointed by this announcement.

"Wow, I thought you would be here until your leave was finished. Who's the guy in New Jersey?"

"His name is Tony Fignoni, and we were in the same unit over there and became friends. He's a great guy. I tried to get him to come up here, but he had no interest in coming to Maine. We were jointly involved in rescuing two wounded soldiers in a firefight. We are good friends, and I want to see him stateside." Bruce looked at Jack, hoping that he understood it was important for him to see this guy.

"Did this guy also sign up for a second tour?"

"Hell, no. He couldn't wait to get out of Nam," Bruce said laughingly.

"Well, in that case, he sounds smart," Jack said without a trace of a smile.

Jack thought about how out of character it seemed for Bruce to sign up for the second tour, as well as for him to decide to move on to New Jersey halfway through his leave. The service and the war had changed his friend a great deal. He was not comfortable with the changes, nor was he happy about his friend's early departure.

"Well then, I guess this is it. I won't be seeing you for while!"

"Yeah, it will all be over in September of 1970 when my hitch is up. Then I'll be back here and things will return to normal."

Jack was not sure about a lot of things—Bruce's future and his own future being among them. One thing he was sure of though was that things were not going to return to normal, at least not to the normal that he had in mind.

Monday morning, Bruce took a Greyhound Bus to New York City. He called Tony Fignoni from the bus station in Bangor to give him his arrival time so he could be there to pick him up. Upon his arrival at Port Authority, Tony was waiting with a driver and a Lincoln Continental. When Bruce saw the welcoming committee he was taken aback. A Lincoln and a driver?

"What the fuck is this?" Bruce expressed his surprise at the entourage that greeted him as they shook hands.

"You have your own driver and a Lincoln?"

"Hey, what did you expect, a fuckin' army jeep?" They all laughed, including the driver who was a hulk of a man. Well over six feet and a solid two hundred fifty pounds or better. Bruce took note of the lack of a neck. He was obviously more than just a driver. He expected that the guy also served as a bodyguard. Why his friend Tony would need a body guard was not clear to Bruce.

"Well, I wasn't expecting this. You come from a hell of a lot more money than little Bruce King, I can tell you that."

Tony laughed out loud at his friend's surprised tone. He had intentionally put on the dog a little bit to surprise his friend.

"You ain't seen nothing yet. Welcome to the Big Apple." Tony had a broad smile as he made a sweeping motion with his right arm to demonstrate the breadth of the city. Bruce's first trip to New York had left him in awe of the size of the city. He was also in awe of the wealth of his friend.

It turned out he was right when he said that Bruce hadn't seen anything yet. When they arrived at Tony's home in Secaucus, New Jersey, Bruce was blown away. The fourteen thousand square foot home was on a beautifully landscaped ten acres with pool and tennis courts. Coming from Old Town, Maine, he had never seen the likes of this place. You didn't pay for a place like this on mill workers' pay.

"Holy shit, Tony. Your old man must be loaded. How did someone with your bread end up in the army?" Tony had given no indication during their time in Vietnam that his family had any money. This setting smelled of a great deal of money and caught Bruce totally by surprise.

"My rich old man's idea. He thought it would teach me a little discipline so I would stop being a royal pain in the ass. In his line of work, he can't have a son embarrassing him."

"What is his line of work?" *An innocent question*, Bruce thought. The two were walking from the Lincoln to the front door of the Fignoni home as he asked it. Tony's reaction indicated it was not a simple question.

Tony stopped walking, turned, and looked at Bruce with a very serious expression. "I think you can probably guess, Bruce, but while you're here, don't ask, okay?" The seriousness with which this line was delivered told Bruce he better leave it alone.

"Yeah, okay."

Bruce stayed in Secaucus for three more days. His bedroom was roughly the size of his house in Old Town, and he had his own bathroom. He ate and drank in style. He only saw Mr. Fignoni twice, and he followed Tony's advice not asking any questions. Mr. Fignoni was not a big man, about five feet, ten inches tall and maybe one hundred ninety pounds. Nonetheless, he was an imposing figure who was obviously in charge of things. A number of bulky men like Tony's driver moved in and out of his office. They all wore expensive clothing and drove expensive cars. The same was true of his friend Tony, who dressed very well, and when he drove his own car, it was a Corvette. To a man, they were all obviously following whatever directives came from Mr. Fignoni. Tony had a driver take the Lincoln into the city as he showed Bruce around a number of popular night spots. They ended the evening checking into a hotel with a couple of girls they met while nightclubbing. The Lincoln was back the next morning to bring them back to Secaucus. Tony made sure that he and Bruce had female companions each night. On his last day there, Bruce talked to Tony about going back for a second tour.

"Bruce, I told you when we were still in Vietnam, I think you made a bad decision. That place is a hellhole. I wouldn't go back even if they paid me."

"Well, I'm headed back, Tony, so wish me well."

"I wish you well, but I think you're a sucker."

He stayed away from the subject of the Fignoni family business, but...

By the time Bruce said goodbye to his friend, Tony, he had a pretty good idea what his father's business interests entailed.

He took the bus back to Fort Devens, thinking that his friend Tony was certainly destined for the same line of work.

Chapter VI

In Maine

IN APRIL, JACK TRAVELED TO New York City to join in a huge anti-war protest. He and three other U.Maine students went down in a van. They arrived the night before the planned demonstration and all slept in the van. There were planned protests for the same day in major cities around the country. The protest took place in Central Park on a beautiful spring day with tens of thousands of participants. Being from Maine, the size of the crowd was awe-inspiring. It struck Jack that there were ten times as many people at this rally as there were in his hometown.

The atmosphere was festive with music and rallying cries against the war. It was easy to get a contact high just walking around as pot smoking was the order of the day. Speaker after speaker stirred up the crowd with fiery speeches. There were rumors Bob Dylan would be showing up, but that never happened. The protest remained peaceful throughout the day. The police stayed vigilant, but there were few arrests.

As Jack sat on the grass listening to a speaker, he felt a tap on the shoulder. When he turned to see who was after his attention, his eyes fell on a beautiful young lady who was passing him a joint. He was so taken with her looks that he sat too stunned to accept the offered joint. He thought she was the most attractive woman he had ever seen. She sat cross legged, looking at him with beautiful wide eyes as she offered the joint. A long moment passed as she held out the joint while Jack stared at her.

Finally, she blew the smoke out and said, "Hey, do you want a hit, or would you prefer to sit there looking stupefied?" She looked at him with an expression that said, "Are you really this numb?"

Jack took the dooby from her and took a hit while never taking his eyes off her. He passed it back and she took it while breaking into a smile. He held the smoke in his lungs while marveling at what he felt was the most bewitching smile he had ever seen. This girl was like something out of a dream.

"Either you have never seen a girl before or you've never smoked a joint before. Which is it?" She was shaking her head and laughing as she said this.

Jack blew the smoke off and answered, "It's neither. I have smoked before, and I've seen girls before. I've just never seen a girl that looks like you."

He could not take his eyes off this lady. Stunningly beautiful with a fabulous body and incredible smile. She was literally the perfect-looking woman.

"What the hell is that supposed to mean? Am I that strange-looking?"

"No, you are stunningly beautiful. I have never seen anyone as beautiful as you." Jack was surprised at his own bluntness, but he was speaking honestly. He could not help himself from his giddy, slobbering praise. Certainly he was not the first to say something of this kind to her.

"And you are as full of shit as a Christmas goose," she said while shaking her head. "Does that kind of bullshit line usually work for you?"

Jack laughed but kept his eyes on this girl. She had brown hair with auburn highlights, brown eyes, and the most incredibly captivating smile. He judged her to be about five feet three or four and hundred and ten or fifteen beautifully formed pounds. She was wearing a very well-filled-out pair of jeans, sandals, and an orange pullover shirt with the peace sign on the front and back. He had been so focused on the speaker that he had not noticed her moving in next to him. They sat side by side on the grass, Jack forgetting all about his three friends, the current speaker, the music, and basically the entire rally.

"I will admit to being full of shit, but in this case, I'm being honest. Can I get your name?"

She thought for a moment then answered, "No, not a chance, you're too creepy."

Jack had never before been called creepy. He had been called a lot of things but never creepy. Nonetheless he continued. "Well, if I guess it, will you tell me?"

She laughed at this and took another long hit on the joint while looking Jack in the eye. She held the smoke while passing him the joint. He took another hit himself as they continued to stare at each other. They both blew smoke out at the same time.

She smiled at him before answering. It was a smile that took Jack's breath away.

She said, "Okay, Champ, go ahead. I will give you three tries. If you guess it, I will give it to you. If you don't, I'm going to kick the shit out of you."

"Okay," Jack said as he looked her up and down getting ready for his first guess. Apparently, his look was a bit more lustful than he thought.

She narrowed her eyes and, with a suspicious look, said, "Somehow I get the feeling that you are looking me up and down more because it gets you off than because you are working on a name."

He had to laugh at that statement because she had hit the nail on the head. Looking her up and down was definitely a pleasurable experience he could spend all day enjoying. "Maybe I'm looking you up and down trying to judge whether or not you actually could kick the shit out of me."

"There's no doubt about that, Champ, so don't push your luck or I might do it even if you do guess my name."

"Debbie." Jack gave his first answer.

"Wrong, dick weed, try again." She took another hit off the joint, looking at him with a bemused look.

Jack was sure he was falling in love with this smart-ass beauty even as he laughed at her insulting remarks. "Okay. Susan." He gave his second-guess. He noticed her eyes widen at this guess, so he figured he was close.

She looked at him in silence for a moment then blew out some smoke and smiled and said in her best Ed MacMann voice, "You are correct, sir."

Jack laughed and winked at her. He sensed a momentum shift. He had come up one time on top of this little smart-ass. It felt good to be getting a bit ahead of her.

"Okay then, I guessed the first half so you have to give me the rest."

She hesitated, going back to that narrowed-eye suspicious look. Then she nodded as if to indicate he was right and she had to live up to the deal.

"Okay, it's Susan Frazier."

Ah, the ice was broken. He had her verbally back on her heels. He pressed on.

"Where are you from, Susan Frazier?"

"Not so fast, dill weed. You tell me your story first."

So she was not on her heels and back on offense. He could see it would be difficult to stay ahead of her. He decided to try a bit of humor.

"All right, my name is Jack Dillweed."

Now she laughed at his smart-ass remark. "You know, I may have misjudged you. Could be you're not creepy. You do look like a dill weed, but I'm sure it's not your name. Now tell me your real name and the rest of your story, or I will beat the tar out of you right in front of all these people leaving you bloody and humiliated."

Jack was thinking he might actually enjoy that. Any physical contact with this girl would have to be great even if he were on the losing end of a beating.

Jack confessed his real name as well as his student status at U. Maine. Then it was her turn to open up. It turned out that Susan Frazier was a junior at NYU. She hailed from Burke, Vermont, she was not currently seeing anyone, hated the war as well as the Nixon administration. She was majoring in communications and had no idea what she wanted to do after graduation. They spent several hours talking, losing any thoughts of the protest, until finally the rally was breaking up. She had agreed to meet him for a drink before he had to head back. Jack told his three friends he would meet them at the van in an hour, then he and Susan walked together to a small café near the NYU campus, got a table, and ordered a couple of cups of coffee. They talked politics, college, the war, and life in general. The conversation was easy for both of them. After just two or three hours, Jack felt as though he had known this girl all his life. Every time she broke into that smile, he felt himself being overtaken with her charms. Superficially speaking, he could not help being attracted to her perfectly shaped body, including the best pair of legs he had ever seen. He didn't want the encounter to end.

"So when are you headed back to the woods of Maine?" she asked as they walked out of the coffee shop.

"What do you mean, 'woods of Maine'? Vermont's not exactly cosmopolitan."

"Okay then, when are you headed back to the great state of Maine?"

"That's much better. We are supposed to leave tonight, but after meeting you, I would like to stay here permanently."

"Still full of shit. Where are your travelling mates?"

"I suppose they're back at the van waiting for me to show up." Jack was hoping that they were waiting, rather than having left without him. He had told them he would meet them in an hour three hours ago.

"If you want to spend some more time in the civilized world, I share an apartment not far from here with three other girls. You're welcome to the couch. I will put myself out to show you around the city."

This, of course, was the kind of answer he sought. He just couldn't believe he got it. There was no way he was not going to accept, even if his three friends ended up hating him. It was truly an offer Jack couldn't refuse. "Let me go to my friends and make arrangements. Can I meet you back here in ninety minutes?" As he waited for her response, he could not believe he was actually making progress with this girl. She was absolutely beautiful, and he was absolutely taken with her.

"You have a deal, but remember, if you stand me up, I will find you and beat the shit out of you."

"You are so violent, but you don't have to worry. I will definitely be here. I'm not sure you could beat me up anyway."

"Don't bet the farm on it, Creepy," she said as she smiled at him.

Jack hurried back to where they had left the van to find his three friends waiting for him. They had agreed earlier to rendezvous here after the protest. Jack was late, and they were not pleased.

"Where the hell have you been, Jack? We've been here waiting for you for three hours," was the greeting from Steve Kane, the driver. His two other travelers looked equally pissed off. He knew he was late, and he knew it hadn't made him any friends.

"I know, guys, I'm sorry, but I met a girl." The three friends moaned collectively. Jack was pleading with them. "Okay, I know, but she's offered to put me up for the night. What can I say? she's the most beautiful thing I've ever seen." Again, collective moaning. "Okay, boys, this is the latest of Jack's most beautiful things. What are we supposed to do, Jack? Stand here until morning? Sleep in the van again another night?" Steve Kane, again the group spokesman, but all three were looking at him with disgusted expressions. He was thinking as he looked at them that he might get the shit kicked out of him, but not by Susan.

Jack understood their anger. He had thought ahead of a way they could leave without him.

"Look, I have thirty-two dollars. If you can all lend me twenty each, I can have enough money to stay in New York a few days then get a bus back to Bangor Sunday. You guys can head home now without me."

They all just looked at him in silence, obviously reticent about his proposal.

Jack pushed on as his friends seemed to be undecided.

"I know it's a lot to ask, but I'm begging you, she's gorgeous." He was pleading even harder now. His friends noted that he was pathetic, an assessment to which he could not argue. His desire to be with this gorgeous woman had left him weak. He could tell that he was convincing them in spite of their resistance. They wanted to head home bad enough that they would provide the finances that he had requested.

The three fellow travelers assessed their finances to see if they would still have enough among them to get home if they lent Jack sixty dollars. They ended up being able to give him forty-seven dollars, while retaining enough among them to get home. Jack thanked them all and headed back to the café with seventy-nine dollars in his pocket. His three travel companions headed back to Maine in the van. Jack figured they would be talking about him all the way back and how right he was. Susan Frazier was waiting outside the café as Jack approached. She smiled when she saw him, a smile that would always leave Jack weak. She was looking at her watch as he approached.

"Well, you made it back just in time. I was about to begin a search-and-destroy mission."

"I told you there was no way I would not show."

"Yeah, well you just saved yourself a severe beating."

Sue Frazier brought Jack back to her two-bedroom apartment two blocks from the NYU campus. On the way, they stopped at a drug store so Jack could buy a toothbrush and other essentials. She shared the apartment with three other girls, two to a bedroom. She introduced Jack to her roommates, Carol Tate, Kathy Sawyer, and Carol Anderson. The three roommates were all very attractive, but Sue Frazier was attractive beyond any comparison.

"This rather ragged, pathetic-looking, homeless man from Maine is Jack Roach," was her introduction. She had cleared his staying on the couch with her roommates earlier while Jack was explaining things to his friends. At that time, she had given him a far more flattering description, but in his presence, she was not prone to be handing out compliments. The four girls welcomed Jack into their home then fixed a dinner consisting of soup and a salad, setting an extra place for Jack. After eating, they all sat up talking until the wee hours of the morning. Jack learned a good deal about the roommates, and they learned about him. As the roommates began making their way to bed, it finally left Jack and Sue alone. She was sitting on the couch next to him. All night, as the five of them talked, Sue and Jack had exchanged glances, held hands, and basically transmitted messages between them that they wanted to be alone. She leaned over, placing her hands on either side of Jack's head; she gave him a long passionate kiss. It was by far the best kiss he had ever shared with a woman. She was not only drop-dead gorgeous, but she was also extremely passionate.

"I have been wanting to do that all day," Sue said, looking into Jack's eyes.

"I hope it wasn't a disappointment."

"Not at all," she said as they kissed again.

As things got more serious, Jack suggested that Sue join him sleeping on the couch.

"Not tonight, Jack Roach, but I definitely share your feelings. We can talk tomorrow." She gave Jack one last kiss and headed to her room. Jack watched her walk to the hallway, thinking she had to be the most spectacular girl he had ever met. He settled onto the couch, trying to sleep, but found it very difficult as he could not stop thinking about this girl. Finally, after two hours of tossing and turning, he fell into a restless sleep.

The next morning, Jack was awakened by a kiss. As he opened his eyes, he saw Sue standing over him dressed in just an oversize New York Yankees T-shirt. The T-shirt only came down to the top of her thighs. The outfit was very difficult for Jack to handle. He once again made the mental note that she had the greatest legs ever.

"You know I'm a Red Sox fan and we hate the Yankees," he said in a half-asleep voice. "But I must admit I have never seen a Yankee shirt look any better."

"I knew you weren't perfect, and I would begin seeing major faults. This Red Sox thing is only the beginning." With that, she squeezed down onto what was left of the sofa. As she leaned over him, kissing him, he thought he might explode with emotion. She mercifully sat up straight and began a serious conversation about what they could do for the day. As he listened, he was sure he would be unable to get from under the one blanket she had given him for quite a while.

It was Saturday, so she had no classes. After breakfast, they took a walk to the NYU campus with Sue guiding the way, pointing out the more important highlights. They held hands as they walked around the campus, which was something Jack never did with anyone else. He was so taken with this girl that all the usual standoffishness was broken. He was never much for public displays of affection, but with her it was different.

They had lunch, Dutch treat, at a Greek restaurant, then went to the Bronx so Jack could see Yankee Stadium. He hated the Yankees, but being a baseball fan, he wanted to see the iconic park, and this was his first trip to the Big Apple.

She took the opportunity to point out how many World Series had been played there, as opposed to Fenway Park, just a little jab at him. He found that he even enjoyed her consistently getting one up on him. She was obviously as bright as she was beautiful.

They made their way back to Sue's apartment by late afternoon, and only Carol was there, studying at the table. Jack whispered, "I was really hoping the place would be empty."

"Don't worry, Tiger, Kathy is going to take the couch tonight, leaving the bedroom to you and me if you behave yourself."

Jack smiled at this revelation and began counting the minutes before they could retire to the bedroom. They had a light dinner after the other two roommates showed up. Everyone knew the plan so very early in the evening Kathy said, "We are headed to a party so you two can have the place to yourselves for a while. Please don't make so much noise that you cause us trouble with the neighbors." They all laughed at this as Jack's face turned red. He had been waiting for this opportunity since he first laid eyes on her. The anticipation was killing him.

The three roommates left, kiddingly wishing Sue good luck. As soon as they were out the door, Sue grabbed Jack, giving him a kiss, and then took his hand leading him down the hall to the bedroom. They stood next to the bed, kissing and undressing each other. When they lay down in the bed, they were both naked. Jack took his time exploring the taut, shapely body with his hands. Sue did the same. Jack worked his way down her body, giving her oral sex that led her to a noisy climax. When he couldn't wait any longer, she surprised him by rolling on top of him. She guided him into her, and they made passionate love together. Jack had been with a number of women, but he felt that this was the first time he had ever truly made love. The emotional experience was unlike anything before for him.

They spent the night together, making love four different times. Jack knew it was by far the best sex he had ever experienced. Sue felt the same as Jack repeatedly brought her to multiple orgasms.

As they woke the next morning, Jack knew he would have to head back to Maine. He would miss his Monday classes and could not afford to miss two days of classes. As they lay in bed together, leaving New York was the last thing he wanted to do. He did not want to leave her, so he expressed that to her.

"I don't want this weekend to be the end, Sue. I've never met anyone like you. Anyone who makes me feel the way you do. I want to see a lot more of you."

"I think you've seen all there is of me," she responded laughingly. Then she got serious.

"I feel the same way, Jack Roach," she said while looking him in the eyes. They embraced, holding each other for a long time, neither one wanting to let go. Finally, they surrendered to the inevitable.

They showered and dressed while the three roommates, who got in late, slept. They had coffee and a bagel, then Sue went with Jack to the bus station where Jack bought a bus ticket to Portland. He lacked the funds to go all the way to Bangor, so he bought a ticket to Portland. He figured he could hitchhike from Portland with twelve dollars still in his pocket. Sue offered to give him money to get to Bangor, but Jack refused.

They parted company as Jack's bus was ready to leave. Vowing to get back together as soon as possible, Jack watched her from the window of the bus as she waved good bye, feeling sick to his stomach that he had to leave her. He knew this could not be the end.

He would pursue a long-term relationship with this girl. She would never be out of his thoughts. His first order of business, however, would be to patch things up with his three travel companions.

Chapter VII

Vietnam

BRUCE ARRIVED BACK IN VIETNAM in May of 1969, assigned to Tiger Force in the 101st Airborne First Battalion 327th infantry regiment. Tiger Force had been formed for the express purpose to "out-guerilla the guerillas." They employed guerilla warfare tactics, operating for the most part in Vietnam's Central Highlands. They employed hit-and-run tactics, laying out the same type booby traps as the VC. They operated deep into enemy territory, employing both sniper and reconnaissance work. They disrupted supply lines and food lines to cause as much havoc as possible. A small elite and highly decorated unit that saw heavy action and sustained heavy casualties. They often met the enemy face to face, employing hand-to-hand combat as well as the hit-and-run tactics. The members of this unit were among the best and bravest fighters in the US Armed Forces. They were well trained and in excellent physical condition.

This unit had run Operation Wheeler in the Song Ve Valley from May to November 1969, for which they would much later be accused of heinous war crimes, including murder of unarmed civilians, mutilating dead VC, and wearing necklaces made of human ears. The investigation would happen years later, and the actions took place before Bruce arrived as part of the unit. However, even while Bruce served in the unit, he was quickly made aware that all the proper rules of war were not always followed. The unit was made up of hard-driving soldiers who were taught to take no prisoners. They were encouraged to run up body counts. Taking prisoners was not a practice they ever employed. Their operation often employed close in fighting, bayonet actions, and hand-to-hand combat. Each man knew that casualties in the unit were expected. One operation to rescue a platoon of soldiers pinned down by the enemy resulted in more than half of the forty-five Tiger Force combatants either killed or wounded. Their missions were dangerous, so the unit was made up of soldiers like Bruce King, who would thrive in dangerous situations. It was a fierce unit that constantly pushed the envelope of what would be considered proper military practice. He was told all the stories stemming from Operation Wheeler in order to indoctrinate him into how things were done in Tiger Force.

In the summer of 1969, Bruce had a fellow Tiger Force comrade take a series of three pictures of him slitting the throat of a VC who was on his knees in front of him. The Viet Cong soldier was badly beaten and barely conscious. Bruce had heard the stories of fellow Tiger Force soldiers sending pictures, as well as cutoff ears, to people back home. He wanted the pictures to send to Jack to show what it was really like to be in Vietnam. He also wanted to show his fellow Tiger Force comrades that he was one of them. His three months with Tiger Force had changed him from a heroic, solid, good soldier to a vicious killer. It was a subtle change over time that Bruce did not fully understand while it was happening to him. He somehow felt far less noble, and his basic sense of right and wrong would often take over, making him feel sick, but the change progressed. Sleepless nights and sick feelings notwithstanding, the Tiger Force experience was making him cold, ruthless, and vicious. The fact that he wanted to send his best friend proof of this change may well have been a subconscious cry for help. He mailed Jack a letter, including the three pictures that captured the atrocity. He did not anticipate what a position his friend would be put in receiving such pictures.

Back in Maine, Jack received the letter from Bruce, opening it hurriedly, expecting news about his friend's plans to come home in the spring. Instead, three pictures fell out along with the letter. He picked up the pictures and was revolted by what he saw.

In the first picture, a smiling Bruce King was holding an obviously beaten and bruised Viet Cong soldier by the hair of his head. He held a knife in his right hand as he looked straight into the camera. In the second picture, he had applied the knife to the throat of the Viet Cong, and Bruce's face was strained as he was obviously putting pressure on the knife. In the third picture, he had completed slitting the throat of his captor, and blood had flowed everywhere, and the life had been taken from the Viet Cong soldier. The worst part of the picture was that Bruce was still smiling. It was an obnoxious display of brutality.

Jack went gagging into the bathroom, afraid he was going to vomit. What had happened to his friend? How had he been transformed into this cold-blooded killing machine? Did he no longer have any feelings, any moral compass? Is this what war did to a person? It couldn't be—he knew other friends and relatives who had served in wartime, and he could not imagine them doing something like this. This was barbaric, way beyond any rules of war.

He was able to hold off any vomit. He went over to the sink, splashing water in his face. He went back to the kitchen table and opened the letter. All it said in big printed letters was "Greetings from Vietnam." His stomach turned again as he held back vomiting. What could he do with these damn pictures? *Take them to the army recruiting station*, was his first thought. The army needed to know what was going on with one of their soldiers. Were these types of atrocities common in war? Would reporting what his friend had done just get him in trouble? Should he just destroy the pictures pretending he never saw them? Jack wrestled with his decision. The entire drama made him sick. He wished Bruce had never sent the pictures.

He decided to talk it over with the man whose opinion he relied on the most. A man who had also seen the effects of war. His father. He waited until the restaurant closed, and his father came home from work. He asked his father to join him in the den so the two could talk alone. When they were settled into the den, he began telling his story, hoping his father could tell him how best to handle things.

"Dad, Bruce sent me some pictures from Vietnam that showed an American soldier committing an atrocity." He held back the knowledge that the soldier was Bruce, not wanting to admit it to his father or really, not to himself.

"What do you mean, atrocity?"

"An American soldier was slitting the throat of a helpless, defenseless, beaten Viet Cong."

His father nodded but remained silent, so Jack went on, "Is this type of thing common in wartime? To kill an absolutely defenseless man who could just as easily be taken prisoner? Is this what American soldiers do?"

Jack Sr. considered the questions for a long time before answering. "A lot of things happen in a war that are unsavory. It happens on both sides. War is nothing like what you see in John Wayne movies. It's ugly, it's mean, and it's sick. Still, in my experience in World War II, I did not witness anything of that kind. US soldiers are people just like us who get called into service. They are trained to be professional, and in my experience and opinion, they are the most professional, moral fighting men and women in the world. Having said that, like anything else in life, there are soldiers that go bad during the experience. The army will deal with them, they always have." It was the kind of straight, no-nonsense, well-reasoned answer Jack was used to getting from his father. Still, he did not know what to do with the pictures.

"Should I take these photos to an army office? Is it my responsibility to report this type of action to the army?"

Again, a pause before answering. He closed his eyes momentarily, scratched his head, then looked at his son. "That decision is totally up to you. You have not said that the soldier involved is Bruce and I'm not asking. If you turn those pictures over, whoever the soldier is will be in trouble with the army. It could have dire consequences for him, ranging from a dishonorable discharge to time in jail. So you decide what you want to do, but understand that there may well be consequences."

Jack nodded and thanked his father. He went back about trying to concentrate on studying for an upcoming test but found he couldn't concentrate. He gave in, poured himself an Irish whiskey on the rocks. He sat for a long time, wrestling with his decision. He finally went to bed, still not sure what he would do about the pictures. He spent a restless night without much sleep.

As he awoke the next morning, he decided to just throw them away and never discuss the matter again with anyone, including Bruce himself. He hoped that Bruce would never bring it up. He also hoped that when he got out of Vietnam, Bruce would be the person he had always been before his time there, not the person in the pictures.

Chapter VIII

In December of 1969, as Jack was finishing his third semester, college deferments ended as the draft lottery was established. Depending on the month and day of your birth, you were arbitrarily assigned a number for draft purposes. The numbers ran from one to three hundred sixty-six to account for Leap Year. It was an unpopular change because of the possibility that doing away with college deferments might result in more wealthy sons ending up in the service. It was a fear that proved unfounded as the wealthy continued to find ways to keep their little darlings out of harm's way by claiming flat feet, bone spurs or some other made up malady while the poor fought the war. It seemed to Jack that in the United States, the wealthy always seemed to find a way around life's little annoyances. Jack was lucky as he drew number 179, which proved to be high enough that he was never called into service. Given his thoughts about the Vietnam War, he had no intention of enlisting.

As his sophomore year came to a close, the event that pushed him over the edge, in terms of his anti-war and anti-establishment leanings, happened at an antiwar protest at Kent State University. In May of 1970, four college students were shot dead by National Guard soldiers who had been brought to the campus during a peaceful protest. The number of college campus protests against the war had caused many campus officials to overreact to protests on their campus with extreme caution. Bringing in the National Guard was unusual but not unprecedented. The event sent shock waves around the country and once again intensified sentiments against the war and against the government. To Jack it was the proverbial straw that broke the camel's back. Having attended protests himself, he could not imagine how a peaceful demonstration had resulted in this horror with college students actually shot dead.

He joined a late-night protest march on the campus president's house. Several hundred students got the president of the University of Maine out of bed at one in the morning and demanded he cancel classes for the rest of the semester. That was followed two days later by the largest rally on the campus to date as over one thousand students rallied on the library steps. It was ten times the size of the crowd at some of the earlier rallies. Even the quiet University of Maine campus had been stirred to action. The actions remained peaceful in nature but there were obviously high emotions involved. While not all classes were canceled, a good few were, and those that were not were taught by professors who could not wait to see the school year come to a close. Many of the faculty felt the same as the students.

Unlike a number of students who simply left school early, Jack finished his classes. He was working his way through school and the money for tuition, and books came hard. He was not going to waste it by leaving early and risk receiving incomplete grades for some key classes. His preoccupation with the campus unrest during finals week resulted in his lowest grade point average in his four years at Maine.

Before classes ended, Jack got more active in the campus chapter of the Students for a Democratic Society, the SDS. This was a national organization active on many campuses across America. It was viewed as a radical anti-establishment organization, and its leadership was constantly on the FBI's watch list. It was generally believed that its membership would find future employment possibilities adversely affected by their participation in the SDS. Jack didn't care about these or any other warnings. He was hell bent on joining the movement to end this war and to bring new transparency and accountability to the US government that seemed to becoming ever more corrupt. It was the Nixon years when the White House was home to the nation's most corrupt administration.

Even with all these things going on, Jack's thoughts were never far from Sue Frazier. They exchanged letters and phone calls, trying to keep as close to one another as possible. As the semester ended, they agreed to meet in Portland on the fourth weekend in May. Jack had finished his finals and was through his spring semester. Sue had one final left to take on Wednesday of the following week. Jack could not wait to see her again. Since he left New York, not a day had gone by that he did not spend half his time thinking of her. The memory of his time spent with her was his last thought every night before he fell asleep.

Sue arrived in Portland by bus, around noontime on Saturday. Jack had driven down in his 1963 Pontiac Tempest that he purchased three months before, for two hundred fifty dollars. All the way down to Portland from Old Town, he said silent prayers that the car would make it. He met her at the bus station, and they embraced like two long-lost lovers. It felt like heaven to have her back in his arms. "This is my favorite place in the world, Jack, in your arms," was her opening line.

"It feels like years since I've seen you, but it's only been months," Jack said as he broke away from a kiss.

"I know, I've missed you every day. I could not wait for this weekend." Jack had spent a lot more money on hotel reservations than he could afford. Plus, he took money with him for meals and other expenses, determined to show Sue a good time whatever the cost and however broke it left him.

"Well, I will give you a tour of Portland's Old Port, but first, I have made reservations for tonight and tomorrow night at the Holiday Inn by the Bay. I think we should go there first to make sure the beds are the way we like them." Jack said this while looking her in the eyes and smiling.

She smiled and nodded her approval. "I'm sure, Jack, that whatever shape that bed is in, it will be in a lot worse shape when we leave." They headed for Jack's car. Parked next to his clunker was a new Lincoln Continental. Jack made as if he were going to the driver's door of that car. "Wow," Sue said with an impressed tone.

Jack chuckled and said, "Just kidding." She snapped her fingers in a motion to show mock disappointment.

With that, he moved to the Tempest, and they both chuckled. "This is more in line with what I expected from you, Jack. Actually,

I like this better. For a minute there, I thought I was hooked up with some pretentious asshole."

"Now you know it's just an asshole with no money."

"That's correct," she answered, reminding Jack of her smart-ass wit.

They drove to the hotel, checked in, and went right to their room. Jack unlocked the door of their room then surprised Sue by picking her up and carrying her across the threshold. As soon as he put her down, they began undressing each other as they kissed. The passion between them had not lessened over their time apart. In fact, it seemed to have increased dramatically.

They fell on the bed, both of them naked. They made love hungrily and passionately, after which they lay next to each other, exhausted.

"Making love to you, Jack, is a real workout. Even though it goes on for a long time, I never want it to end. It's almost magical how great it is."

"The pleasure is all mine," Jack responded.

"Like hell it is. The pleasure is mutual."

Jack smiled at this, continuing to lie next to her. He reached over and held her hand, and the two of them lay like that for an extended period, simply taking in the pleasure of each other's company. Finally Sue moved over and began kissing Jack while fondling his genitals. After a short time, he was erect again. She climbed on top, guiding him into her, and they made love again. The two of them could not get enough of each other. Neither had ever experienced anything quite like this intense, insatiable desire.

That night, they walked the Old Port, they ate at the Italian Village, listened to live music at the Old Port Pub, then settled back into their hotel room. They talked about school, they talked about war, but mostly they talked about the tragedy at Kent State. They shared shock and sadness about the incident. They both felt the anti-war protests would intensify again, and they both wanted to be a part of it. It was the only way they felt they could have any effect on the tragic direction their country was taking.

"I can't believe that four students were shot dead for protesting a war," Sue said. "The National Guard soldier wasn't any older than the kids that were shot. You can't help but feel sorry for them being put in that position."

"I know the whole thing is insane," Jack answered.

"It shows how raw the emotions have become in this country. We have to keep at it, Jack. We have to keep active."

"The protests are important, Sue, but we really need to get involved in the elections to put people in Washington that want to end this thing. We need to get Nixon and his crooked cronies out. Replace him with someone who will bring this country back together."

"Agreed. Especially the next presidential campaign. You have a candidate from Maine that we could get behind. They say right now he's the front runner for the Democrats."

"Yeah, Ed Muskie should be the vice president right now," Jack observed. "If people had been smart enough to vote against the crook currently in the White House, Muskie would be our VP today."

"We should get involved in his campaign. It will give us something to do together in addition to making love. Don't get me wrong—we have to continue making love as often as physically possible."

Jack smiled, nodding his agreement. "If we are as good at campaigning as we are at making love, Muskie's as good as elected."

They agreed to explore the possibility of volunteering on the Muskie campaign once it shifted into high gear. It was another area in which they could work together for constructive change.

They repeated the routine on Sunday, making love several more times around walks and meals. As Sunday night came, they knew their time together was winding down.

"I hate to have this weekend end," Sue said as they walked back into the hotel lobby late Sunday afternoon.

"I know. It's been one of the greatest times of my life being here with you. Why don't you transfer up to U. Maine for your senior year?" Jack made the suggestion tongue in cheek, knowing it could not happen.

"I can't do that. You know I can't do that. Maybe you should transfer to NYU."

"I guess I do, it's just wishful thinking, and I could never afford NYU. I can only afford U.Maine because I live at home."

"What about this summer, Jack, can we get together? We have to, we should make plans now to see each other over the summer."

"I have to work for a construction company all summer to pay my tuition. Maybe we can get together on weekends or something. But the problem there is, I work weekends at our family restaurant. Maybe you can get up to Maine."

"It's your turn to come to Burke, Vermont, now that I have come up to Maine. We have a beautiful state, you need to see it."

"Well, you stuck your big toe into Maine. I mean, you only came to Portland. Many of us further north think of Portland as part of Massachusetts. Still, I agree and I would like that. I have never been to Vermont. I hear it's a beautiful state. That would involve meeting your family, I assume?"

She looked at him while nodding. "Yeah, that's probably true, but they don't bite."

"Tell me about your family. I know nothing about them."

"Well, my father died young. He's been gone for five years now. So my mother has raised me and my sister Gail. My sister is older than me. She is married with a son and lives in Nashua, New Hampshire. So I live alone with my mom. She is still young enough that she's as much a friend as she is my mother. We do a lot of things together."

"I'm, sorry to hear of your father's passing. It must have been hard on all of you to lose him so young. And it must be equally hard on your mother being left alone.

"Well, he left her quite wealthy, so finances are fine, but she is alone. She has been seeing someone, but I don't think it's serious. At least not yet."

"Well, I will definitely get to Burke, Vermont, this summer as many times as I can."

"There should also be a protest or two we can hit together. I don't want you to get rusty, Jack."

They continued to explore the idea of participating in any scheduled events of political unrest.

They agreed to make every effort to get together as often as possible throughout the summer, whether it be in Burke, in Maine, or at planned protests.

On Monday morning, Jack dropped her off at the bus station. They said their sad goodbyes as she headed to New York, and Jack headed back to Old Town. Again, he worried all the way back that his car may not get him there.

Over the summer, Jack was indeed tied up working for a local construction company ten to twelve hours a day, Monday through Friday, then Friday night and Saturday in the restaurant. He did manage to get a friend to cover his restaurant duty so he could get to Vermont three times, but they never got to any anti-war protests. It was difficult enough getting the time to get to Vermont.

In Vermont, they hiked some mountains, swam in some of Vermont's pristine lakes, and generally spent the weekends ecstatic to be in each other's company. Jack fell in love with the relaxed rural nature of Vermont. They spent Labor Day weekend together in Vermont knowing it would be the last one for a while. They would both be headed back to school on the following Tuesday.

Jack met Sue's mother, Elaine. She was a very young-looking fifty-something, and it was easy to see where Sue got her good looks. The large three-bedroom home they lived in bore out the fact that the widow was left well-off financially. She was dating a local man who ran a large bed-and-breakfast resort, so Jack and Sue got a good bit of alone time. It seemed to Jack that Elaine's relationship with her male friend was a bit more serious than Sue thought it to be. Jack enjoyed Elaine's company very much, so the alone time with Sue was great, but having Elaine with them was also pleasurable. She treated Jack like he was family.

As the summer was ending, they were both headed back to school, Sue for her senior year, Jack his junior year. Jack was sure that for the first time in his life, he was in love.

* * * * *

Vietnam

Bruce continued his activities with the Tiger Force. He was surprised and a bit disappointed that he got no response from his best friend after sending the pictures. It did not change the way he was operating.

He was keeping a running count of the number of Viet Cong he had killed. Within the Tiger Force, there was competition around the question of who had killed the most enemies. Bruce ranked in the top three and worked hard to maintain that status. It provided him with top standing among his peers.

At one point, they evacuated a small village suspected of providing food to the VC troops. It was part of their function to interrupt supply lines. The village occupants were obviously reluctant to leave. Bruce threatened several with his weapon. These were unarmed civilians. Old men and women and young kids. He had all he could do to resist shooting some of them, but he had not yet sunk that low. Still, the fact that the urge was present was bad enough. A couple of his fellow Tiger Force comrades did not resist the urge, so four older villagers, three male and one female, were shot to make an example for the others. At one time, he would never imagine himself shooting defenseless civilians. That had changed. He reflected on this in some of his more thoughtful moments. He knew innocent civilians had been killed by some of his fellow Tiger Force comrades in the past. It was a bit troubling that he was no longer repulsed by the idea. In September, after four Viet Cong had surrendered, dropping their weapons, six Tiger Force soldiers opened fire on them as they stood unarmed with their hands in the air. It was the first time he had opened fire on an unarmed enemy. It would not be the last.

His slide away from the moral compass he once had continued unabated. The killing of surrendering Viet Cong soldiers, as well as unarmed civilians would continue throughout the remainder of his tour.

In the spring of 1970, as Bruce was wrapping up his second tour of duty in Vietnam, he was once again approached by an official looking to recruit him. This recruitment would prove to be even more of a life change than the last.

Chapter IX

Vietnam

ON APRIL 22, 1970, COLONEL David Haywood was in his office when he was approached by a CIA official named Coleman Young. Young was in Vietnam for the purpose of reporting the progress of the war and the progress of accompanying CIA operations to CIA headquarters in Langley, Virginia. He reported directly to the Directorate of Operations in Charge of Covert Action. His function in Nam was to cooperate with military field activities, gather intelligence, and report to military intelligence as well as CIA headquarters.

On this occasion, his purpose was completely different. He was meeting with the colonel on a recruiting mission. The agency had followed closely the activities of Tiger Force, focusing particular attention on several key members of that unit. His purpose in meeting with Haywood was to discuss several of the soldiers under his command in Tiger Force. One of these soldiers was Bruce King. He was questioning Haywood to get his opinions on the soldiers Young had decided might be CIA material. As he wrapped up his questions on the first two prospects, he moved on to King.

"Okay, so tell me about Private Bruce King," Young asked.

"Like the rest of my force, he is a hard-driven soldier. A tough individual who knows how to follow orders. Knows how to accomplish objectives. He is one of our best men."

Haywood had no hesitation in praising Bruce as a soldier. A quality individual that you could count on in a tough situation. The kind of man you would always want to have on your side.

"That has been my impression in watching from a distance. Would you describe him as one of your more disciplined recruits? As a loyal member of the force?"

Haywood did not have to think long about his answer. "Private King is a loyal American. He has tremendous courage as well as tremendous discipline. He is the kind of soldier you would want covering your back in the most intense situations."

"Colonel, you know what I would want from a recruit, and you know where I would send him. Is Bruce King a good prospect for what I have in mind, and would you recommend him?"

With no hesitation Haywood answered, "A resounding yes to both questions."

With that, the meeting ended, Coleman Young shook hands with the colonel, leaving the meeting with Private Bruce King on the top of the list of soldiers he intended to meet with next. The colonel had just confirmed Young's own impressions about Bruce King.

Bruce was working toward the finish line of his second tour of duty. He had less than a month to go on the tour and a bit over three months to finish his entire hitch in the army. His problem, as he approached the end, was that he didn't know what he wanted to do when it was all over. Up until the past few months, he had always planned on returning to Old Town, Maine, finishing high school and finding a job. Now he wasn't sure how that plan fit into what he wanted for a future. He was considering seriously staying in the army. He had come to like the excitement, the danger he was experiencing. He was unsure now if he would be happy with the rather humdrum life that Old Town had to offer. The rather boring existence that civilian life had to offer. He liked the danger, the excitement, the adrenaline flow it all gave him. He could not imagine civilian life providing any of that.

By the same token, a life in the army after Vietnam may hold no more excitement than a civilian job. As sad as it all seemed to him, he had become accustomed to war and actually thrived on the danger of it all. The realization of how his feelings had changed actually scared him at times, but he had come to accept it as the reality of his life. He had spent two full years fighting against a people who Uncle Sam identified as the enemy. It was now his lifestyle, and he did not think he wanted it to change. He was totally indoctrinated to the life of a soldier at war.

On April 27, Bruce was summoned to headquarters. He assumed he would be meeting with Colonel Haywood. When he arrived, he was greeted by a civilian who was a stranger to him. As Bruce approached him, the civilian extended his hand for a hand-shake. Bruce was so used to saluting that he automatically brought his right hand up to a salute. The civilian returned the salute and introduced himself.

"Private King, my name is Coleman Young, and I appreciate you taking the time to meet with me."

Bruce stood at attention out of habit and answered, "It is good to meet you, Mr. Young, but frankly, I thought I was coming to meet with my colonel."

"Okay, so I did not intend any trickery in getting you here. I apologize for the confusion. Please take a seat, soldier, and be at ease." He motioned to a chair as he invited Bruce to take a seat. Bruce had no idea what this could all be about, and he was anxious for some answers.

They each took a seat at a small conference table in the colonel's office. Bruce took the opportunity to take stock of the man across the table. He stood at 6'1" or 6'2". He wore a gray suit with a shirt and tie, but the suit did not hide the fact that he was obviously in top physical condition. He had a military-style buzz cut, and Bruce estimated his age in the midforties range.

"So I imagine you are curious as to the purpose of my asking to meet with you," Young said in opening the conversation.

"I assume we will get to that immediately." Bruce made no attempt to hide the fact that he expected to get right down to business.

"You don't want to waste time with small talk. I appreciate that. Let me tell you who I am. I have been with the CIA for eighteen years. I operate within the Special Activities Division. The CIA is the head of our nation's intelligence community. We are focused on over-seas intelligence gathering. We are authorized by law to carry out and oversee covert action on behalf of our nation. One of my functions here in Vietnam, along with providing intelligence to the military, has been to observe soldiers like you and recruit them into service with the agency. In a nutshell, that is the purpose of my request to meet with you today."

Young stopped here, looking for a reaction from Bruce. There was not one coming as Bruce sat silently looking at Mr. Young. His expression gave nothing away, so Young had no clue how his remarks were being received. After a time, Young continued, "You have no reaction at all, Private King?"

"I have spent most of the past three years learning to never volunteer information. I would like more specifics on what you have in mind before I give you a response."

"Fair enough. The CIA has use for loyal, disciplined patriots with your skill set. We operate an assassin's training facility that is intended to cultivate discipline and a killer instinct. You have seen firsthand, Private King, that there are enemies of the United States that need to be dealt with by us. We do not always have an opportunity to deal with them in the context of a war zone. That duty falls onto the CIA, and we train people to accomplish what needs to be done. We would be looking to train you to serve in the capacity of field agent for the CIA. Duties would include missions in foreign countries, dealing with situations in those countries that endanger United States interests."

Again, Bruce sat silent while he contemplated his response. He was not naive and was well aware of the reputation of the CIA. He answered, "So you are looking for an assassin, basically?"

"That's correct. Does that shake you?" This was an important question to Young. He needed to know if Bruce would have a taste for the kind of duty he would be asked to perform.

"No, I've heard of black ops and covert operations. I realize what the agency has to do to protect the nation."

This was the type of answer Young was hoping to hear. A trained soldier with full appreciation for the dangerous world in which he lived. A soldier who understood what needed to be done to keep the nation safe.

"I'm not sure that being a trained assassin is what I want for the rest of my life."

"I don't want you to get too hung up on the term *assassin*, Private King. Basically, you will go through a type of training that is necessary for that type of work, but you will be an agency asset that will be asked to perform a variety of duties."

"Let's take first things, first, Mr. Young. Explain to me the training that you would expect me to go through." Bruce had already had more than his share of difficult training sessions. He was looking for an honest answer with no sugar coating.

"Those who go through CIA assassin training must be disciplined, loyal, courageous, and secretive. You will be trained in the martial arts and in the use of explosives, as well as various other weapons. The training is extremely rigorous and can take anywhere from six months to two years. When you have finished, you will be in the best shape of your life, and your body will be as lethal as any of the weapons on which you have received training. During the training, there will be no outside communication. You will be tested physically as well as mentally. We will see what you are made of, and you will find out as well."

Bruce mulled this over as he continued to size up Coleman Young. He had received the honest, straightforward answers he was seeking. After a time, he asked, "When I'm finished, I'm a trained CIA asset for how long of a commitment?"

"It's not like joining the army, Private King. Our operatives put CIA missions above all personal relationships and duties. I will not sugarcoat it—you will be required to live a life of secrecy and to risk your life on a regular basis. You will not be able to confide in anyone outside the agency, even to divulge who you are working for. It is not an easy life. It is the ultimate way to serve your country, and that is the major reward."

Bruce sat thinking of his options. He was concerned that a return to civilian life would no longer suit him. He was equally concerned that army life state side would be much the same as civilian life. He did still desire to serve his country but was unsure of this particular type of service. Did he really want to make the commitment to become a CIA asset and spend the next twenty years or more following orders from people like Coleman Young? He decided he would have to take his time considering this proposal.

"I will give this some thought, Mr. Young. How do I get in touch with you?"

"I will get back to you, Private King, one week from today. I will require an answer then. My intention in saying so is not to pressure you. I simply must know in one week so that if your answer is no, I can move on to other options. Your inclination will be to discuss this with others. I will caution you not to do that as secrecy is a prime requirement of the job. You will have to be your own council."

Young stood and extended his hand to Bruce, who shook it this time. "I will meet you right here one week from today at the same time."

With that, Bruce walked out of the office with a lot to think about. Over the next six days, he went over his options as he saw them. A high school dropout by necessity, he had no expectation that private sector employment would be lucrative or enjoyable. The requirements of CIA life as laid out by Mr. Young seemed arduous but really not much more so than army life. He came to the conclusion that his misspent youth had really left him with few attractive options for his future. As many times as he went over it, he seemed to end up in the same place. As unsure as he was that life as a CIA operative was what he wanted, he was equally unsure that any of his other options would be fulfilling. As Young had pointed out, it was not like joining the military. Presumably he could get out if it was not working.

He went back to meet again with Coleman Young right on schedule, prepared to give his answer. He was greeted again by a handshake and then offered a chair.

"It's good to see you again, Private King," Young said as he sat down in a chair opposite Bruce.

"I have a couple of questions for you, Mr. Young. I have roughly three more months to serve in the army. I assume that if I accept your offer, I finish my service in the army."

"No. If your answer is yes, you will be leaving here within one week, headed to our training facility with an honorable discharge. There will be no requirement for you to finish your army hitch because you will still be serving your country."

Bruce thought about this for a moment. He wanted some time for himself before entering their training. He followed with another question.

"Can I ask where the training facility is located?"

"No." A direct, curt answer with no apology for the bluntness.

"The leave time I have accumulated is lost?"

"That's correct. We would allow you a brief R&R in Hawaii before training begins, but a two-week leave back in Maine is out. As I have explained, we do not want you discussing this with friends or family. If you choose to be a CIA agent, it is a profession that is kept secret from those outside the agency."

Again, absolutely no attempt at niceties.

"What am I to tell the folks back in Maine who are expecting me?"

"You tell them you have signed up for additional duties with the United States army and that you will be out of touch for some time. No more than that."

Bruce sat contemplating these answers that were harsher than expected. He did want to return to Maine for two weeks, and he did not like all the secrecy. He also did not like Coleman Young, and he wondered if everyone in the CIA was this big of an asshole. He usually appreciated straight talk and blunt responses, but this guy seemed to take it a bit too far.

Young spoke up again before Bruce had responded.

"I know what you're thinking, Private. You're thinking you could take your two-week leave in Maine then give me an affirmative answer. That won't work. I need an answer in the affirmative today, or it's the last you will hear from us."

The pre-army Bruce would have responded to this ultimatum with a firm "fuck you." The Bruce who sat here now was not as cock-sure of his future. Not so easily dismissive of things because he was far more inclined to take matters more seriously. He had made up his mind to move onto the CIA, but he did not care for the browbeating he felt he was taking from Young. He spoke after a long silence.

"I have one nonnegotiable requirement. While I am in training, I want to be able to finish the high school education the court and the army took away from me. I want a high school diploma."

"That can be arranged."

Bruce hesitated for a long moment then said, "I will take you up on a four- or five-day R&R in Hawaii and agree to join the CIA." There it was, the commitment Young was looking for, and Bruce was still unsure it was the right thing for him even as he made the statement.

Young stood up again, extending his hand to his new recruit. "You will make a great addition to our agency. This will provide you a tremendous opportunity to continue to serve your country."

They shook hands and parted company. That night, Bruce wrote two long letters, one to his mother and one to his friend Jack Roach. He explained that he had signed on for more duty with the army and would not be coming home on leave. He left everything quite vague out of necessity. He did make it clear that it would be some time before they heard from him again. Three days later, he was in Hawaii on R&R. Four days after that, he was in a secret CIA training facility in Georgia.

Jack Roach received the very perplexing letter and immediately sent a response, looking for some clarification. He posted the letter to the army return address provided by Bruce. His letter, as well as the next two that he addressed to the Army, came back "return to sender."

Chapter X

JACK WAS MILDLY CONCERNED ABOUT Bruce when his first letter to him came back "return to sender." Through the summer, as two more letters were returned, he became more concerned. The letter he had received from Bruce had been very vague. It required far more explanation, but none seemed to be forthcoming. He had no access to him and no way of getting any clarity to his situation. He had discussed it with his army veteran father who also felt it was peculiar.

He discussed it with Sue on a couple of occasions, explaining to her the entire situation of how Bruce ended up in the army. She had no explanation as to what was going on and no suggestions of how to proceed. Jack did not tell her about the pictures Bruce had sent. He saw no point in poisoning her impressions of his best friend before she even met him. He thought, given the pictures, that perhaps Bruce was in some type of rehabilitation program because of all he had been through. He ran that idea by his father, who agreed it was a possibility, but thought even if it was the case, he could still answer a letter. It was all very troubling, but life still goes on, and Jack was entering his junior year of college.

In late September, Jack and Sue were able to spend a weekend at a campground near Old Orchard Beach. They spent days on the beach, swimming, joining in on volleyball games, and relaxing in the sun. Jack had the camping equipment, so they stayed two nights in a tent. He brought two sleeping bags, but as it turned out, they only used one. While they were together, they made plans to both participate in a planned anti-war protest in New York on the first weekend of October. It was another opportunity to get together as well as a chance to express their opposition to the war. Jack took a bus down to New York after classes on Thursday and stayed at Sue's apartment

Thursday night through Sunday. They spent Friday walking through Central Park and visiting the American Museum of Natural History. The protest rally took place on Saturday, organized jointly by the SDS chapters on Columbia and NYU campuses. The large crowd included a good contingent from both of those schools, but there were plenty of other schools represented.

It started as a peaceful protest in Central Park, but late in the afternoon, a small group of counterprotesters showed up, and some fighting broke out. Arrests were made by New York's finest, none of which involved Jack or Sue. On Sunday, after sharing breakfast at a New York café, Jack took the bus back to Bangor. The two of them made plans to have Sue come up to meet Jack's family during Thanksgiving. Things were getting quite serious between them. Jack was sure he had met the perfect girl and wanted to spend time with her as often as possible. He could not wait to have the rest of his family meet her.

On October 19, the Nixon administration sent then Vice President Spiro Agnew to the quiet University of Maine campus. The idea was to put on a little dog and pony show on a campus that was relatively peaceful. It would show the public that the majority of college campuses were not anti-Nixon or anti-war.

The audience that gathered in Hauk Auditorium to hear this great man was handpicked by the more conservative faculty and administration officials in cooperation with the campus republicans. As his helicopter landed, the five hundred or more protesters, including Jack, were cordoned off behind police barricades a good three hundred yards from the helicopter pad. Protest chants were hollered loudly, but neither Agnew nor the press could hear them. He, of course, waved to the crowd as if they were there to be his friendly greeters. Inside, the handpicked crowd cheered, and the entire staged show went as planned. Jack couldn't believe what a staged bit of bullshit the whole thing was. His distaste for the hypocrisy of American politics was once again enhanced by yet another phony display. His desire to see the end of the Nixon administration was enhanced by the spectacle.

The Wednesday before Thanksgiving, Jack picked Sue up at the Bangor bus station in the late afternoon. It was her first trip to Bangor, Maine. Indeed, it was her first trip north of Portland. She was extremely nervous about meeting Jack's family. She stepped off the bus and fell into Jack's arms. As they embraced, she said, "Jack, I can't believe how nervous I am about meeting your family. I'm so nervous I'm shaking."

"Oh, come on, where's that smart-mouth wit of yours, that swagger, that confidence?"

"Back in New York where I left it."

Jack laughed then looked her in the eye and said, "Sue Frazier, you have nothing to worry about. My family is not judgmental or difficult to get along with. They will love you like I do."

With that, he kissed her then went to get her luggage. When he walked back to her, carrying her bags, he said, "The big problem is, we won't be able to sleep together. Good Irish Catholic family, you know." She put on a pouty face at this news, showing her displeasure.

"So what are they going to do, put me outside in a tent?"

"Of course not, they will put you in my sister's room. After one night with my sister, you may ask for a tent. In any case, you two can sit up all night telling each other stories about me."

"What a fathead," she responded.

"Now there's the smart-ass Sue Frazier we all know and love."

Jack's oldest sister, and the family's only conservative, was married to an army major stationed in Kansas, so she didn't make it home for Thanksgiving. His other three sisters were there, two with husbands, plus his younger brother. It made for a full house with ten adults present on Wednesday night. The restaurant closed at eight and stayed closed on Thanksgiving Day. So the entire family was together for meals, and Sue got the full flavor of Jack's family. On Wednesday night, she had her first exposure to the clan.

Being a good Irish family, Jack's mother's maiden name was O'Grady. They were a group that did not shy away from a good drink. They enjoyed talking, laughing, and poking fun at one another. All present except Jack's younger brother, who was too young, were gathered around the kitchen table enjoying a lively conversation, as well as a late-afternoon cocktail. Jack Sr. was still at the restaurant, and the evening meal of lobster, steamed clams, and salads would be held up until he got home. Jack and Sue walked in to the middle of things, and Sue was introduced to his mother, three sisters, and two brothers-in-law.

"So this is the Vermont beauty we have heard so much about," was Jack's brother-in-law, John's, first remark made with a broad smile.

"Now try not to be a complete horse's ass embarrassing this young lady before she even sits down," responded Jack's mother.

Jack grabbed a couple of beers for him and Sue and brought her over a chair. Sitting down, in an effort to set the stage, he told them all, "Susan Frazier is the prettiest young lady to ever come out of Vermont. Let's just get that out of the way. She is also a first-class smart-ass who is currently holding her tongue trying to be polite, but if you pile on her, you will be doing it at your own peril."

Jack's other brother-in-law, Chris, chimed in, "Well I just have one piece of advice for you: don't walk away from this family. Run, run like your hair's on fire and your ass is catching."

This comment brought a good round of laughter, after which Sue, who had yet to speak, said in a quiet, humble voice, "Very nice to meet you all." This brought more laughter.

As the evening wore on, Sue Frazier was a big hit. She drank along with the rest of them, her progressive liberal leanings fit right in with everyone, and her sense of humor won everyone over. Jack's father whispered to Jack as they headed for the dining room for dinner, "She is a real knockout, you should hang on to her." It was easy to be impressed with her looks, but her personality was equally enchanting.

After dinner, the conversations went on, shifting from business to sports to politics. When the topic was sports, it came out that Sue was a Yankee fan. In this house filled with Red Sox fanatics, this knowledge did not go over well. Jack switched topics to politics so she could survive the evening. Music playing in the background would occasionally result in an impromptu sing-along. People did not head to bed until after 1:00 a.m. True to Jack's prediction, Sue was shown to the room of Jack's sister rather than Jack's. He did kiss her good night, a kiss he had to sneak because open displays of affection were frowned upon in the Roach family. Hugs were few and far between, and holding hands was something that never happened.

Thanksgiving Day went much the same way, with another late night with plenty of food and drink. On Friday, Jack took her on a tour of the University of Maine campus. Being a rural campus, it was quite a change from her NYU campus, but she had visited the University of Vermont while deciding which college to attend, so she was familiar with a rural setting. She was very impressed with the beauty of the Maine campus. While at the campus, Jack took her to his fraternity house so they could finally have some privacy and share an intimate moment.

On Friday they had lunch at the Roach family's restaurant. Sue exclaimed with some surprise that her pastrami on rye was as good as anything in New York. Jack Sr. bragged that she should next try the corned beef because that would also be as good as any New York deli. After lunch, he drove her around the area, reliving a number of stories about his misspent youth with his friend, Bruce. These stories required no embellishment as the raw truth of them was shocking enough.

"You two were absolute terrors. Are these stories really true, or are you embellishing them?"

"I assure you, these stories require no embellishment. They are the truthful accounts of two friends who took life as a joke and enjoyed every moment of their misspent youth."

She could only shake her head in astonishment of some of the escapades she was hearing. He had told her that he and Bruce had pulled some capers, but now, receiving the full accounts with reference to where they occurred, was shocking. He also relayed the story of how Bruce ended up in the army. Still, the new stories she was hearing were quite revealing as to exactly how misspent his youth had been.

"Unbelievable," she said then in a more serious tone. "You were really close, weren't you?"

"Just like brothers since the sixth grade. We raised a bit of hell, but we had a great time doing it. We worked together, lived together, and partied together."

"You're worried about him now, aren't you?"

"Yeah, I have not been able to reach him since last spring. Three letters returned to me and nothing, not a word from him. It's not like him, and it's not like the army to have a soldier so out of touch, so difficult to reach."

"You have no idea what is going on with him?"

"The last word was the he had signed up for another tour of duty with the army. That makes no sense because even when he was in Nam, we wrote back and forth. Now there is no contact. Yeah, I'm concerned about it. I don't even know if he's alive or dead."

"I don't blame you." She reached over and held his hand as he drove. "I'm sure there will be an explanation at some point." She was doing her best to comfort him.

"I hope so," he said.

They returned to the Roach home in time for another fabulous dinner along with late night fun. Sue had the impression that Jack came from a very close, fun-loving family. They enjoyed each other, and they enjoyed a good time. They made her feel welcome and treated her like family. She not only felt she was welcomed by them but that she was part of them. Jack had been correct when he told her they were not judgmental. They were all progressive, liberal thinkers, and she felt right at home with them.

On Saturday, Sue had to head back to New York. She needed all day Sunday to finish work on a paper that was due on Monday. She hated to leave.

"This has been a great weekend, Jack," she said as they drove to the bus station. "Your family is great, I enjoyed every one of them."

"Well, that's because my oldest sister, our token conservative, was absent. Anyway, how could I not have a great family, being as great a person as I am?"

"Here we go. Little Sir Fathead tells it like he sees it, even though nobody else sees it that way."

They both laughed at this, but the farewell at the bus station was a sad affair. After giving her suitcase to the driver to store beneath the bus, they embraced. "I always hate to leave you, Jack. This weekend was great. The only thing missing was that we had to sleep in separate rooms. The trip to the frat house was good, but it didn't make up for three nights that I couldn't sleep with you."

"Maybe it will do us some good to abstain. Remember, I'm Catholic."

"Well, with your Catholic upbringing, it might have done you some good, but it didn't help me. We will need different arrangements for Christmas break."

"Agreed. We will have to work on that." With that, they had a long goodbye kiss and final embrace.

She boarded the bus, and once again, they waved goodbye, her from the window of the bus, him standing at the station. They both were headed back to college, knowing they would be missing each other.

Chapter XI

Bruce King started his CIA training in June of 1970. The training had been described to him as extremely difficult, and that quickly proved to be an understatement. Physically, he was put to a very demanding test on a daily basis. Long training runs, obstacle course runs, survival training, plus martial arts training on a daily basis tested his physical as well as mental endurance. He had been told that in the end, he would be in the best physical condition of his life. He had only been in the camp for a month when he concluded that to be an accurate prediction. The weight training and martial arts work were combining to add hard muscle to his five-foot-ten-inch frame. The same training was increasing his quickness and agility. He could see the effects of the hard work on a daily basis.

He was being trained on every form of weaponry designed for taking out a target. His army training on firearms paled by comparison to what he now went through. He had been shown dozens of ways to kill a person with no weapon other than his highly trained hands. Conventional weapons training, explosives training, chemical weapons poisons, and training on devices recently perfected that he had never even heard of before. He would emerge from this course a one-man death machine with an instilled killer instinct. Just as advertised. He had many moments when he questioned the wisdom of his decision.

It concerned him that he had been unable to contact the people back home in Maine. He knew they would be worried about him. He wished he could at least contact them to tell them he was all right. He found the secrecy annoying as well as unnecessary but accepted it as part of his new life.

It was a seven-day-per-week ordeal for fourteen long months until October 1971 when he was deemed fit to graduate. He walked out a twenty-one-year-old CIA agent assigned to Langley, Virginia, ready to perform whatever duties were assigned to him.

He rented an apartment in Alexandria, Virginia, close to CIA headquarters. Once he settled in, he felt it was time to make a few calls to try to explain the long period of absence. His first call was to his old friend, Jack Roach. He called the Roach house at seven at night, thinking it would be a good time to catch Jack at home. He fully expected to be confronted by an angry Jack Roach because of the extended period of silence. He expected the same from his family. He wanted to make the calls, face the music, and get it over with so he could move on.

By this time, Jack had finished his junior year, worked through the summer of 1971 on construction, and was working through the first semester of his senior year. He had all but given up on the idea of ever hearing from Bruce again. It had been fourteen months since the letter from him and the three "return to sender" letters Jack had sent. At the Roach home, Jack's sister Cathy answered the telephone.

"Hi, this is Bruce, and this sounds like Cathy."

Cathy was stunned to hear that familiar voice. All the members of the Roach family were well aware of Bruce's fourteen months of silence.

"Bruce King, you must be kidding. We had given up on you. Where the hell are you?"

"I'm in Virginia. I'm sorry about the long period of silence, but I will explain it to Jack if he's there, and then he can explain it to everyone else." Bruce obviously did not want to say his lying explanation more than once. Cathy did not push the point figuring Bruce was probably much more comfortable talking to Jack.

"Okay, hang on, and I will get Jack. He's here someplace."

After a few minutes, Jack came on the line, "Bruce King, where the fuck have you been, and why has nobody heard from you?" Exactly the response he had expected to receive and actually delivered with less anger than he expected. He tried to respond in a nonchalant manner that might defuse things a bit.

"Well, it's nice to hear your voice too."

"Come on, this is no joke. It's been over a year with no word. My letters to you came back 'return to sender.' Your mother hadn't heard from you. Come on, Bruce, what's been going on?" Jack seemed to be getting madder the more he talked. Bruce again tried to lighten things up with his response.

"Well, I'm sorry if my latest assignment has inconvenienced you people." This was Bruce's attempt to put Jack on the defensive. "But I've been a tad busy."

"Okay, big shot, busy doing what?"

Now he had to get into the specifics of his explanation. "I have been a training instructor at a top-secret army facility involved in training special forces. It is a very secure facility, and I really can't tell you more than that. While you are there either as an instructor or a cadet, you are totally closed off from the outside world. So I'm sorry for the extended silence, but I had no choice."

"Jesus, Bruce, have you signed up for life with the army or what?" A calmer Jack Roach.

"Again, I can't tell you much about my status, but I will be assigned to the Pentagon here in Washington for a while."

This was the story he was given to tell his family and close friends by way of an explanation for the past fourteen months. He was instructed to be as vague as he could be and to respond to requests for further explanations by simply saying that he was restricted on how much he could divulge. It was a lie, but Bruce figured lying would also be part of his new CIA life.

"So it will be a long time before you will be back in Maine?" Jack's question was in reference to when Bruce would be moving back for good. Bruce answered on a more short-term basis.

"Actually, the good news is that I have some time off and will be in Maine in a week or so." Bruce did not want to tell him that his next phone call was to Tony Fignoni and that he would be spending some time in New Jersey on his way to Maine. He assumed he would still be welcome at the Fignoni home.

"Well, that is good to hear. Will you be staying with us, Bruce?" Jack was thinking that he might get a fuller explanation when he saw Bruce in person.

"Maybe a night or two if that's all right, but I should spend a few nights with Ma. What's been going on with you, Roach? Have you flunked out of college yet? I always figured it was a matter of time."

Jack first thanked him for the vote of confidence then explained that he was in his senior year looking to graduate in May. He also told Bruce about meeting Sue Frazier, explaining how serious their relationship had become.

"Jack, that doesn't sound good. You sound a bit pussy whipped. Does this mean we are done sharing our women?"

Jack laughed at this, saying he had no intention of sharing Sue with anyone. They talked for another twenty minutes while Bruce explained that he now had a vehicle of his own, so he would be driving to Maine. He gave Jack an estimated day of arrival, and they ended the call. By the time the call ended, Jack had calmed down and the anger had left his voice. Bruce was pleased with the way the call ended, but he was unsure whether Jack bought the explanation.

He then called his mother and gave her the same explanation. His mother seemed less skeptical than Jack. He also gave her an estimated day of arrival, and she expressed her unhappiness with the fourteen months silence as well as her joy in knowing she would soon see her son. Most of all, she was happy to hear that he was all right. She had been worried sick. After that, Bruce made his third call, this one to Tony Fignoni. The Fignoni household had a private unlisted phone number that Tony had given Bruce on his last visit. He was pleased to find that it was still a good number. It took a few minutes but he finally got Tony on the line.

"Bruce, you son of a bitch, where the fuck have you been, jail? Nobody hears from you for months on end, then a phone call out of the blue. What do you need? Bail money, a woman, drugs—name it."

"Given your usual circle of friends, Tony, I can see why you would arrive at the jail conclusion, but actually, I have been busy making the world safe for democracy. How have you been, my man?"

"Making the world safe for democracy. What a line of bull shit. Are you telling me you are still a GI? I can't believe you would be stupid enough to still be in the army."

Bruce went through the same canned explanation for the third time. To him, it sounded less believable every time he told it, but it was all he had by way of explanation. Of the three calls he had made, he figured Tony was the least likely to buy it, and he was right. "That's the biggest load of bullshit I've ever heard."

Bruce figured changing the subject would work better than trying to press Tony into believing the lie. "So listen, I'm headed up your way. If you want to spend a couple of days catching up, I would like to stop in and stay with you, that is, if you want me."

"You know you are always welcome here, Private King. When will you be presenting that ugly puss of yours at my front door?"

"Well, I will be driving up, leaving the DC area tomorrow, at your front door by mid-afternoon unless that's too soon."

"Hell, no, I will be looking for you. I'll alert the security people so they don't shoot your stupid ass by mistake."

They laughed off that comment, but Bruce's laugh was a bit strained. Knowing Tony's line of work, it was not all that funny. They talked a bit longer then ended the phone call. The next morning, Jack headed for Secaucus, New Jersey.

He arrived at the Fignoni home at 2:00 p.m. Not much had changed in terms of the business operation. There were still a good number of oversize staffers patrolling the place and going in and out of Tony's father's office. The only big change was that Tony seemed to have taken on more responsibility in the organization. Like his father, he kept an office in the house and had a few of the oversize staff bouncing in and out of his place as well. This was no surprise to Bruce. He had expected Tony would move into the family business. No doubt he would someday take it all over from his father.

He spent the afternoon catching up with Tony, who was obviously a busy man since leaving the army. In the evening, Tony had made arrangements for a couple of very attractive women with rather casual morals to take care of his and Bruce's more primitive needs. It was absolutely classic Tony Fignoni and exactly what Bruce had expected. After spending fourteen months virtually in prison with no contact with anyone, including any female companionship, Bruce was more than ready.

The next morning, Tony began a conversation by stating that he doubted Bruce's explanation for the fourteen-month silence.

"Bruce, my old friend, I don't believe the army kept you completely out of touch with the world for fourteen months. That's not the army's style. As I've thought about it, that sounds a lot more like the CIA. I don't expect you to answer that, but remember, I was in the army with you, so we both know enough about how they operate." Tony said this with an air of confidence that left the impression that he had some inside information.

Bruce took a long moment before saying, "Tony, what I'm doing is top secret, so like you told me on my first visit here about your father's business, don't ask."

"Touché, my man, touché." Tony knew that his old army buddy was in a position that he could not talk about, so he left it alone. He did, however, make a mental note to find out more about what Bruce was up to through his family's various government contacts. However top secret it might be, Tony had the means to find out the truth.

So after that exchange, the subject was not brought up again. Bruce stayed two more days with Tony before heading to Maine. As was to be expected, Tony made sure Bruce had plenty to eat, drink, smoke, and plenty of women. Tony hugged him as he was about to get in his car to leave and said, "We covered each other's ass in Nam, Bruce, and whatever you are into here, if you need your ass covered again, remember, I'm here." He looked Bruce in the eye as he said this.

"That goes both ways, my man."

With that, Bruce was in his car, headed up I-95 to Maine. He had the feeling that his friends in Maine may be just as skeptical as Tony of his explanations, but he would stick with it anyway.

He arrived in Old Town after eight and a half hours of driving and went straight to Jack's restaurant. As was the case so many months ago, when he walked in, he received the warmest of welcomes from the staff and Jack and Polly Roach. They all commented on the added pounds of muscle, which were hard to miss. He took a bit of a scolding from Polly, "What the hell do you mean not being in touch with us for a year?"

Bruce went into his canned explanation, but he was cut off by Polly. "We heard that from Jackie, but I don't care what the army says, don't pull this shit again." Jack Sr. just smiled at his wife's scolding, then he talked with Bruce about the army, asking what kind of commitment Bruce had made for his stay in the service. Bruce was very vague with his answer. He thought he sensed a bit of skepticism from another man who had served in the army. Maybe it was just that he was getting paranoid, but the more people he told this canned explanation, the less they seemed to buy it.

They told him Jack was up at the house, so he headed up to see him. It was quite a different reunion than past times. Bruce had changed considerably. He had put on twenty pounds of muscle, and his facial features had hardened noticeably. Jack looked different as well, not as dramatically as Bruce, but he had matured. It had been over two years since they had last seen each other. Both were somewhat shocked at the changes as they both grew into manhood. Bruce had changed more because of all he had been through, but Jack was noticeably changed as well. They had both gone from teenage boys to young men.

Bruce explained that he would be living in northern Virginia for a while, doing work for the Pentagon. For his part, Jack explained that he was headed for graduation from the University of Maine in the spring. His plan was then to attend law school. He would be taking the law school admissions exam in November. Bruce found this all very interesting but moved right into the subject he was most interested to hear about.

"So what about this girl I hear you are so smitten with?"

Jack had a grin as he answered, "What can I say? She seems like the perfect girl. Witty, intelligent, beautiful, and she loves me. What more could I ask for?"

"Now when you say beautiful, are we talking that goofy inner beauty, or is she a bona fide fox?" The kind of question Jack would expect from Bruce.

"She is incredibly beautiful inside and out. I'm lucky she gives me the time of day."

"Built well? Does she have the kind of body that turns heads when she walks in a room?"

"Like nobody I have ever been with before. I'm telling you, Bruce, she got it all."

"Well, this sounds serious. You actually see yourself having a life with her?"

"Yeah, I do. We've talked about getting married once I'm settled into a position that makes it possible."

This news struck Bruce as way out of character. "Wow, where is she now? I want to meet this beauty?"

Jack explained that Sue had graduated from NYU last spring with a degree in communications. She immediately landed a job on the news team at a Portland television station. She lived and worked in Portland, and if Jack got accepted at the Maine Law School in Portland, he intended to move in with her, Jack was staying with her a lot already because he was a volunteer on Senator Ed Muskie's presidential campaign and spent a lot of time in Portland working for the campaign. Jack's political involvement was shocking enough to Bruce, but the female involvement blew him completely away.

"Man, my old buddy getting this serious over a girl. Never thought I would see the day this would happen." Bruce was more than a little surprised by Jack's commitment to this woman he had not seen yet.

"I must say I never thought I would see the day that my old drinking buddy would be working in the Pentagon. I guess nothing stays the same." With that, they both picked up their glasses, and they clinked them together.

Bruce spent four days in Old Town, two at the Roach's house and two at his mother's. He and Jack spent a lot of time reminiscing with each other as well as with other longtime friends. He did not get to meet Sue Frazier, but he did talk with her over the telephone a couple of times. He tried to tell her what a thug her boyfriend used to be, but she cut him off, telling him she had already heard all the stories. He was disappointed that he didn't meet her but admitted to Jack that in conversation she certainly seemed as witty, intelligent, and charming as she had been described.

As the time came for him to head back to Virginia, everyone in his family, as well as the Roach family, made it clear they expected him to keep in touch. He answered everyone that he would, especially Jack.

"We have been through way too much together for us not to keep up with each other," was one of his final statements to Jack before he left.

He invited Jack to come visit him in Virginia, and Jack promised that he would. Bruce headed back, and Jack continued in school. A very short time ago, neither of them would have believed that they would have gone their separate ways and been so much out of touch with each other and on such different paths in terms of their futures. They were both still young enough to find life's changes a bit shocking. As they parted company, they both had this same sad thought. Life had changed dramatically for both of them.

Chapter XII

As 1971 ROLLED INTO A new year, Jack was in his final semester. He had scored a 671 in his LSATs and filed his application for admission to the Portland Law School. With a strong undergraduate record, including six trips on the Dean's List, coupled with a good score on his LSATs, he felt confident of acceptance. He had decided in his freshman year in college that he wanted to go to law school. Now his dream was close to becoming a reality. He waited nervously to hear from the admissions office.

Meantime, he was working on the Muskie for President campaign, getting to Portland as often as possible, both for the campaign work and to see Sue. He stayed with her over the Christmas vacation, except for two days on either side of Christmas, which he spent at his family's home in Old Town. Christmas was a big deal with the Roach family. All six siblings plus their spouses and children gathered in Old Town at the family homestead. It was a lively time with plenty of food, drink, and merriment. He asked Sue to join him there, but she had planned to go to her own home in Burke, Vermont. Jack was beginning to sense that something was wrong between them, but he convinced himself it was just his paranoia. She had struck up a friendship with a chiropractor who recently opened a practice in Portland. She insisted to Jack that he was, in fact, just a friend, but Jack had his suspicions. Jack didn't have much use for chiropractors anyway, and this situation was not enhancing his opinion of them.

In January, Jack spent some time canvassing for Muskie in New Hampshire. He knocked on doors, put up signs, and made phone calls in New Hampshire, the site of the nation's first primary. He stayed with Sue, using it as his base. Though she also supported Muskie, Sue could not join him because of her job in the newsroom.

Muskie was the leading candidate in the Democratic Party heading into the New Hampshire primary. Jack was intent on defeating Nixon, and Muskie seemed the most likely Democrat to pull that off. Every chance he got he spent time on mailings, phone canvassing, putting up signs, and basically any role he could play to enhance the Muskie campaign. Once the spring semester started back in Orono, Jack's campaign time was reduced considerably. It became very difficult to find the time to get to Portland.

Two weeks before the New Hampshire primary, on February 24, a forged letter was printed in the Manchester Union Leader, indicating Muskie was prejudiced against Americans of French Canadian descent. It became known as the Cannuck Letter. The owner of the paper had also made some unkind remarks about Muskie's wife. Both the forged letter and the attack on his wife came about for one reason: he was the front-runner most likely to defeat Nixon. He became the first target of the Nixon dirty tricks campaign.

A visibly angry Muskie held a press conference outside the paper's offices. While defending his wife and calling out the paper's owners, Muskie appeared to cry. He later claimed it was snow melting on his face, but the press dubbed it the crying speech. This led to claims by his opponents, especially the Nixon camp, claiming he was not stable enough to be president. He won the New Hampshire primary but only by nine percentage points over George McGovern. It was the beginning of the end for the Muskie campaign as after a fourth-place finish in Florida in March, Muskie withdrew. It was a sad event for Jack, and all the Muskie supporters.

In October of that same year, the FBI showed that the Cannuck Letter was the work of Donald Segretti and Ken Clauson and part of the dirty tricks campaign of the committee to reelect the president. It all worked to sour Jack completely on the world of politics. He would never volunteer on another campaign. To see a candidate of Muskie's caliber brought down by a dirty tricks campaign led by a scurrilous lowlife like Nixon was all he could take. He always exercised his right to vote, but that would be the extent of his political activities in the future.

Jack had other problems mounting in his world. A fellow cam-paign worker and friend whom he and Sue had double-dated with reported to him in early February that Sue and the new chiropractor seemed to be more than friends. It was not that he had not had his own suspicions, but this was the first confirmation of them.

"Jack, it's not my place to be a gossip, but you're a friend, and I want you to know that I've seen the two of them together a lot."

The announcement chilled him to the bone. His legs actually went weak on him, almost giving out.

"What do you mean together, doing what?"

"I've seen them out to dinner together as well as at the movies. Also, I know she has been running errands for him."

"Are you sure?"

"I'm not just trying to make trouble, Jack. I'm just alerting you to watch your back." She helped him move into his office and basi-cally spends a lot of her free time helping him.

Jack confronted her with questions about her relationship with this man, but she insisted they were just friends. She pointed out that Jack was not always in town, so she had gone to the movies with him, but only as a friend. Jack wanted desperately to believe her so he let it go. Then in the middle of March, two days after he received his acceptance to the Portland Law School, he got the letter from Sue while he was in Old Town.

It was not common at this stage of their relationship for him to get a letter from her. So he opened it with some trepidation. It was his worst fear. She announced that her friend, the chiropractor, was moving in with her. She expressed her sorrow that things were over between them but hoped Jack could "move on with his life." The news dealt a crushing blow to Jack. He was in love with this girl. He was saving up for a diamond engagement ring that he planned to give her upon his graduation. He could not remember ever crying in his life, but he broke down reading the letter. The fact that it brought him to tears was more shocking to him than the letter. He had never been given to this type of emotional breakdown.

His inclination, given his past, was to drive to Portland and beat the hell out of her friend. He knew it would accomplish nothing, but he also knew he would feel better after. And beating up a chiropractor might actually be good for society in general. He did not want to confront her. It would not be in his nature to whine or beg for her to come back. All a confrontation with her would accomplish would be a screaming session to get things off his chest. He saw nothing good coming from a confrontation for either of them. What he needed to do was cool down and be rational in his response.

In the end, he waited two days without doing anything, then he answered her letter with one of his own. The letter was a large piece of white typing paper with no greeting and no signature. It simply had one word printed in large block letters: goodbye. It killed him to lose her, but he refused to get into any kind of debate with her about it. The one word was enough. It said all he had to say.

He posted the letter swearing to himself that he would forget her. He had been dealt a double blow with the eye-opening dirty dealings of politics and that abrupt hurtful end to what he thought would be a lifelong relationship. It was the kind of one-two punch that would leave him thinking he couldn't trust or depend on anyone. He went through a major bout of depression that he dealt with by working more hours to get ready for law school. He was trying to save up enough to pay his first year's tuition and books and rent housing somewhere in Portland. He would use the money he had been saving for the diamond, but he also needed to increase the hours he was working. Between that and his studies, Jack's social life was almost nonexistent. But in reality, he was not really in the mood for any social life. When graduation day finally came, his father, who had been watching him struggle with his loss and was worried about him, sat him down for a talk.

"Jackie, I know the past few months have been tough, and I know you have dealt with it by burying yourself in work. You need some R&R."

As always, Jack appreciated his father's concern and his advice. But he had other commitments.

"I know, Dad, but I start work on construction in a week. I will need the money. I don't want to show up late and lose the job."

With five other kids to take care of and not a lot of money to work with, Jack knew he could not ask for a lot of help from his dad.

"Understood, but why don't you take my car and drive down to Virginia to spend some time with Bruce? Your car may not make it that far, so take mine." His father was smiling as he said this. Jack's 1963 Pontiac seemed to be approaching the end of its life. His father handed him four one-hundred-dollar bills, saying, "You and Bruce have a couple of beers on me." Four hundred dollars was a lot of money for Jack's father and he appreciated the gift.

Jack considered the offer for a moment then nodded in agreement. "Okay, I will call Bruce to see if he can get a couple of days off from whatever in hell he does."

Bruce was well aware of Jack's break up with Sue Frazier. The working relationship he had with the CIA did not require him to come in every day. It was an arrangement whereby they sent him on assignment as necessary. When Jack called, he was in Alexandria with no indication he would be called out. So he told Jack he would get a few days off from his Pentagon job, so Jack headed to Virginia. He made it driving straight through for twelve long hours. He was anxious to get there. As he drove it became even more obvious to him that his father was right.

When he arrived at Bruce's apartment, his first words pleaded for the old Bruce.

"Bruce, I need to spend some time with the old Bruce King. Not the army version, not the guy that disappeared for fourteen months. I need a couple of days with the guy who left Bangor juvenile court in 1967 because I need a couple of days being the old Jack so I can forget that bitch. I can't be the old Jack unless you are the old Bruce."

Bruce looked at him for just a moment and replied, "You got it, Jackie Boy. What we are going to do is head for Georgetown and do some bar hopping. We can start at Murphy's Pub. Just the medicine for an Irish boy like yourself."

They started early doing the best they could to don the carefree, nothing is serious attitude they left behind. Jack even picked a fight in the Irish bar called Murphy's. Two guys at the bar were giving a hard time to the waitress. Jack noticed it as he came back from the men's room, so he got involved.

"Hey, if you two assholes want to give somebody trouble, why don't you start here?" he said as he stood directly behind them.

The two patrons swung around to look at him as he stood behind them. "Well, little Sir Gallahad wants to defend a damsel in distress. You figure you can handle the two of us?"

"Oh, I don't think I'll even work up a sweat. I've beat up assholes like you two all my life, just for exercise," Jack responded as he stood ready to throw the first punch as soon as one of them made a move to get off their stool.

"I'm damn sure that the two of us can handle you two without breaking a sweat," Bruce chimed in as he walked up behind Jack. The two loudmouths took one look at Bruce, who was five feet, ten inches of chiseled muscle, and decided they should move along. Not before Jack insisted they apologize to the offended waitress, which they did. She thanked Jack for his troubles, which began a conversation that ended with Jack and Bruce taking her and a friend out for the evening. All four ended up at Bruce's apartment for the night. It was the first time Jack had been with a woman since Sue Frazier. He enjoyed every minute of time he spent with this lady. Being intimate with a woman again was just what the doctor ordered.

After breakfast the next day the two girls left, agreeing to get together again if the guys wanted to stop by Murphy's that night. Jack told them he and Bruce would show up at the bar around nine. As soon as they were out of earshot, Jack said, "I need to stand them up." He looked over at a surprised Bruce, waiting for a response.

"Why, the sounds from your bedroom seemed to indicate you were enjoying her company and she was enjoying yours." Jack smiled, knowing that the two of them had been quite noisy.

"Oh yeah, she was great. Still, I need to stand them up just to regain my perspective on women."

"You need to be on the top of a relationship is what you're saying. You need to be the one being a dink instead of the girl." Bruce stood with hands on hips, smiling from ear to ear.

"Right you are, Bruce. I need to feel like I'm the one calling the shots."

They both laughed at this, and Jack felt like it really was like old times. They rode Bruce's motorcycle into Baltimore, checked into a hotel, and made the rounds to some Baltimore watering holes. Bruce won fifty bucks breaking wrists in a redneck honky-tonk. Once again, at the end of the evening, they were back in their hotel with two local women they met at the hotel bar. Once again, Jack was reminded what it was like to have a great night with a woman with no obligations and no broken heart at the end.

It ended up as three full days of the old Bruce and Jack. Raising hell, not worried about any consequences. Just carefree hell-raising. At 5:30 a.m. on the fourth day, Jack was awakened by the sound of Bruce's phone ringing. Bruce answered it in the next bedroom and Jack heard one side of the conversation. Bruce's voice was muffled and Jack could not make out the words, but he could tell by the tone that it was an important subject being discussed. He surmised that it was a work-related call and that Bruce would be headed to the Pentagon or wherever he actually worked. He lay in bed awake, waiting to hear what came next for Bruce.

After hanging up, Bruce came into Jack's bedroom with a real sense of urgency.

"Jack, I've been called in on a very important matter. I have to leave immediately. Listen, take your time leaving. Just lock the door behind you."

Jack, while half asleep, looked a bit stunned by this turn of events, so Bruce went on. "Look, I'm sorry about this, Jackie, but duty calls."

Jack shook out some cobwebs. "No, that's fine, man, it's been a great couple of days, really. Just like old times and really just what I needed. You do what you have to do. I'm going to get a little more sleep and then head home."

They slapped each other five, and Bruce headed for the shower while Jack went back to sleep. He slept until eleven, got up, made some coffee, and took a shower. He left Bruce a note thanking him for the good time while promising to stay in touch. By noon, he was on the road back to Maine, ready to go to work for the summer and then law school. It had been a great couple of days with his old pal. It had helped his state of mind tremendously. It was great being with the old Bruce again. The one he remembered. Still he wondered driving home if he would ever see the old Bruce again. He had one other feeling as he drove, and that was that he knew he did not want to see Sue Frazier again. He was done thinking about her and what might have been. She was now with someone else and good riddance.

Chapter XIII

As Jack left for Maine, Bruce was being briefed at CIA headquarters for a mission concerning Haiti. The twenty-year-old dictator, son of the late "Papa Doc" Duvalier, Baby Doc Duvalier, was being backed by the CIA. As usual, Duvalier was friendly to United States' business interests, so even though his was a bloody reign, like his father, the CIA gave him total backing. They helped put him in power and worked to keep him in power. CIA backing made staying in power in a small nation a much easier task.

Like any ruthless dictator, he had developed no shortage of enemies. Because of his iron-fisted rule, he dealt with all those who opposed him in Haiti; without trial, they were either jailed or executed. The focus of the CIA briefing for Bruce was an enemy who was not living in Haiti. A very popular ex-patriot named Victor Perez was living in St. Martin on the French side of the island. It was not an easy undertaking to send some of Duvalier's henchmen to St. Martin to deal with him. They would be well noticed as soon as they hit the island. Word would spread fast that they were there and Perez would be on guard. Perez was busy plotting against Doc Duvalier, and the dictator considered him a real threat. Not only was he a very popular figure, but he was also a very intelligent operator capable of putting together a workable plan to overthrow the regime. Bruce was assigned to travel to St. Martin to take out the threat. He was given intelligence reports on where Perez lived as well as his daily habits and who he had with him for protection.

This was not his first assignment, but it was his most dangerous. Perez was no fool, and he kept himself protected at all times. Bruce flew from Dulles Airport to Miami, then from Miami to St. Martin. He rented a car and checked into a hotel on the Dutch side of the island. His briefing at Langley had given him all he needed to know about Perez. He caught a night's sleep then went over to the French side to check out his target.

He was staying in a small beach house that was barely visible from the road. It was located very close to the famous nude beach on the French side. Bruce could not get a good look from the road so he drove to the nude beach, parked, took his clothes off in the men's locker room, and walked down the beach with a towel. Even among an entire beach full of nudists, his toned, chiseled body got attention as he walked to the end of the beach closest to the Perez house.

At the end of the sand, there was a hill between the beach and the house. He could not get a good look at the house from the beach. Bruce did not want to be too obvious, so he laid his towel out and caught some sun. After a half hour of that, he went in the ocean, swimming out far enough to get a look at the house. Swimming back in, he had the lay of the land. He would have to get to the top of that small hill to have a good spot to observe his target. That could not be done in the daytime without raising suspicion. He got back to the beach, toweled off, and headed back to his car. He would come back at night under cover of darkness.

That night, wearing dark clothing and bringing binoculars, he parked in a public lot a half mile from the beach and walked to the hill. He climbed up from the road staying on the beach side until he got to the top so that he could not be seen from the house. He lay on his stomach watching the house through binoculars from 9:00 p.m. until 3:00 a.m., observing every movement. He did this four nights in a row until he was sure of a plan. The occupants of the house did not exhibit any set routine, but they did retire for the evening without posting a guard, and Bruce saw no alarms except on the house itself. There were no security cameras or trip wires that he could see around the perimeter.

There were four people living in the house, three bodyguards and Perez himself. They had one car in the yard. The car was used to travel to and from the town to get supplies. They usually used it in the morning. The rest of the time it sat in the yard. Perez never left in the car, and one or two bodyguards always stayed back with him. He decided on a plan and made a list of what he needed.

After the fourth night of observation, Bruce notified headquarters what he would need. He wanted C4 plastic explosives and a Winchester rifle, the same model he used in Vietnam. He also required over the water transportation giving specific detail of where and when it would be needed.

On the fifth day, Bruce checked out of the hotel and turned in his rental car. He was picked up by boat at the pier on the Dutch side of the island. The boat that picked him up rendezvoused with another boat four miles out to sea at 7:00 p.m. The second boat carried his requested items, the explosives and the rifle. They were packaged in a waterproof pouch. Bruce had received training in scuba diving, he put on a wet suit and air tanks while the boat was positioned a half of a mile offshore from the nude beach. At 10:00 p.m., Bruce swam the half mile with the pouch and was on top of the hill by eleven fifteen. The boat stayed anchored in position through the night, waiting for the signal to move in closer.

Bruce watched the house until he was sure everyone was asleep. He had made sure, watching the previous four nights, that no guard was posted through the night. Still wearing the dark wet suit, he crawled to the car parked outside the house and planted the explosives on the car. He set them to go off when the car was started. Then he crawled back to his position and waited with his Winchester. He waited patiently for more than four hours. Finally, at seven fifteen the next morning, two of the bodyguards came out of the house. They stood and talked for a moment on the steps while one lit a cigarette. Then the one with the cigarette proceeded to the car followed by the second one. When they started the car, the explosives ignited and the car blew up. Bruce readied his rifle.

As he had hoped, the third bodyguard as well as Victor Perez came out of the house, Perez in his underwear, to see what happened. The third guard, suddenly realizing the man he was supposed to be protecting might be in danger, turned, hollering at him and pointing for him to get back inside. It was too late. Bruce squeezed off a shot that hit him square in the chest. The guard turned to look where the shot came from just in time to catch the second bullet in his chest. Two shots, two hits.

Bruce fired a second shot into Perez as he lay on the ground, just to make sure. The boat, having heard the explosion, was headed in to pick him up. As he ran to the shore, he put the rifle back into the waterproof pouch. Reaching the shore, he donned his tanks and was in the water, unseen, long before the arrival of the authorities.

When he reached the boat, he was taken aboard. They notified headquarters that the kill was made and headed for a US Navy ship four miles away. Bruce was taken by the navy ship to a point outside Miami then to shore by helicopter.

He flew back to Washington, briefed his superiors at the CIA, and was back in his own apartment ten days from when he left; mission accomplished.

Chapter XIV

JACK WAS FINDING LAW SCHOOL both more difficult than undergraduate work, as well as more interesting. The learning was approached differently. Classroom participation meant nothing, and there were no exams during the semester. Each course had a final exam at the close of the semester. That exam would determine your grade. He was taking six courses, and that would be the same course load for all six semesters until graduation. His studies took up a great deal more time than had undergraduate school studies, but he still had to work part-time to help defray costs. He had taken out his first student loan as he started his first of three years. He would have to take one or maybe even two more in order to finish. Not only did he have to pay for tuition and books as he did in undergraduate school he also had to pay for housing. He was living in a one-room, third-floor walk-up apartment and tending bar two nights a week at a popular watering hole on Forrest Avenue. Between work and study, his social life was pretty much nonexistent. He had made a few friends from his fellow classmates as well as at the pub where he worked. He even went out on a Saturday night with them from time to time, but mostly, he studied. As interesting as he found the coursework, he could not wait for the grind to be over.

He made every effort to avoid seeing Sue Frazier. She was on the local news broadcast every night, but Jack watched the other channels on his small black-and-white television, if he watched anything at all. He kept himself close to the law school at all times in order to avoid running into her by accident. The last thing he wanted was to run into her and her chiropractor friend in some social situation. He was not totally confident that a chance meeting would not result in his beating up a chiropractor.

At the Thanksgiving break, he made his first trip back to Old Town, spending some time with his family. Even as he took that brief three-day break, he brought work with him and spent time studying up at the University of Maine library. He returned to Portland on the Sunday after Thanksgiving, ready to face the last three weeks of his first semester.

The following Tuesday night, as he was working his shift at the pub, a familiar face walked in and sat at the bar.

Sue Frazier was alone, sitting on a barstool, staring at Jack Roach. Because it was his job, he walked over to wait on her even though he would rather have had an ice water enema. He approached the task with as cold a tone in his voice as possible.

"Can I help you?" he asked.

"Yes, could I have a glass of chardonnay and moment of your time?"

"Is the house chardonnay all right, or is it too low quality for your taste?"

Jack couldn't resist a sarcastic response even though he did not want to talk to her at all.

She blanched a bit at this obvious sarcastic dig but answered, "The house chardonnay is fine."

Jack poured a glass of the wine and placed it on the bar in front of her. "That will be four twenty-five."

He stood in front of her, waiting to get paid.

"Do you want me to pay now?"

"It's customary to pay for drinks in a bar." More sarcasm.

She dug in her purse for the money. "You did not answer the other request about having a few minutes of your time."

"I'm very busy here, ma'am. I don't have time for idle chitchat with every two-bit customer who wanders in off the street."

"Look, Jack, I would like to sit with you at your convenience for half an hour or so and discuss what happened with us."

Jack stood, waiting for the money, saying nothing. She had stopped digging in her purse for the money, simply staring at him, waiting for a response. Finally, he broke the silence. "That will be four twenty-five, please."

She went back to looking for the money, finally pulling out a five-dollar bill, handing it to Jack. He took it without a word, ringing it in the cash register. He brought her the change. She opened her mouth to say something, but he cut her off, saying, "Thank you, ma'am, enjoy the wine." Having said that, he walked away. She sat and stared at him as he walked away, frustrated by the exchange.

As he continued to work, he occasionally glanced over at her from the corner of his eye, trying not to make it obvious. He noticed she was writing something, and he considered that it might be something for him. He made every effort to stay away from the section of the bar where she sat so that he would not have to talk with her again. Unfortunately, he had to wait on two young men who sat in her section of the bar. He took their order, and as he walked away, she said "Excuse me" to him, but he walked away ignoring her. This was repeated when he brought them their drinks and he ignored her again.

Finally, he saw her get up to leave. She noticed him looking at her, and she waved. He did not respond as she stood up waiting, so she left. Jack went over to clear the bar. She had left a half glass of wine, a five-dollar tip, and a note. He shoved the tip and the note into his pocket, resisting the urge to throw the note away. He came to the conclusion he should hang on to it and read it when he got home. He finished his evening shift, walked to his apartment, undressed for bed, placing the note on the table next to his bed. He looked at it for a long moment then decided he would sleep better if he didn't read it, so he turned in, figuring to read it in the morning. He did not sleep well, doing a good deal of tossing and turning. The encounter with her, as brief as it was, had left its mark. He could not get it or her out of his mind.

When he awoke in the morning, he sat on the edge of his bed, looking at the note for a long time before finally picking it up and opening it. The note read:

Dear Jack, I know you probably hate me now, and I don't blame you. Still I would like to talk with you. Could you please give a half hour of your time? I will be in the coffee shop in Luther Bonney Hall at seven, Thursday morning. Please meet me there. If you don't, I will understand. Sue

Short and to the point. Jack sat thinking about it with questions running through his mind. Did he really want to give her any time? Did he want to get involved with her at all? Did he have the strength to resist her if she wanted to get back together? Did he want to take the risk? These questions ran through his mind one after another in rapid order.

He had all day to think about it, so he took a shower and got ready for school. It ended up that he did think about it all day, and he thought of little else. She had not lost a thing in terms of her beauty. He had no idea if she was still with the chiropractor, but if she was, did she just want to rub it in a bit? He decided he would meet with her but would do so keeping his guard up. He spent a second restless night as he could not put the pending encounter out of his thoughts.

The Portland law school was contained in one seven-story building across the street from the University of Southern Maine campus. Luther Bonney Hall was part of the university campus. At seven the next morning, Jack walked into the coffee shop in that building and saw Sue Frazier sitting alone at a table drinking coffee. He walked over and sat down across the table from her without saying a word.

They looked at each other during a long silence until she finally said, "Thank you for coming." Jack did not immediately respond, creating another awkward silence. As much as it hurt even to admit it, she was breathtakingly beautiful. Finally, he said, "I really don't know why I'm here, and I don't have much time, so speak your piece."

"Okay, I guess I did not expect a warm fuzzy greeting, but I hope you came here because you still love me." She looked at him pleadingly as she made this statement.

Jack rolled his eyes at this but did not answer. He simply looked at her for another awkward silence until she went on.

"Jack, I made a terrible mistake. I left the man I love because I thought I was in love with someone else. I knew shortly after I sent you that letter that I made a terrible mistake, and I was so, so sorry. I did not dare to approach you about it because I knew you would be angry, so I have stewed about it for months until I went into the bar the other night, finally confronting you. It took all the nerve I could muster to do that, but I had to try and meet you to explain myself."

She stopped here and looked down at her coffee cup, waiting for a response. Jack let her wait for a time before saying, "What are you looking for now, Sue?"

"Jack, I'm hoping you can find it in your heart to forgive me. I'm hoping we can get back to the way things were between us. I'm hoping you can understand that I made a mistake and that I still love you. I'm hoping you still love me."

Jack was absolutely stunned by this attempt at reconciliation. It had crossed his mind that this might be her reason to get together, but he truly did not expect it. He thought for a moment before saying, "Are you still living with the chiropractor?"

She hesitated before answering, "No, he has moved out."

"When did that happen?" Jack snapped back.

She stuttered a bit with her answer, finally being very vague in saying, "A while ago."

Jack knew she did not want to get into this so he pressed on. "A little while ago, or a long while ago?"

She hesitated then said, "Does it matter? It was a while ago."

This pretty much told Jack all he needed to know. She did not want to tell an outright lie that would be too easy to prove as a lie, but the departure of her live-in was most likely a fairly recent event. Jack sat in silence for a bit, summarizing the situation as he saw it. He decided to completely end any chance of a relationship between the two of them.

"You threw me aside for what you thought was a better deal but it didn't turn out that way. After all the things you said to me, all the fake passion and lies, you dumped me. You really had me fooled. I really believed you loved me but you were only playing me for an idiot. I won't be played any longer. I guess love really is blind because I never really knew you, did I?"

He stood to leave, giving a parting shot. "What I said in my last letter to you still stands. Goodbye."

With that, he walked away as she sat in silence. Every word he had spoken hurt because the truth was that he did still love her. Regardless of that, he was not about to be played for a fool any longer. He left the building with tears in his eyes but resolved to move beyond her. He figured his parting speech had ended any possibility of them every reconciling. Now he had to work on forgetting the only woman he had ever loved.

Chapter XV

OVER THE NEXT TWO AND a half years, Jack worked his way through law school. He established himself as a solid student, graduating fourth in a graduating class of fifty-three. The good news was his academics and that he saw no more of Susan Frazier. He knew from watching the news that she had left Portland for a bigger market job. He hoped to never see her again. He could not even find it in himself to wish her well. By the time he finished law school, he could finally think about her without all the troubling emotions.

The bad news was that he had to take out a second student loan. He graduated with a debt of twelve thousand dollars. In 1975, that was a fair-sized debt for a man with no assets except a twelve-year-old car worth maybe fifty dollars to a junk dealer. He would have to make retiring that debt a top priority. He hated owing money. The years of law school were pretty routine with work, studies, and holiday trips home. Every summer, he found full-time employment, and during the school year, he was tending bar two nights. He exchanged phone calls with Bruce on a monthly basis, but they saw very little of each other. Over the two and a half years, Bruce had been to Portland four times, and Jack had visited Washington only twice. When they did get together, it was great fun as always, but neither one seemed to have enough time for the other. As busy as Jack was, Bruce was just as strung out. The biggest political event as those years passed was the Watergate scandal and resignation of President Nixon. That entire episode served to make Jack ever more cynical about politics and politicians. He wondered if there were any people in power in the United States that were still honest, still trying to do the job of serving the people, the job they were elected to do. He had made up his mind to explore working for the American Civil Liberties Union.

In spite of the student debt he had to deal with, he thought the work the ACLU was doing would make the low earning tolerable. The more he looked into that organization, the more appealing was the idea of working with them. They provided legal assistance in cases when civil liberties were at risk. They were a nonprofit organization with a stated purpose: "To defend and preserve the individual rights and liberties guaranteed to every person in the country by the constitution and laws of the United States." A mission that, given the stench of events like Watergate, was looking pretty good. The problem was he also needed money to pay off his loans and establish a decent living arrangement.

Watergate also had a direct impact on Bruce. The team that engineered the Watergate break in had a distinct CIA flavor. James McCord and E. Howard Hunt, two principles in the affair, had extensive CIA histories. They were working for the same organization, the Committee to Reelect the President (CREEP), that sabotaged the Muskie campaign. What's more, CREEP was financed in part by a CIA front, The Mullen Company. The entire ugly mess inspired James Schlesinger, the newly appointed CIA director in 1973, to send a memo directing staff to inform him of any and all operations carried out that were outside the agency's legal charter. The folder became known as the "Family Jewels," and it gave details on sleazy CIA operations going back years. The folder was a poorly kept secret within the agency, and Bruce was well aware of it, knowledge that would play a big part in later events in his life.

Meantime, Bruce was establishing himself as a very valued asset for the agency.

In 1973, Bruce was the chief CIA operative in Chile as the agency worked with the Chilean army and its commander-in-chief Augusto Pinochet to overthrow the democratically elected Socialist leader Salvadore Allende. Allende had made what American industry felt was the unforgivable sin of nationalizing American owned firms. It was a major objective of American industry to end Allende's rule. That being the case, it was also a top CIA objective. The coup was a success, putting Pinochet in power, who promptly tortured and murdered thousands of his own countrymen in a crackdown on labor leaders and left-leaning politicians.

The coup ended with the death of Allende on September 11, 1973. The official version was death by a self-inflicted gunshot wound. This explanation was not accepted by many Chileans who insisted he was assassinated. Bruce never divulged what really happened or if he was responsible for Allende's death. Even his superiors at the agency were left in the dark on the matter, but several suspected Bruce was involved. He was very good at keeping such details to himself.

Bruce was also involved in a subsequent bloodless coup in Australia. By working with longtime CIA collaborator Governor-General John Kerr, they successfully used an archaic never-before-used law to topple the democratically elected government of liberal Prime Minister Edward Whitlam. Whitlam had made the mistake of running afoul of American business interest. This being a bloodless coup, Bruce was not the lead CIA operator. He was there to make use of his special talents of arm twisting and beating malcontents to get them in line with the program. His talents here came in handy to CIA objectives.

In Angola, Bruce truly earned his stripes as a CIA asset. As Portuguese troops pulled out of Angola, three factions struggled for control of an independent Angola. The MPLA, Peoples Movement for the Liberation of Angola, a left-leaning group led by Agostinho Neto, had its base in the capital city of Luanda. The other two factions were the FNLA led by Holden Roberto—their power base was in the north—and the UNITA faction in the south led by Jonas Savimbi. The three factions met in Portugal and agreed to a democratic election to settle things, but that idea was soon scuttled with some CIA help.

The agency was afraid that if the left-leaning MPLA got control, it would result in an expansion of Russian influence in Africa. So they got involved, sending over a team led by John Stockwell, first backing the Roberto-led FNLA. Roberto had a plan to cripple the MPLA by taking out its leaders through assassinations. This was right up the alley of team member Bruce King.

Working with a select group of FNLA soldiers, Bruce joined in the efforts to eliminate MPLA political leaders. They were unsuccessful in two attempts to take out the very well-protected leader, Netto. The team was successful in assassinating a number of lower-level leaders with Bruce taking out three of them himself. Overall, the strategy did not seem to have the desired effect as political leaders eliminated were soon replaced. Nonetheless, Bruce had made his mark on the agency effort to keep the MPLA faction out of power.

As time went on, the agency was lending support to both the NFLA and UNITA. In the view of the CIA, anything would be better than an MPLA government. A United States troop commitment was out of the question, so the assistance of South Africa was worked out by a CIA team that included Bruce. Cuba had gotten involved on the side of the MPLA. Even though there was no apparent Cuban/Russian collaboration, the agency always looked at Cuba as an extension of Russia. They used the Cuban involvement to justify the agency's ongoing efforts. So the entire struggle was a microcosm of the Cold War.

The following year, a war-weary congress cut off funding for the CIA effort in Angola. The Angola effort was not the only CIA activity that congress had grown tired of supporting. A published history of the CIA entitled "The CIA and the Cults of Intelligence," written by two former intelligence officers, prompted a congressional investigation led by Senator Frank Church. The Church committee led to a number of reforms intended to make the CIA more accountable. The reforms proved ineffective as the CIA proved to be very adept at ignoring Congressional concerns. However, the increasing congressional oversight into the CIA activity was making times difficult for black ops operators like Bruce. They continued their involvement in Angola on a more limited and more clandestine nature. Still, when the funds were cut off in 1976, Bruce returned to the United States. The agency had other plans for his talents. He was one of a number of clandestine operators who worked under the radar screen virtually invisible to congress or the executives.

In between his various assignments abroad, he found time for his occasional get-together with Jack. Given his occupation, his social life in the DC area was all but nonexistent. So he looked forward to the trips to Portland; he just had very little time to get away. He did have the occasional rendezvous with Tony Fignoni in the D.C. area. They maintained their relationship in spite of the nature of Tony's business. It was relationship that would eventually prove to be problematic.

Chapter XVI

JACK'S PLANS TO JOIN THE ACLU were waylaid when he was recruited by a major Boston law firm, Morrison, Jenkins, and Lowe. They were a firm with over a hundred lawyers operating in various fields of law from corporate to international business, with a small division of criminal defense lawyers who dealt exclusively with white color crime. Jack had long since decided he wanted to be a defense attorney. He envisioned himself in the ALCU defending clients abused by the system. However, the offer from the Morrison firm was too financially attractive to pass up. *After all,* he told himself, *you have a student loan debt to pay off.* Plus he was tired of living in a third-floor one-room apartment and driving a junk car. At the end of the day, in spite of his high ideals, he went for the money.

So he took an apartment in Boston, three blocks from Fenway Park and his beloved Red Sox. He sold his twelve-year-old car for sixty dollars, and on August 3, 1975, he took the subway to the Franklyn Street offices of Morrison, Jenkins, and Lowe to begin his career as an attorney-at-law.

As a junior associate, he initially did most of his work as co-council on some of the bigger cases. This involved assisting the more senior lead council by researching case law relevant to the case in chief. His court appearances were few, and when he was in court, it would be as second or third attorney at the defense table. He understood that this was how things worked and he would eventually work his way into the position of being first council. At this point, it was important that he perform well in a second council role. He worked diligently to perform at a high level to prove his capabilities.

The Boston Red Sox were in the 1975 World Series, and the law firm had season tickets along the third base line. Jack had won the office drawing to use the tickets to attend game six. He was in the stands to witness Carlton Fisk's extra inning walk-off home run. That alone made it totally worthwhile to be with a Boston firm even if he was the low man on the totem pole in a large law firm. He had invited Bruce to come up for the game, and he flew into Logan just in time. They spent a couple of days together, catching up on things, one of the few times they were able to get together.

By the spring of 1976, Jack was taking the lead on cases involving minor offenses. A wealthy client of the firm had his son caught with half an ounce of cocaine. On another case, a client of the firm was arrested for operating a motor vehicle under the influence of alcohol. He did well with these smaller offenses, pleading them down to minor fines or, in some cases, getting them dismissed on technicalities. Even as he took the lead on these cases, he still worked as second council on the larger offenses. The bottom line was that he was involved in a good mix of legal defense work that was training him well.

In November of that year, he drew the lead on his first major case. Immediately after that, another big case fell in his lap. A major client of the firm was charged with tax evasion. The case had been under IRS review for months before actual charges were filed. The case was tried in federal court with the government, arguing that the client had taken a series of deductions illegally as well as underreporting their income. Jack, with the able assistance of the firm's tax attorneys, was able to work through a long list of charges, ending up with convictions on a few minor offenses and an ultimate fine that was a fraction of the original IRS assessment. His courtroom demeanor and case preparation were quickly impressing the partners in the firm. He was working long hours, billing out sixty to seventy-five hours a week. He was establishing himself as an up and comer in the firm after less than two years on the job.

Needless to say, with all that work his social life was not real active. Furthermore, he and Bruce were growing ever more distant from one another. During his three years of law school, they had exchanged phone calls on a fairly regular basis, and Bruce had made a couple of trips to Portland. Except for the World Series game, it had been some months since Jack had heard anything from him. Bruce would virtually disappear for months at a time with no word of what he was up to or where he was. He had no way of knowing Bruce was in a foreign country. It all reminded him of the fourteen months with no word from Bruce a few years back. Finally, he got a message at his office that Bruce King had called and left a phone number. Jack returned the call immediately upon entering his office.

"They told me I had a message from Bruce King, and I had to scratch my head trying to remember who the hell that was."

"Oh, how soon we forget now that you're a bad-ass lawyer in a bad-ass firm."

"Well, it's quite easy to forget someone whom you never hear from. Where the hell have you been?"

"I had to go through two secretaries to get to you. I've been out of the country for a while, so I had no idea you had become so fucking big-time."

"I don't know about big-time, but I do finally have a job that pays. So what were you doing out of the country?"

Bruce explained that he couldn't really talk about it because it was still work for the Pentagon. Jack pressed him a bit, so Bruce told him he was headed up to New Jersey to see Tony Fignoni and he would like to keep going up the coast to visit Jack in Boston. What he didn't say was that he had a couple of weeks off because of his extended stay in Angola. His vagueness in explaining his where-abouts and his duties in general were no longer believable to Jack.

"Of course, you are welcome here. I even have an apartment now with a spare bedroom, so unlike Portland, you will have a place to sleep."

"Sounds good. I will call you when I leave Fignoni's so you will know when to expect me. Give me your phone number at the apartment."

Jack did as he was asked, and they spoke for a few more minutes before hanging up. Jack had been suspecting for some time that his old friend was not being honest with him about his duties in Washington. He was determined that on this visit he was going to get to the bottom of it and find out exactly what Bruce was into. It was obviously something he was told not to talk about, but Bruce knew full well that he could trust Jack to keep a secret.

Bruce spent three days in New Jersey with Tony Fignoni and family. It was obvious from day one that Tony had moved into an equal role with his father in running the family business. Bruce was kept away from any discussions about that business for obvious reasons. When Tony was working, Bruce spent time at the poolside, relaxing. They went into New York City in the evening for the usual entertainment. On those trips, they were driven by and accompanied by the proper amount of "muscle" to ensure there were no unfortunate incidents. Bruce told Tony he was a bit uncomfortable with the "goons" hanging around, but Tony told him it was necessary.

At breakfast on the third day, as Bruce prepared to leave for Boston, Tony brought up the subject of Bruce's employment for the first time.

"So I'm seeing all this shit on the news about investigations into CIA activities. Congressional inquiries, Senate hearings, special recommendations, blah, blah, blah. What's going on with your outfit?"

"I have nothing to do with any of that. I work at the Pentagon."

"Come on, Bruce. This is Tony you're talking to. You can't bullshit me, fess up. I know how the Army works, and I know you ain't working for the Army."

Tony looked at Bruce with a smile on his face, expecting an answer.

Bruce just looked at him with no comment. After a long pause, Tony broke the silence. "Okay, my man, you will tell me when you're ready. Just remember that I'm here to cover your ass when you need it. Something tells me you are going to need it eventually."

Bruce smiled and thanked his friend for the thought. They parted company as Bruce headed for Boston without any further discussion on the subject. When he arrived in Boston, it was late afternoon, so he went right to the offices of Morrison, Jenkins, and Lowe. He was instantly impressed with the very high-class office his pal worked in. Jack was in court, so he sat and waited for just over an hour when his friend made his entrance. Bruce had been reading a magazine outside Jack's office. He stood to meet him, and they high-fived one another as Jack introduced him to his secretary as "his best friend."

Jack showed him around the office, made introductions to the appropriate people, then took him to his favorite watering hole for drinks before dinner. Unlike Tony, Jack did not wait two days before bringing up the elephant in the room. As they sat at a private table sipping their first drink, Jack broke the ice.

"Bruce, we have been friends since the sixth grade, Jack began. We have never kept secrets from one another because we trusted each other's ability to keep our mouths shut. You know I would never breathe a word to anyone about a subject you wanted kept secret. So quit fucking with me and tell me what the hell you are doing in Washington, and please don't give me the Pentagon story—it insults my intelligence." Jack said all this with a tone of authority. It was clear he expected an honest answer and would accept nothing less.

Bruce sat looking down at his drink during this entire speech. After a time, he looked up at Jack and said, "Okay, I will level with you with the understanding that it goes no further, that this conversation never happened, and that we both know you have no intelligence to insult."

Jack smiled at the last comment but agreed to the requested silence on the subject. With that, Bruce opened up and told him he was working for the CIA. "Having told you that, I would ask that you not ask me about any specifics because it's all top secret. Everything I do, every trip I make, is top secret. The congressional oversight committee does not even know I exist. You can't talk about this with anyone, and I mean anyone—not your family, your girlfriend, your coworkers, no one."

"Okay, I won't ask about specifics, but I will tell you that I suspected you were with the CIA. While I won't ask for specifics, I will ask if any of your activities are part of the current investigations."

Bruce thought before answering. He had to be careful here not to divulge things that would be trouble for both him and Jack. "Look, I have been involved in some shit, okay? Stuff that some would think we should not be involved in, but I have done what I have done for my country. There have been investigations on specific areas in which I have worked. I will ask you, Jack, to leave it at that."

Jack raised his glass to Bruce and said, "Agreed, no more discussion on the matter." Bruce had confirmed what Jack had suspected. Knowing he was CIA answered a lot of questions about the long periods when he was unable to be reached. Jack didn't need to know the specifics.

Over the next two days, the subject did not come up again. Bruce had arrived on a Friday, so they had the two-day weekend spending time making the rounds of Boston nightclubs and spending time with some lady friends of Jack. Friday and Saturday were both late nights filled with wine, women, and song. Much like the time they had spent in Virginia.

On Sunday evening, Jack had to go into the office to spend a couple of hours preparing for court on Monday. Bruce stayed in the apartment patiently killing time until Jack returned. He got back to his apartment just before ten and apologized to Bruce for having to leave early Monday morning for court.

"No problem, Jack. I will have some coffee and head back to DC."

They had a nightcap together, promised to do a better job keeping in touch, and retired for the evening. In the morning, Jack was already gone when Bruce got out of bed.

Chapter XVII

As TIME MOVED THROUGH THE late seventies, Jack Roach's responsibilities in the firm increased exponentially. His cases now involved major white-collar crimes, money laundering, SEC violations and EPA violations. He took the lead when a client of the firm was charged with manslaughter for a motor-vehicle death. His client was charged with driving while impaired, causing the death of the other car's driver. Jack was able to win the case, proving that the field sobriety test was faulty. The case was based solely on the officer's field sobriety test with no accompanying blood test.

As his caseload became more involved in serious crime, his reputation as a defense attorney grew and his services became more in demand. His earnings were well into the six-figure level growing more every year. In late 1979, the firm was being coaxed by a judge to take a court appointment on a murder trial. Jack volunteered to take the case. He wanted the experience of handling a murder trial. After two and a half weeks in court, Jack was able to get an acquittal. He was able to explain away the circumstantial evidence and discredit the testimony of the key witness who claimed his client wanted the deceased out of the way.

The problem with it all was that Jack was working so many hours he had no time to enjoy the money he made. He had purchased a home in an exclusive Marblehead neighborhood. He drove a Mercedes and basically enjoyed all the creature comforts of the wealthy. With all that, as he moved into his thirties, he had begun to ask himself if it was all worth it or should there be more to life. He was working six and, sometimes, seven days a week. His home state of Maine with its more relaxed lifestyle was looking better and better to him. He often went back to thinking of work with the ACLU which was so far removed from his current casework. He felt like he had become the type of money hungry workaholic he had always hated.

He got a call one July night in 1981 from a friend from law school named David Kerry whom he had not heard from in years.

"Roach, this is David Kerry calling, how you doing?"

"David Kerry, I would have assumed you died a long time ago. What in hell prompts this call…no, wait, let me guess—you've finally been disbarred."

"No, but I'm sure that's in my future. Listen, I'm coming to Boston this weekend to see a couple of Sox games, let's get together."

A rather surprising call and a surprising invitation.

They had been friends in law school, but there had been no contact since graduation.

"I'd love to. Do you have tickets already?"

"No, I was going to call for them tomorrow."

"Don't do it. I have two season tickets on the third baseline. Meet me in my office Friday night at six, and we will go to the park from there. Also, don't make any hotel reservation. You can stay with me at my place in Marblehead." David objected to this offer, but Jack insisted. David suggested that a poor Maine kid would not be allowed into swanky Marblehead, but in the end, he agreed to stay with Jack.

They caught up with each other a bit before ending the call, but plans were set for Friday night. They were in their seats at seven to catch the opening pitch of a game against Baltimore which the Red Sox won 5–3. After the game, they headed to Jack's Marblehead home. "Jack, you've got it made. A home in Marblehead, a Mercedes, a key position in a major firm, what else is there in life?"

"It's not as sweet as it seems. All work and no play is making Jack a dull boy. What's up with you, Dave?"

David explained that he was a partner in a small nine-lawyer firm in Portland. One of the lawyers was another classmate of Jack's. Gerry Conley was a defense attorney in the firm, and he was also a good friend of Jack's in law school. The entire scenario sounded so refreshing to Jack. It wasn't just the nostalgia of hearing about two old friends. It was the more relaxed and simpler lifestyle.

"Of course, Gerry's not handling murder trials like you are, Jack."

Jack was a bit surprised that David was following his career. The murder trial was not that high-profile for the news to reach Portland.

"How did you know that?"

"We read the Boston papers and talk to members of the Massachusetts bar. You've made a hell of a name for yourself."

Jack just shrugged at this remark, trying to look humble.

"Yeah, I suppose, but it's a hell of a rat race in Boston. The money is great, but there is more to life, isn't there?"

"Well, anytime you want to trade it all in for a quieter practice, let us poor folk in Portland know."

Jack was a bit surprised by this offhanded remark. He had actually been thinking of just such a move but didn't expect an offer to pop up.

"Are you serious?"

"Of course, I am. We would love to have someone with your ability and reputation."

"Be careful what you wish for, David, I might just take you up on it."

The rest of the evening was spent discussing the possibility. Jack was curious to know the types of cases that were common to the firm. David explained that they handled about everything from real estate to wills to corporate work and defense work. The criminal defense work would be a good deal smaller crime than Jack was currently handling. However, with Jack's ability and reputation, they would probably start getting more criminal work involving major crimes.

They attended the game together on Saturday afternoon, also won by the Red Sox, went to dinner in one of the North Ends great Italian restaurants, then hit the town a bit before heading back to Marblehead on the train. All through the game, dinner, and later at Jack's home, he was asking David questions about the firm in Portland. David told him that he couldn't guarantee it without discussion with the other partners, but he thought Jack could come right in as a partner.

They parted company on Sunday, with David headed for Portland and Jack headed to his office to start another workweek. They agreed that Jack should at least visit the Portland office of the firm. As he drove to his office in Boston, Jack was wondering if lawyers in Portland were stuck working every Saturday and Sunday. He rather doubted it. One more thing that looked better than Boston.

During the same time span as Jack was establishing himself as a first-rate defense attorney, Bruce was continuing his clandestine work for the Agency. In El Salvadore, a group of young military officers overthrew a right-wing government known for its massacre of the poor. The CIA immediately got involved with a plan to convince the inexperienced officers who were taking control to include many of the old guard in key positions in the new government. Essentially, this would put elements of the overthrown regime into key positions in the new government. The resistance to this plan came from a thirty-seven-year-old civilian political operator named Oscar Sanchez. He was dead set against the CIA plan to involve some of the people associated with the very regime they had just overthrown. Bruce King was brought in to resolve the situation by removing the obstacle.

Bruce had to be careful to avoid getting CIA fingerprints on the assassination. Sanchez had a rival among the civilian reformers named Manual Ortiz. Ortiz was also not a fan of the CIA proposal, but he was a rival of Sanchez in the battle for who was in charge. The two had jockeyed for leadership positions among the reform group. It was no secret that they harbored ill feelings toward each other.

For the CIA to succeed, it was essential to get rid of both of them.

A forged CIA memo with Sanchez's signature was presented to Ortiz. It claimed that Ortiz was in league with the officials of the overthrown regime. The memo had the desired effect of igniting the well-known temper of Ortiz, who proceeded to rail against Sanchez in front of a number of military officers. That gave Bruce King an opportunity to put a plan into action to get rid of both. He had a well-paid plant spend an evening with Ortiz. When Sanchez returned to his home that same evening after spending several days away, Bruce was waiting in the dark. As Sanchez entered the room,

Bruce wrapped his arm around his neck and drove a twelve-inch blade into his back. He stabbed him intentionally a number of times so it would look like a murder committed while the perpetrator was in a rage. The murder weapon was hidden in Ortiz's home the next morning.

Ortiz vehemently professed his innocence, but the person he spent most of the evening with, the well-paid CIA plant, denied being with him. Thus, he had no alibi and the knife matching the stab wounds perfectly was found in his home. The agency used the killing of one civilian reformer by another as proof that the young military leaders needed the experienced, steady hand of some of the old guard involved in the new government, an argument that worked.

With Sanchez and Ortiz removed, they prevailed in the argument, and soon things were back to normal with a right winger running the government, repressing and killing poor civilian protesters.

Bruce's involvement covered the globe. He was in Afghanistan running American weapons into local tribal leaders fighting the Russians. He was in Nicaragua after the fall of Anastasios Samoza, the CIA-backed dictator. He was active in organizing the remnants of Samoza's personal army, the National Guard, into a unit to fight the communist leaning Sandinistas who had taken over the government. The reorganized unit would be called Contras. In 1981, the CIA would begin an illegal sale of arms to Iran at very high marked-up prices using the profits to fund the Contras efforts against the Sandinistas. This activity would result in a scandal that would nearly take down the Reagan presidency.

Bruce King was involved in it all. Political assassinations, torturous interrogations, blackmail, bribery, gun running—you name it, he participated in it. He carried out every black op order he received. He did it all successfully while operating under the radar screen, invisible to congressional oversight. He knew the inside story on CIA operations and where all the bodies were buried, the type of knowledge that would become useful in Bruce's future. The downside to his success as a field agent was the gnawing feeling that he had completely lost any moral compass. He pushed these feelings aside and moved on, but they wouldn't go away completely.

Chapter XVIII

TONY FIGNONI SAT ON THE oversize leather couch in his father's office pondering his father's last question. The two of them were discussing a new rival for their narcotics and prostitution market in New York and New Jersey. A Columbian group had moved into their territory more than two years ago. At first, their impact on the Fignoni's business was so small it hardly mattered. They were bringing in drugs from their native Columbia, selling them in the same areas claimed by the Fignoni's, but their impact was small. Gradually, they had grown to a point where they were crowding the market, taking business away from the Fignonis at an alarming rate. Competition for market share was not something the Fignoni family tolerated. They had already let it go on too long. It was past time to do something about it, and they both knew the longer it went on the more difficult it would be to address the issue.

To add insult to injury, the Columbians added prostitution to their business line and began taking some of that business away from the Fignoni's in prime areas. The Fignoni family was in the business of very high-priced prostitutes. They relied on the staff in many of New York City's finest hotels to provide a steady stream of clients. Now the Columbians had even taken a good chunk of that business. Tony's father had asked what are our options to deal with the Columbians. He could no longer sit by while his market share shrunk.

"One thing is for certain," Tony answered. "We have waited too long. We have been too fat and lazy, thinking they could never get big enough to have a great impact. Now we are dealing with a large, strong, well-financed foe."

The senior Fignoni looked at his son with a dismissive expression. "That's stating the obvious, and it doesn't answer the questions," his father responded. It had been a long time since the Fignoni family business had to deal with an unwelcome competitor. They were out of practice after years of having the market in their area to themselves.

"Well, the options are simple. We either meet with them to try and work out a cooperative agreement or we start a war with them to try to take them out."

Both options carried their share of problems. Trying to cooperate would signal a weakness to their competition as well as resulting in sacrificing a good deal of their market share. Showing any weakness in their business was never a good option. Reducing the operation ran against everything the senior Fignoni believed about operating any business, whether it's a legal or illegal business. He often said, "You're either growing or you're dying."

The second option was also fraught with problems. The Fignoni family no longer had the muscle available to wage war with a rival. Over the years, it had become unnecessary to carry a payroll loaded with hired guns. They could bring it in from outside, but in those cases, loyalty was always questionable. Also hiring from outside was expensive. A long, drawn-out battle with the Columbians would cripple both operations, causing huge losses of business for both. While the two fought with each other, it invited other players to move in to fill a void. It may just be a mutually assured destruction with neither side coming out a winner. It was a no better option than negotiation.

"I have no doubt that now that they have moved into prostitution. Gambling will be next for them. So we will lose market share there as well," the senior Fignoni said in breaking a long silence. "They are very aggressive, and they have shown us no respect." He looked at his son for a response.

"What we need is a quick devastating strike that blows up their entire operation," Tony observed.

His father shook his head, saying, "Again, you state the obvious. Give me a fucking plan. This is your future we are talking about here. I'm really too old to even be worried about these beaner fucks."

Tony thought for a moment then got up from the sofa saying, "Okay, I have an idea. You know the friend I made in the army, Bruce King." His father nodded. "He may well be in a position to help us. I will travel down to DC tomorrow and talk to him."

"Your solution is to have law enforcement take care of our problem? You must be out of your mind. If you get the feds in here, we will all end up in jail."

Tony walked to the door to leave then stopped, turning to his father. "Give me a little credit, will you. I have the beginnings of a plan in mind. I just need to run some ideas past Bruce. Just give me a couple of weeks, and I will have a plan that will work."

His father dismissed him with a sarcastic wave of his hand, figuring he would have to deal with the problem on his own terms. Tony walked out of his father's office to call Bruce. Lucky for him, Bruce was not out of the country, and he answered on the third ring. Tony told him he was headed for DC on business and wondered if Bruce was going to be around so that they could get together. Bruce told him he expected to be around and would be glad to meet with him.

"Do you have something on your mind, or is this just a social call?" Bruce asked.

"It's a bit of both, but believe me when I tell you, Bruce, that the discussion will be interesting." They ended the conversation at that, leaving the specifics for the meeting.

Tony flew down to Washington, checking into the historical landmark, the Willard Hotel that same afternoon. He called Bruce, inviting him to come into town and have dinner together. They met at the dining room at the hotel and after brief small talk, Tony got right down to business.

"Bruce, you need to understand that my family has a lot of connections outside of New York and Jersey. We have them here as well. I know you are in the CIA and I know what you do for them. You don't have to confirm it or deny it. Your activities with the agency have provided you with some very unique specialty training. We are having our problems in our business, and I believe with your training you can help us solve them."

Bruce started to respond, and Tony put up his hand to stop him. "Let me finish. We would be looking to pay you and pay you very well for your services. It would be work outside your CIA duties but of a similar nature. I need to know if you would have any interest in taking on a task to help an old combat buddy. A task that will pay you a lot of fucking money." Tony finished and looked expectantly at Bruce for an answer. He looked across the table for any sign that would give him insight into his friend's reaction. Bruce had a poker face that gave nothing away. So Tony went on. "Well, can I at least get an answer, a nod, a smile, a frown, something?"

Bruce took his time, leaning back in his chair, looking across the table at Tony.

"Tell me what the problem is and how you think I can help."

He took encouragement from the fact that Bruce asked the question.

Tony went into a long, detailed explanation of the problems they were facing in dealing with the Columbians. He explained that the only real option was to destroy the Columbian operation but that the Fignoni family lacked the resources for a long, protracted war. What was needed was a bold, quick, devastating strike that crippled their competition's entire operation.

"With your experience operating in the CIA, I think we can come up with a plan to deal with the situation. You have been involved in a number of intricate CIA operations that have accomplished similar objectives. We need you, Bruce. I don't think we can do it without you."

Obviously this was a very unique kind of proposal. It had the potential to get him involved in illegal activity on behalf of a criminal enterprise. It also had the potential to provide him with a large cash reserve that would make an exit plan from the CIA viable.

Bruce sat for a time before responding. Finally, he said, "Are you looking for me to design a plan that you will carry out, or am I expected to carry out the plan myself? It would make a difference both in terms of my interest and the money I would require if I'm just passing a plan on to you, or if I'm carrying it out."

"I would accept any help you feel comfortable giving us but ideally a plan that we carry out together. This will involve illegal activity putting me at risk, so what kind of money are we talking?"

Tony was pleased at this point that his proposal was not rejected out of hand. As long as Bruce was still talking, he had a good chance to bring him into the deal.

"We will deposit $125,000 in a Swiss bank account in your name as soon as we agree on a plan of action. We will deposit another $125,000 immediately after the successful completion of the operation you design."

Again, Bruce digested all that had been said before answering. "Let's order dinner, talk about this no more this evening. Give me forty-eight hours to think it over and meet here again two nights from now at the same time and I will give you an answer."

"You want me to spend two more nights in this shithole town?" Tony delivered this line with a smile.

"I'm sure you can keep yourself occupied for forty-eight hours unless you've changed a lot."

The two ate dinner while talking over old times, consumed after dinner drinks, then parted company.

Bruce spent the next two days deciding if he really wanted to get involved in this matter. It was not only well outside his CIA government duties, but it was also illegal activity. Still, it would involve similar activities to his current job simply with a different master. Plus, in this case, he would be paid handsomely, unlike his government job. He had been thinking recently that it would be nice to leave the CIA. Having built up a nest egg in a Swiss bank account would make the exit easier. He decided he would devise a plan, offer it to Tony at a price, and decide later if he would participate in carrying it out.

They met two nights later right on schedule at the Willard as agreed. This time, Bruce started the discussion telling Tony what he had decided. He would need a couple of weeks to put together a plan of operation. "It will cost you more than $125,000. If you like the plan, I will expect $200,000 to be deposited in a Swiss bank account. I will tell you after we agree on a plan whether I will participate in carrying it out. If I do agree to participate, I would expect another $300,000 to be deposited upon the successful completion of the plan. This will be a difficult task, not to mention illegal work you are asking me to perform. I won't do it for short money. We are longtime friends, Tony, but this is a business arrangement. An illegal business arrangement. If I'm in, it will cost you."

Tony sat back and considered the proposal. Leaning back over the table, he said, "You are demanding quite a lot of money, Bruce. Do you think you're worth it?"

"Of course, I am. If you didn't already know that you wouldn't be here. So put up or shut up."

Tony smiled at this. "You're pretty brazen talking to a made man like this. I will agree but keep in mind I will have to run it by my father. He would make the final decision. The price is high, but if the plan impresses him, I will be able to bring him along."

With that, Bruce said he needed certain information delivered to him. He needed to know the number of men in the Columbian organization they would consider key people. He needed their names and positions. He needed a map detailing the locations the organization operated from. If possible, he wanted to know how their supply of narcotics came into the country and how it was delivered to them in New York. "Get me that information, and I will have a plan in two weeks."

Tony agreed he would provide all the information they had available.

They had dinner together with Tony telling him he was catching a red-eye flight back at eleven thirty. Bruce gave him a ride to the airport where they parted company, with Tony saying he would have his father's answer within twenty-four hours.

The next day, Bruce returned to his apartment in Alexandria at six thirty in the evening to find an envelope had been slipped under his door. He opened it to find the list of names of key men in the Columbian organization, the requested map, a statement that they did not have the information about how the narcotics were delivered, plus a note from Tony saying his father approved the payment plan as long as the proposed plan looked good to him. All systems looked like a go. Bruce began working on a plan of attack that same evening.

The Columbian organization was relatively small. There were basically only eight key people. Their drug trade was handled out of a warehouse two streets up from New York's commercial docks. They also ran a trucking company out of the same warehouse as a cover for their illegal activities. There were warehouse workers as well as truck drivers, but the key people were the eight office workers. They contracted out the long-haul trucks to various companies, hauling a host of products to different locations around the country, all very legal activities. They owned a fleet of six tractor trailers that they kept busy as independently contracted haulers. This operation, as well as the drug business, was basically handled by a half-dozen key people who worked in the offices on the second floor of the warehouse. In addition, two other key people ran a rapidly expanding prostitution ring out of the same location. The eight office dwellers included six males and two females, all from Columbia. This was the nerve center of the entire operation.

Street distribution was handled by subcontracting with local gangs. The Columbians supplied the narcotics, sold them to local gangs for street sales. Essentially it was a wholesale drug operation. They were operating in New York and New Jersey as Tony had initially said, but the information provided to Bruce indicated they were making plays to move into Philadelphia and Baltimore. They were organized, aggressive, and looking to grow by expanding into other markets.

The head of the organization, Carlos Hernandez, stayed in a large waterfront home in the Hamptons with several women friends and his righthand man, David Garcia. He only came into New York to visit the warehouse operation two or three times a month. He worked out of the Hamptons in an office he set up in the house. All the key people working in the offices, as well the warehouse, answered to Carlos Hernandez. He was the direct link between the North American operations and Columbia.

Bruce spent a couple of weeks going over the information and designing a plan of attack. He viewed this operation much like a

CIA operation, approaching it the same way. Careful planning and execution was the key just as in the case of CIA black ops. It would be as requested, a bold quick hit that would devastate the Columbian operation. After two weeks, he had a plan, but to execute it, they would need some inside information about how the narcotics came into New York and when a large shipment would be due.

Given the location of the warehouse, delivery by ship would be very possible. However, given the trucking company operation, delivery over the road also seemed a logical assumption. They would have to nail down the system of delivery and get some planned dates. Bruce had a plan how to obtain the needed information. He called his friend Tony to set up a meeting to go over his plan. They agreed to meet in Secaucus in two days.

Chapter XIX

JACK HAD MADE HIS DECISION. The six-figure income, the prestige, the name he had built for himself in the very big Boston market was all great, but he felt like a gerbil on a wheel in a cage. His original idea of working for the ACLU had long since been forgotten. It was time to go back to basics. His discussion about going back to Maine, to Portland, had struck a nerve, and he had decided to pursue the change. He picked up his phone after a long day in the courtroom and made the call to his friend, David Kerry, to set up a meeting with him as well as the rest of his partners. They set up an appointment for the following Saturday afternoon in Portland. It would mean a Saturday in which he wasn't stuck in his office working. So he left his home in Marblehead Saturday morning, heading north.

He arrived at the downtown Portland law offices of McCarthy, Kerry, and Conley at two o'clock on Saturday. He was greeted by the three partners in the firm. Kerry and Conley had gone to law school with Jack, and like him, they were in their thirties. McCarthy was the senior partner who had been running his own three-person firm before being joined by the two younger partners nine years earlier. At fifty-two years old, he was still young by Portland lawyer standards. He had decided in his early forties that he wanted to grow his small firm. He fed off the youthful enthusiasm and aggression of his younger partners. The firm had grown in size as well as reputation since the two young, aggressive junior partners had come on board. The three had discussed extensively what it could mean to bring in a lawyer of the caliber of Jack Roach. A young lawyer who had quickly made a name for himself in a big market. While only nine years out of law school, Jack had built an impressive reputation as a defense lawyer. He had worked in a big firm and quickly moved to the top of his department. The three partners felt that adding Jack to the defense team headed by Conley had the potential to elevate the firm's status to a whole new level among Maine defense lawyers. They were also encouraged by his youth and his aggressive nature. They saw nothing but positives in having Jack on board, but still the interview process was necessary in order to judge the chemistry between Jack and the partners. No matter how talented Jack might be, the chemistry in the firm was important.

The three partners all shook hands with him as he entered their conference room. He was offered coffee as pleasantries were exchanged among them. Jack was well acquainted with his two former classmates, but it was his first time meeting with McCarthy, who had a solid reputation as a lawyer who specialized in estate planning. Jack knew McCarthy was well respected within the Portland legal community.

McCarthy opened the discussion around the subject they were all there to explore. "So, Mr. Roach, you have very quickly established yourself as a top defense lawyer in a big market with a ton of competition. We've seen you handle high-profile, white-collar crime cases as well as a manslaughter case and a murder case. How have you managed so quickly to establish yourself as a rising star in a city lousy with lawyers?"

"It's nice of you to open with a compliment, although some in Boston might not like the characterization that it's lousy with lawyers," Jack said as a joke. "I will try to answer the question with humility."

Jack explained that he was fortunate to go into a large firm with a small defense attorney staff. They broke him in on a fast track over just two years. Then when he started taking the lead on cases, it just happened that a good number of high-profile cases landed at the firm. The murder case was kind of a favor to a judge who had leaned on the firm to take the case and Jack wanted the experience, so he volunteered within the firm to take the case.

Further questions involved the inner workings of a large, big city firm. They asked how much Jack was making there and if he felt he could have eventually become a partner. He answered all their questions and was finally asked by McCarthy, "Why would you be interested in coming to Portland to work for a piddly-ass firm like ours? You will be taking a pay cut, and if you did make partner in Boston, your earnings would be enormous. This was the question all three partners wanted to have answered. The two younger partners were envious of Jack's position in Boston. Why he wanted to come to Portland was a bit of a mystery to them that they wanted solved.

Jack answered, "I bill out a minimum of sixty hours a week, often ballooning to ninety or more. I work most Saturdays and Sundays. I make a shitload of money, but I have precious little time to enjoy it. I'm a bit tired of that rat race. I'm tired of having no time for myself. Also, I love Maine, and I miss living here."

"Well, we may be a bit more laid-back here," Conley said. "But we put in plenty of hours as well. I hope you're not looking to semiretire."

"Absolutely not. I have been working since I was thirteen. I'm a hard worker and will be until I die. The pressure in a large, big city firm is very difficult to describe to someone who has not experienced it, but believe me when I say it's much more than just hard work. It's pressure that is with you every minute of every day. It's impossible to escape it or ever leave it behind."

The three partners were very satisfied with Jack's answers as well as his entire demeanor. Having gone through law school with him, Conley and Kerry had no doubt about his work ethic.

"Well, Jack, you must also have questions for us, and we have given you no chance to ask," commented McCarthy, "so please ask away."

Jack asked questions about their firm in terms of what areas of law they worked, how the division of labor was handled, and if they wanted to grow the firm larger.

Basically, as a small general practice firm in a relatively small market, they would handle every area of law. However, all nine attorneys had an area in which they specialized. McCarthy and one of the associates, Joe Dugan, handled primarily estate planning and corporate law. Conley and another associate, Patrick Crowley, concentrated on criminal defense. David Kerry, as well as John Merrill, handled mostly real estate work. Karen Foster handled family law and was considered Portland's toughest divorce lawyer. She usually represented the wife and was the husband's worst nightmare. Thomas Delahanty concentrated on government permitting and regulations as well as workers comp claims. He also did some lobbying at the state level. Cory Higgins, the newest associate, still learning the ropes, worked in all areas assisting where needed. The partners were unanimous in wanting to grow. Kerry and Conley were young aggressive lawyers with big plans, and McCarthy supported them. All three felt that Jack Roach would team with Conley and Crowley to make them a leader in criminal defense.

With all questions having been answered, they offered to bring in Jack as a partner with a salary lower than his Boston salary but generous by Portland standards.

After being offered the partnership position, Jack agreed to the deal. He said it would take him sixty to ninety days to wrap up his work at his current firm, so he would start in three months.

The three partners and their new fourth partner then went to DiMillo's Restaurant, where they would be joined by the three wives for dinner. Over drinks, before the wives arrived, Jack asked the very important question of whether his new firm wanted to pick up the cost of his two prime location season tickets to the Red Sox. McCarthy had little interest but was quickly outvoted by his two original partners.

Jack stayed in Portland overnight, heading back on Sunday morning. On Monday, he announced his decision to the managing partner of the firm and called a realtor to put his Marblehead home on the market. He knew that the money he would get for a home in Marblehead would buy a quality home in the Portland area. He promised to help make the transition as smooth as possible but noted that he would have to take a number of trips to Portland over the next few months to get settled. His fellow attorneys were genuinely sorry to see him go but said they understood. He went to bed Monday evening feeling good about his decision. He looked forward to returning to the state he loved.

Chapter XX

BRUCE DROVE UP TO SECAUCUS and met with Tony, Tony's father, and a trusted Fignoni family lieutenant named Johnny Bartonni. He laid out his plan of attack which, if successful, would finish off their competition in one devastating move. What's more, the attack's effects would be so profound, so stunning, that it would send a message to any other would-be competitors. He would be working as an informant to the DEA and FBI to bring the law down on the Columbians, to crack down on their entire operation. In addition, he would make his own strategic hit at the heart of the operation using military-type weapons. As he laid out the plan, it was enthusiastically received by the Fignonis. It was exactly the type of operation they wanted with devastating immediate impact.

There was, however, one problem. In order for things to work right, they needed to know how narcotics were delivered to the Columbians and they needed to know when a shipment would be coming. Bruce had a plan for that as well. He suggested that they grab off one of the key people working the warehouse and torture him to get the information they needed.

"These guys are pretty tough, Bruce," Tony said. "I'm not sure you can get one of them to talk."

Bruce smiled at his old friend and responded, "I have a few ideas on how to make him talk. Don't forget whom I work for in my day job."

The confidence of the statement impressed the Fignonis. The senior Fignoni was beginning to think they had the right guy. He was still a bit leery about bringing in the FBI, but the way Bruce explained their involvement eased his fears.

The next night, Bruce and Johnny Bartonni sat in a van across the street and a half block down from the warehouse, watching for an opportunity to follow one of the Columbians as they left. Johnny knew the key players by sight but he was less recognizable to them than Tony would have been. Of course they had no way of knowing Bruce.

Finally, after three hours of waiting, two workers pulled out in a Ford Mustang at seven thirty. As they drove past the van, Johnny recognized them as two high-ranking members and he pulled out to follow them. They drove four blocks to a popular nightclub, pulled over and parked. They got out of their car laughing and walked into the club. After the van was parked, Bruce told Johnny to wait in the van while he went into the club. "Stay here until I come out with one of them."

Bruce entered the building, walking around until he spied his target. He stood at the bar and ordered a drink, while keeping an eye on the two. They were sitting at a table, trying to strike up a conversation with two women at an adjacent table. They did not seem to be doing well. The body language from the two women seemed to indicate that they were not going to pull it off. Eventually, the two women picked up their drinks and walked to another table obviously the two Columbians had no rap.

Bruce continued to watch them as they discussed their performance with the two women. One of the two women walked past their table, headed to the ladies' room. The Columbian on Bruce's left got up, said something to his friend, and headed after her. They both walked past Bruce standing at the bar. He followed, thinking the man was leaving and this was too good to be true. It wasn't, he was not leaving, he was headed to the men's room, which he entered right after the woman he was following went into the ladies' room. Bruce had not noticed when he came in that the bathrooms were on your right as you entered the building. Still a perfect opportunity. He followed him into the men's room.

In addition to the two of them, a third patron was washing his hands as Bruce came in. He stood at one of the urinals, pretending to be using it until the third person left. His target finished his business and walked behind Bruce headed for the sinks. With amazing quickness, Bruce turned and wrapped his right arm around the Columbian's neck, applying pressure to cut off the oxygen to his brain. He struggled for a time until he lost consciousness Bruce put the unconscious man's right arm over Bruce's shoulder while holding him up with his left arm around his rib cage. He walked him out that way, telling the bouncer at the door that his friend had a bit too much to drink, given the drugs he had taken before coming into the club. The bouncer nodded his understanding as Bruce walked past him out the door.

Johnny had taken an opportunity to move the van closer to the door, so it was a short walk for Bruce.

Getting him to the van, Bruce put him into the back and proceeded to tie him up while Johnny drove away. They drove to Secaucus to a garage on the Fignoni estate. Bruce had set up a make-shift table there using sawhorses and boards. They laid their captive, whose name Johnny told Bruce was Ivan Velez, on the table and tied him down. "We don't really want to hurt you, but we need a bit of information that I think you can help with," Bruce addressed his captive.

"You can go fuck yourself. You will get nothing from me."

"Well, I would not be so sure of that if I were you," Bruce responded as he laid out a terry cloth towel next to his captive. He looked down at the Columbian, giving him a smile as he made sure the ropes were secure.

"You don't know who you are fucking with, asshole. I will tell you nothing no matter what you do to me, and you will pay for fucking with the wrong people."

Bruce laughed at Velez, whom he knew was scared in spite of his bravado.

"I have fucked with the wrong people all my life, pal, and I haven't paid yet. By the way, you speak very good English for such a dumb-looking asshole."

"Go fuck yourself."

"Now, now, there's no need to be vulgar."

Just then, Tony and Johnny came into the garage. Bruce had requested ten five-gallon jugs of water be placed in the garage along with two towels. Tony had asked why and Bruce merely answered, "You will see." Now he explained what he had planned for Mr. Velez to his two accomplices, speaking with some pride in his torture abilities.

"What I'm going to show you here, Tony and Johnny, is a way to get information used by the CIA. It's not new—it's been around for a long time—but we have recently reinstituted the procedure. It's called waterboarding, and believe me, our tough little friend here will eventually sing like a bird."

"You will get nothing from me."

"There, there now, just relax, my Columbian friend. You know those two girls at the bar were never going anywhere with a butt-ugly prick like you."

Before Velez could respond, Bruce began the process. On the third pouring of water over the cloth, Velez lost consciousness. Bruce slapped him several times to bring him back around. Tony said, "I think you're going to kill him before he tells us anything."

Bruce shook his head. "Don't worry, I've done this before. The idea is to bring him as close to death as many times as it takes to get what you want. Eventually he will break, they all do."

With that he began again. After each time, the water was poured. They would pull off the towel then they would ask him how narcotics were delivered to the warehouse. Finally, after six times bringing Velez, within inches of death, he decided he had had enough. He said he would tell them what they wanted to know, just "please stop with the water." Bruce looked over at Tony and smiled. Bruce gave Velez credit for his toughness, but the waterboarded Mr. Velez was ready to talk.

Three of the tractor trailers the trucking company used had false bottoms. Drugs came in by ship at various ports, using a variety of haulers. Mixing up the ships used and the ports of delivery made it difficult for the DEA to track them. Whatever port was used, they would pick the drugs, place them in the false bottom of the trailers then deliver them to New York. It had proven to be a fail-proof system. The false bottoms would only open when triggered by a remote switch hidden under the dash board where nobody could find it. Without using the electronics switch, the false bottom could not be accessed, and to the naked eye, it was undetectable. Bruce made him describe the hidden switch and how to find it.

"When are you expecting the next big delivery?" Bruce asked.

Velez had got his breath by now, and he was regaining some of his courage. He stared up at Bruce, not answering the question. Bruce let out a long sigh and picked up the towel. He placed it over Velez's face, stifling an objection, and poured a healthy slug of water over the towel. It took two more doses of water before he was ready to talk again; he was a tough customer.

"Enough drugs were coming into the Port of Virginia in Norfolk that it took two trailers to pick them up. They will be arriving into the New York warehouse in four days." Having gained the information they were after, Bruce looked over at Tony and smiled. He then resumed his waterboarding, again stifling a cry for mercy. This time, he kept pouring water until Velez was dead from drowning. The cold-blooded killing even stunned Tony and Johnny. Bruce did not seem to care. He told Johnny to dispose of the body.

Bruce's plan of attack was essentially two-pronged. First, he was working with the DEA and the FBI on the shipment of drugs for the organization. He had given them a heads-up that his work in South America for the CIA had gained him an informant who would feed him information about drug shipments into the United States. He met ten days ago with both organizations, telling them that he was expecting information on a large shipment due to come in soon. Naturally, both agencies were anxious to make the bust.

After gaining the information from Velez, he called his contacts in both agencies and a conference call was put together for the afternoon, following the torturing of Velez. A plan was put together whereby the DEA would monitor the Norfolk docks watching for the ship Velez had named and then observe the offloading from the ship to the two tractor trailers. The entire transaction would be filmed from a distance, then after the trucks had left, they would move in to seize the ship.

The trucks would be discreetly followed up the coast to New York. Once they pulled into the warehouse, the FBI would move in with full knowledge of the false bottoms of the trailers as well as how to access them. They would seize the drugs, all the vehicles, and the warehouse, and arrest everyone there. The vehicles and the warehouse would be auctioned off by the government while those arrested would be tried and jailed. The involvement of the DEA and FBI would be limited to the Columbians as they acted on Bruce's tip.

While all this was happening, Bruce himself would take care of the house in the Hamptons, as well as all its occupants. The timing would be set so that the New York warehouse seizure, and the attack in the Hamptons would happen simultaneously. Just like a good CIA operation, good planning and solid execution will get good results. The Columbian operation would be completely eliminated.

* * * * *

Within the Columbian organization, there was immediate concern over the disappearance of Velez. At first, it was thought he had run into the woman he had followed on his way to or from the men's room, been able to convince her to spend the night with him, and he had left with her. When he did not show up the next morning, it was reported to Carlos Hernandez in the Hamptons. It was not automatically suspected that the Fignonis were involved. There were a number of possibilities ranging from the gangs that they used for distribution to the New York City police. Hernandez put the onus on his right-hand man David Garcia to see if he could find out what happened. Garcia was in that process as Bruce's plan kicked into action.

On Thursday evening, September 8, 1982, at 7:00 p.m., the two tractor trailers rolled into the New York warehouse. Within one hour of their arrival, FBI agents moved in and surrounded the warehouse. The occupants did not put up any resistance to the agents as they felt confident that their false bottoms in the trailers were virtually undetectable and the drugs would remain well hidden. They had no way of knowing that the agents were all well informed about their tractor trailers and had opened up the false bottoms within an hour's time. The arrests were made in both New York and Norfolk where the delivery ship had already been seized.

Meanwhile, Bruce King was set up in the Hamptons five hundred feet from the house owned and occupied by Carlos Hernandez. As luck would have it, David Garcia was in the house as well. Bruce had seen him pull his car in and enter the house within the hour. Things were coming together perfectly.

Bruce was perched on a hill behind and across the street from the house. Security cameras, guard dogs, and a fence made it impossible to simply wire the place with explosives. So Bruce had chosen to set himself up with five M72LAW (light anti-tank weapons), a portable one-shot 66 mm unguided tank guns as well as his trusted Winchester rifle. His plan was to fire the 66 mm shots into the house from the hilltop that he reached by motorcycle, destroy the house, and kill everyone in it. He kept the Winchester available on the off chance that anyone would survive and try to flee the house. At five hundred feet, to the old sniper, it would be like shooting fish in a barrel.

He began firing the anti-tank guns in rapid succession. His first hit blew through the back wall, exploding on contact, shattering most of the rear of the building. The second shot followed within seconds, hitting the sidewall closest to Bruce with the same devastating impact. The third shot followed the same path, and the explosion collapsed the entire north end of the house with both floors falling into rubble. To his surprise, a lone male staggered out of the front of the crumbling building. At the distance of his perch, he could not tell who it was, but it really didn't matter. He picked up the Winchester and fired two shots into the staggering body, dropping him dead.

The final two shots from the anti-tank gun collapsed the rest of the structure leaving little doubt that the inhabitants had been crushed or killed by the explosions. That being finished, he stuffed the spent M72LAW weapons into his knapsack, strapped the Winchester over his back, got on his motorcycle, and traveled across country for half a mile to a neighboring street where Tony Fignoni waited in a U-Haul truck. He could hear the sirens in the distance as he made his escape. He drove the motorcycle into the back of the U-Haul, closed it up, and they headed for Secaucus. Mission accomplished. The assets of the Columbians had all been seized along with a huge drug shipment. The principal operators were all in jail or dead. The Fignoni family would not have to worry about them anymore. Bruce had pulled it off with amazing efficiency. The five hundred thousand was money well spent.

Chapter XXI

JACK WRAPPED UP HIS WORK at the Boston firm, sold his house in Marblehead, and moved to Portland. He purchased a home in Falmouth and began work at his new firm. The work was quite different from the white-collar crime defense he specialized in while in Boston. Here he was defending drug related offenses, OUI arrests, and domestic assaults. The volume of cases kept him busy, but the crimes he defended were very different. They were petty crimes compared to his work in Boston. It was a step down that sometimes made him wonder if he had made the right move. He found the office less hectic than Boston and certainly a lot less pressure. Plus, the lifestyle in general was more relaxed, but part of him missed the challenge the larger cases brought.

Still, he was settling in nicely. He enjoyed the people he worked with and the more relaxed attitude of the city in general as compared to Boston. He had begun dating a twenty-eight-year-old Chevrus High School teacher named Elaine Watkins whom he met at a local concert his first week in town. She was a blond, blue-eyed beauty who grew up in Bangor, went to college in Farmington, and was in her fifth year teaching at Chevrus. She had a very independent, self-assured attitude that he loved. Jack was still a bit reluctant to get too serious about any woman after his experience with Sue Frazier, but he really enjoyed Elaine's company. He had to make a conscious effort to stay somewhat under control emotionally. Once burned, always cautious.

It only took a couple of months before he landed a high-profile murder trial. A fellow attorney named Catherine Merrill killed her husband, a financial adviser named Chadwick Merrill. They were both high-profile people in greater Portland. Ms. Merrill grew up in Waterville and met her future husband when they were both attending Dartmouth College. Chadwick came from an old Portland family that was awash in old Yankee money. He grew up protected by a silver spoon and was generally considered by most people that knew him to be a pompous ass. He worked in the well-established family business, providing financial planning to the upper crust. The Merrills all lived in Falmouth Foreside in very high-end homes. They were involved in a number of financial businesses ranging from banking to hedge funds. The Merrill family wealth and influence was well-known to all Portland residents. They were a financial as well as political force to be reckoned with.

Jack got an early morning call at his office from Catherine Merrill on a Saturday when he just happened to be in. She was under arrest, being held in the Cumberland County jail for murdering her husband. She used her one phone call to reach Jack, asking him to come to the jail and act as her attorney. Jack was surprised by the call, having only met her on a couple of occasions. He was not sure why she chose him as her attorney. Surprised as he was, he knew a golden opportunity when he saw one. This would be a high-profile case that would be right up his alley.

Jack dropped everything to hurry to the jail to meet with his potential client. After a short wait, he was ushered into small conference room used for attorney client meetings where he sat waiting for his client. After a few moments, Catherine Merrill was brought into the conference room accompanied by a guard. She was tall at five feet, ten inches and looked much younger than her forty-one years. Her face, as well as her figure, showed no signs of aging. Jack was stunned by the appearance of this woman that he knew to be a very sophisticated, classy lady. It was not just the orange jumpsuit; it was her entire unkempt appearance and her entirely defeated, downtrodden demeanor. The independent, confident woman he thought her to be was not in evidence. She had obviously been crying, and the left side of her face was badly bruised and swollen.

She was led to a chair across the table from Jack. She winced visibly as she sat down, looking across the table at Jack as the guard left the room. Jack reached across the table, patted her hand while looking her in the eye, and said, "You have obviously been through hell. Take a moment to gain your composure, know that I'm here to help, and tell me what has happened. Unless you object, I'm going to record your statement."

She nodded, motioning that she did not object.

Catherine Merrill told the story of what had transpired in the early morning hours at her home in Falmouth Foreside. She and her husband had been at a social function at the Falmouth Golf Club on Friday evening. As usual, her husband had too much to drink, so she had to drive home. On the drive he began accusing her, wrongly, of flirting with several of the other male guests who had been in attendance. This was a common refrain when he was drunk. If there were any other men around, she would be accused of flirting with them. She knew better than to argue with him, so she simply said, "We can discuss it in the morning." This enraged him all the more, and he shouted at her, banging his fist on the dash. When they reached their house, she walked into the kitchen from the attached garage ahead of him. She turned to look at him, and he landed a full-fisted punch to the side of her face, knocking her down. At this point in telling the story, she brought her hands up to her face and began sobbing uncontrollably. Jack waited for a bit, letting her cry out some of her emotions.

Finally, he told her, "Take your time, Ms. Merrill. We have all morning," as he handed her his handkerchief. He sat in silence, waiting for her to regain her composure. Finally, she wiped her eyes, saying, "I'm sorry, Mr. Roach, this is just very hard."

"It's okay. Remember, I'm here to help. By the way, Jack will do fine."

She smiled and nodded as she began again. He kicked her twice in the ribs, which she thought were either cracked or broken. Then leaning down over her, he pulled her up part way by the hair and delivered another crushing blow to the face, which knocked her back down, telling her if she ever acted that way again, he would kill her. He then walked to the portable bar on the other side of the kitchen and poured himself a scotch, which was the last thing he needed.

She struggled to her feet half conscious and leaned over the kitchen sink. Her nose was bleeding, and she felt that it may be broken. She turned around to face him after controlling the bleeding somewhat with a tissue. She told him that she was leaving, and she started for the door. He dropped his glass of scotch and hurried after her, catching her by the door. He grabbed her by the shoulders, spun her around, and pressed her against the counter, driving her head against the upper cabinets. He slammed her head into the cabinets several times. He had his hands around her throat, choking her. He applied more and more pressure. While calling her a bitch and spewing profanities. She could not breathe. He reminded her that he had promised to kill her if she ever tried to leave. She felt that he was going to keep that promise right then in their kitchen.

She tried to pull his hands away from her throat or to get free from his grasp, but he was too strong. As she struggled, she reached behind her and felt on the counter the knife holder that rested on the granite counter and held five carving knives. She grabbed one and stabbed her husband in the side. His face registered surprise, and he momentarily loosened his grip. But he quickly tightened it again, hollering that he would "kill this bitch." She stabbed him two more times, and he finally fell in front of her. After catching her breath so she could breathe normally, she called an ambulance and the police. He was dead when the ambulance arrived.

After completing her story, she nearly collapsed from exhaustion. Jack again told her to breathe deeply and regain her composure. After giving her some time, he asked, "Is this the first time he ever beat you?"

"God, no, there have been a number of times."

"Have you ever called the police to report the beatings?"

"No. He threatened to kill me if I did."

The report of this kind of spousal abuse in this upper crust family was surprising to Jack. He did not know either Catherine or her husband well, and he had heard stories about him that were not complementary, but still this news was a bit shocking.

Jack was taking notes furiously in addition to the recorder he was running.

"Are there records anywhere that will verify these beatings? Pictures, hospital records, family, and friends who knew about them?"

"He was usually careful to hit me where it would not leave a visible mark. Stomach, ribs, legs. But I have been to Mercy Hospital with internal injuries on at least four occasions. Plus, on a couple of occasions, I have gone into work with bruises I could not hide with makeup or my attire, and I've had to make up stories about how I got them."

Jack wrote this all down, knowing he would have to document and verify every incident at trial. He knew immediately that this type of long-term abuse could be a solid defense, but he would have to show proof of the events.

"Have you confided in friends or family?"

"I never told my family because if my brother or father found out, they would kill Chad. They both suspected it, and my brother even brought it up to Chad once. I have told two of my closest friends."

"I will need their names."

She nodded her understanding of this. Jack let her sit for a moment without questions, just for the mental rest.

"I'm going to step out for a moment to call my office. I want to get a camera over here to take pictures of the bruises on your neck as well as your face. I'm also going to insist on an immediate and complete medical exam to determine if your ribs, as well as other bones, are broken. Who is your regular physician? "Chad always insisted we use his cousin as our physician. You should not call him, he will do all he can to protect Chad." "Okay, I will get an exam at Mercy Hospital. A couple of guards will have to go with you, but I will insist it is done this morning." So I will be gone for just a moment. Please wait here and, Ms. Merrill"—he leaned closer, looking her in the eyes—"don't worry, you are going to be fine, I will see to it."

With that, Jack left, called his office to have a camera delivered, and began the process of getting a medical exam ordered so it could be completed over that morning. When he returned, he asked, "I have to ask you why you decided to contact me. Surely there are defense lawyers in town that you have more history with than me."

"I know of your reputation, Mr. Roach, as a defense attorney. But more importantly, you are new to Portland. You haven't yet been completely influenced by the aura of the Merrill family. They control a lot in this town, and you haven't been exposed yet, so you haven't been bought off or intimidated."

Jack had already heard of the Merrill family but paid little attention to the stories.

He thought for a moment then responded, "I can assure you that I'm not a person who can be intimidated. I honestly can't remember the last time I was afraid of anybody."

"That's good to hear, Mr. Roach, but believe me when I say you will be coming under a lot of pressure from the Merrills and their friends, so be ready for it."

Jack just smiled. He was not concerned about the Merrills. When the camera arrived, he took the pictures he needed. The physical exam had been scheduled, and she was up for arraignment on the following Monday. Jack told her he had work to do in the office and would be back to her to discuss her plea at the arraignment. She would have to spend the weekend in jail, but at her arraignment on Monday, he would request bail. She registered her doubts about getting bail, but he assured her that he could make a good case. They parted company, Jack hoping he had helped her feel a bit better. For his part, he already felt good about his position as defense counsel. He went back to his office to put the pieces together for his presentation at the arraignment and the eventual trial.

Chapter XXII

TONY FIGNONI SAT ON THE same oversize leather couch in front of his father's desk that he had been sitting on five weeks earlier discussing the same Columbian drug dealers they had discussed at that meeting. The difference now was that his father was in much better humor than he was then.

"I knew getting you in the army would eventually pay off. Your foxhole pal is one hell of an operator. The half million we paid him we will make back in three months now that the competition has been eliminated."

"Bruce was something of a death machine in Vietnam. Now he has added his CIA experience to his resume. Taking care of our little problem, I knew, would be a walk in the park for him." Toni was very proud of the fact that he had initiated the move that eventually resolved their issue. He had scored major points with his father by proving he could deal with a major problem.

His father was smiling from ear to ear. It was unusual to see him this happy. He knew a job well done when he saw one. "You know, Tony, we could make use of his services on a fairly regular basis. His torture techniques as well as his killer instincts will come in handy in our line of work. We have a lot of times when we need to keep people in line. I want you to stay close to him, let him know we appreciate what he did and that we would want a long-term relationship." Having someone of Bruce King's caliber around to call on when needed would be a great asset, and the senior Fignoni knew it.

"That won't be difficult. Not only are we great friends, but Bruce takes pride in what he does. He enjoys it, and he's good at it. Plus, I'm sure that the money helps."

The two Fignonis continued celebrating their choice of assassins, vowing to use Bruce's services often. Meanwhile, Bruce was back to work at his day job. The battle in Nicaragua continued, and the CIA continued bolstering the efforts of the Contras. Bruce saw front-line combat duty, joining with the Contra rebels in battle. An experienced soldier of his caliber gave the rebels a working example of high performance in the field. He was involved in training exercises for the Contra rebels, all under the radar, out of the sight of congress. In Honduras, Bruce was involved in hands on torturing of leftist dissidents in order to properly train the CIA-inspired "Battalion 316" in torture techniques.

In Haiti, "Baby Doc" Duvalier's presidency was in peril and his life in danger, so the agency saw to it that he was set up in a comfortable retirement in France. They then worked behind the scenes to ensure the election of another right-wing strongman. To support the new right-wing regime, Bruce was dispatched as part of a team to strengthen military support. The agency team helped form and train the National Intelligence Service to lead the effort to suppress revolt and torture and assassinate dissidents. All the usual CIA activity that was done secretly in Haiti. Bruce played a part in all the actions, moving from country to country wherever he was needed.

One particular dissident in Haiti, Francois Badeau, was causing real problems right in the capital city of Port-au-Prince. Badeau had built up quite a following, giving fiery speeches at well-attended meetings. He brazenly spoke out against the regime, figuratively thumbing his nose at their authority. He had been brought in on several occasions by the Haitian military, tortured and locked up to no avail. The public outcry in his defense would eventually lead to him being set free. His followers would protest loudly at any attempts to silence him.

Bruce was called in to address the situation. He met with Haitian general Raoul Calvaire to discuss a plan. He told the general that he should plan on putting his troops in the city on alert in anticipation of Bruce taking action.

"*Si*, and why should I plan to put my troops on alert?"

"I plan to assassinate Francois Badeau, and when I do, I expect some unrest from his supporters. He has a pretty broad following in the city, so your men need to be ready."

The general acknowledged his understanding of the need to be prepared. He pledged his complete cooperation. Three days later, Bruce picked up on Francois Badeau in a downtown café. He waited for him to leave then discreetly followed him to his home. He took note of the location then spent the entire next day, picking out a perch from which he could get a good clear shot. He settled on a rooftop about six hundred yards away. He met again with the general and decided on a day to make the hit. Again, the general promised whatever support Bruce requested.

Two days later, at 4:00 a.m., with the general's help, Bruce got into the building he had picked for his perch. He was let out on the roof again with the general's help. He got himself in position, sighted the Winchester the general had provided in on Badeau's front door, and waited.

He waited for over two hours until Francois Badeau came out of the front door. Bruce sighted him in through his scope on his Winchester rifle. He took a deep breath and blew it out. He closed then opened his eyes then squeezed off the shot, a perfect head shot, dropping Badeau right where he stood. Six hundred yards away and a perfect hit. Still an amazing marksman. To Bruce, it was just like Vietnam. He had not lost his touch when it came to sniper fire. The general had witnessed the whole thing and marveled at Bruce's marksmanship.

A mild protest followed the assassination. It was much tamer than Bruce and the general had anticipated. To Bruce, it was just another day at the office. He went from his rooftop perch to the American embassy to plan his trip home.

When he returned to his apartment in Virginia, he had a message from Tony. Since the initial contract work for the Fignonis, they had used him two more times. They were both torture assignments against Fignoni employees suspected of skimming money. He water-boarded both of them and easily obtained full confessions. It earned him an additional fifty thousand dollars in his offshore account. He liked being able to bankroll so much money, but the idea of working for a crime family was troubling him. He was always able to justify his work for the government, but this was not the same. The guilt feelings were beginning to eat him up. Going back to his days in the Tiger Force, he had begun to have qualms about his frequent acts of killing fellow humans. The CIA camp had erased some of the guilt feelings, but now he found he was being haunted by his conscience. The Fignoni connection was a major source of guilt.

He called Tony back to see what was up.

"About time you got back to me."

Bruce did not like the tone of this greeting. His friend Tony was starting to take him for granted, and it annoyed him greatly. In his mind, he had done the Fignonis a great favor at tremendous personal risk. They needed to show more appreciation.

"Hey, I've been out of town. Don't forget I have a day job."

The tone of his response let Tony know he had aggravated his friend.

"Okay, okay, well, we need to contract with you for a small job."

"That's fine, but don't start thinking I'm some full-time employee. I do this as a side, and I could stop anytime."

"All right, just relax. I didn't mean to stir up a shit storm."

Bruce knew that they couldn't discuss the details over the phone. So he suggested, "Why don't we meet and discuss things? Can you get down here?"

"I will be in Baltimore tomorrow. I will call you and let you know when I get there and where I'm staying."

"Okay, I will be around tomorrow so we can get together."

With that, they hung up. Neither of them knew that the FBI had a phone tap on the Fignonis, and the entire conversation was listened to by the FBI.

Chapter XXIII

JACK MET CATHERINE MONDAY MORNING in a private room used by attorneys to consult with clients at the Cumberland County Courthouse. She was to be arraigned within the hour, and Jack wanted some time with her prior to the arraignment. They had met the previous day at the jail to go over details, but Jack still wanted one more meeting. She obviously had not had any sleep as she looked tired and drawn. Her appearance concerned Jack, but he knew a weekend in jail was not conducive to solid rest and a positive attitude. He had the medical report showing that Catherine did have two broken ribs which certainly added to her discomfort. He was surprised there were no broken facial bones. Apparently, Chadwick didn't pack enough punch.

"How are you holding up, Catherine?" Jack asked by way of opening the conversation.

"Well, having an attorney in the county jail provides a good bit of heckling material for the inmates, but I made it through the two nights."

"Well, I'm going to request bail at your arraignment. It would be quite unusual for a judge to grant bail in a murder trial, so I don't want to get your hopes up, but I believe we can present a strong argument."

"Do you think it's a waste of time?"

"No, you're an officer of the court and a respected member of the community. I think we could have a chance. You also have two children that need to be considered."

"They spent the night on Friday at neighbor's house, and my brother picked them up Saturday, and they are still with him. Can you have them come to the jail if we don't get bail?"

"I will take care of that. A couple of other things. We are obviously going to plead not guilty. Our defense is you acted in self-defense. Secondly, I confirmed yesterday that you have had four emergency room visits for which I will be receiving the records. What's more, given the facts of this case, I can't believe you have even been charged. I intend to talk to the district attorney about dropping the charges."

Catherine Merrill gave a cynical smile to this and said, "You don't understand yet, Mr. Roach, but you will. I killed Chadwick Merrill, in this town, that's an unforgiveable crime. The district attorney would not dare to do anything but prosecute."

Jack looked into her eyes, noting the fear and sincerity in that statement. "I think I told you last night, Ms. Merrill, I'm not easily intimidated."

"Perhaps you are not, but the district attorney is another matter."

Jack assured her that he would battle this case with everything he had, in spite of the Merrills' influence.

At the arraignment, they entered a plea of "Not Guilty" as expected. Jack requested bail, and the assistant district attorney, Kenneth Coleman, instantly objected on the grounds it was a murder trial.

Jack responded, "Your Honor, Ms. Merrill is not only an officer of the court and a well-respected member of the community, but she is also a mother of two children who need her. She is not a flight risk, and she deserves to be bailed if for no other reason than the weakness of the case against her."

"Your Honor, regardless of her standing in the community, the defendant has admitted to murdering her husband. Bail is out of the question," was the incredulous response from Coleman.

"I will decide what is out of the question in my court, Mr. Coleman." The response from Judge Murray, as well as the look on his face, indicated some annoyance at Attorney Coleman. His honor obviously did not like being lectured in his own courtrooms. "You have made a strong case for bail, Mr. Roach. I'm setting a bail of two hundred and fifty thousand dollars, and the defendant will surrender her passport." Judge Murray hit the gavel as he set the bail. Attorney

Coleman looked as if he wanted to object, but it was fairly obvious he had already aggravated the judge.

Jack turned to his client. "Can you cover that bail?"

"Yes, I have the resources. You could call my brother Carl in Scarborough. He will take care of everything." She gave him the number to call her brother.

"I hate to bring up money, but I will require an initial twenty-five-thousand-dollar retainer."

"When I meet with Carl, I will take care of that at the same time as my bail."

"When I leave here, I'm going to make an appointment to meet with District Attorney Rideout to discuss your case. I plan to argue that he should drop the charges."

Again, a cynical smile from Catherine Merrill with no accompanying comment.

Jack went back to his office and called the DA's office, making an appointment for later that afternoon. Before going, he grabbed his friend and colleague Gerry Conley to discuss the case. He explained the facts as presented to him by his client, and he pointed out that he had made an appointment with District Attorney Rideout to discuss the case.

"I just don't understand, Gerry, why the DA's office is trying this case. Unless I'm missing something, it's a clear case of self-defense."

"Two things, Jack—first, you are basing your self-defense argument solely on your client's side of the story. The police investigation may have come to a different conclusion, which you will find out when you see their report. Secondly, this is Chadwick Merrill we are talking about. It's a very high-profile name around town here, so there may be forces at work that are driving Rideout. He may very well be under a great deal of pressure to push this forward."

Jack digested this a bit and said, "I keep hearing about these Merrills. I can't wait to meet the family."

"Don't worry, my friend, I'm sure you will be meeting them."

Jack went about other work until it was time to head over for his appointment with Rideout.

At the DA's office, Jack sat waiting in the outer office for twenty minutes beyond the scheduled time for his meeting. Finally, the secretary who had kept herself quite busy while he sat there, told him he could go in to DA Rideout's office. He thanked her as he got up and walked to the door.

Rideout was seated behind his desk accompanied by Kenneth Coleman who occupied a chair in front of the large desk. Both attorneys stood to greet Jack, offering their outstretched hands by way of greetings.

After a bit of small talk, they welcomed Jack to the community of Portland, as well as to the Maine legal fraternity. All the usual pleasantries for a first meeting.

"I have heard a lot about you, Mr. Roach. You had a very solid reputation in Boston as a trial attorney."

"Thank you. As you know, I will be the attorney in the Merrill trial, which is why I wanted to meet with you. This seems like a very clear case of self-defense, and I'm actually a bit surprised that you are going to trial with it. Admittedly, I have not yet seen the police reports or the coroner's report, but other evidence is quite compelling." Rideout and Coleman exchanged a knowing look between them before Rideout responded.

"Mr. Roach."

"Please call me Jack."

"Okay, Jack, you are new to this area, so I can excuse your naivete in this matter, but you need to understand that your client killed Chadwick Merrill, son of Stanton Merrill and grandson of August Merrill. He was a member of one of this area's most prominent families. His murder cannot be simply swept under the rug." Rideout spoke as Coleman nodded his agreement.

Jack sat in silent contemplation for a long moment before answering, "I see, so given the facts of the case, if it were somebody else involved—say, a Joe Smith instead of Chadwick Merrill—this would be handled in a far different manner. Is that the message I'm getting here?"

The district attorney looked across the desk at his lead prosecutor and shook his head with a look that seemed to say, "This guy has no clue." Looking back at Jack, he said, "Look, counselor, why don't you review the police report and really all the evidence of the case and prepare yourself for trial? This will be a very high-profile trial and you need to be prepared."

Jack was surprised by the condescending dismissal he had just received from an overly smug district attorney. He smiled as he rose from his chair, put both hands on the desk, and leaned into Mr. Rideout to say, "Don't worry, Mr. Rideout, I will be prepared. Your office will be advised to do the same."

Without extending his hand or looking at Mr. Coleman, Jack turned and walked out of the office. He was more determined than he had ever been in any previous cases that he would win this trial and wipe that smug look off Rideout's face. The Merrill family not-withstanding, he felt confident he had the stronger case. He intended not only to win it, but in so doing, to expose Chadwick Merrill for the monster he had been to his family.

District Attorney Rideout watched the departing Jack Roach, then turned to his lead prosecutor, "He's right, you know, we had better be ready for a battle royal."

Chapter XXIV

BRUCE MET TONY AT HIS hotel the next afternoon in Baltimore. Tony let him know the problem.

"We are constantly on the FBI's list of organizations to watch. Lately, the heat from them has become more intense. We have reason to believe they have flipped one of our guys, Michael Veno. We think he is working with them. He needs to be taken out." The mention of the FBI grabbed Jack's attention. He did not intend to find himself on their radar screen.

"That sounds pretty simple, Tony. Why do you need me involved?"

"Because it's not that simple. We want this to look like we had nothing to do with the killing. If the FBI knows we are responsible for hitting an informant, they will be even more intent on shutting us down. This requires some imagination. It needs to look like an accident. An accident in which we had no involvement." Jack knew it had to be an accident that left no questions. Better still, a death from natural causes, leaving no questions.

"Okay, I will have to put some thought into it," Jack said while rubbing his face with his two hands. Then he said, "It's going to cost you, Tony. I don't like doing this, it puts me at risk, plus—" He stopped without finishing. It could not be explained to Tony, but Bruce's involvement in the Fignoni problems was causing a great deal of emotional stress. Night sweats and nightmares were becoming a nightly routine.

"How much?" Tony asked.

"Not a simple job. I will need two hundred fifty thousand if you want this done right."

Tony expressed shock at the requested price. It seemed to him that Jack might be trying to price himself out of doing any work for the Fignonis. He was not entirely off base.

"I will have to clear that figure with my father. I will get back to you tomorrow to confirm a price."

Bruce said he was not comfortable going to the Fignoni home again, not with the FBI watching them so they agreed to meet in seven days at the Park Plaza in New York in the bar at 8:00 p.m.

With that settled, they got down to more typical small talk between two friends. What they did not notice was a young, unshaven, long-haired man sitting on the other side of the hotel bar, reading a paper, sipping his drink. Tony had been followed from New Jersey as the FBI worked to close in on the Fignoni crime family. They had listened in on the phone call, so they knew this meeting was going to happen. The young man in the bar was, in fact, an FBI undercover agent. He not only observed the meeting, but he also took pictures with a tiny camera hooked to the pocket of his shirt. Neither Tony nor Bruce took any notice of him or detected the picture taking.

Bruce headed back to Virginia and Tony to New Jersey. As Bruce drove to Virginia, he contemplated the life he was living and what is was doing to him. In Vietnam, he had a lot of struggles with his conscience about the killings he was involved in. He started having nightmares about the things he had seen and done. He could rationalize them away as part of his patriotic duty in wartime. That became harder to do when he joined Tiger Force. The fourteen months of training in the CIA camp had programmed him enough that he was better able to rationalize what he did. But of late, it was even harder still with the CIA and the Fignonis. Nightmares had become more frequent as well as having more qualms of conscience. Now he was killing for money, and there was no way to rationalize these murders. He would wrestle with these thoughts every morning when he looked in the mirror. He determined that this would have to be the final time working for the Fignonis. Somehow this all had to end. He would do this one and do it right, but this was the final time. He had a lot of thinking to do as he tried to come up with a plan to take care of Mr. Veno, while making it look unrelated to the

Fignoni family. Tony's father hit the ceiling when he heard the price. "Your friend is using us. This price is an outrage." Tony settled him down to the point that he agreed to the price but said, "This is the last time with this guy. We need to find another option then figure out how we deal with your soldier buddy."

"What does that mean?" Tony asked.

"You know what it means. We stop using him then we have to deal with him because he becomes a loose end that needs to be dealt with. It's as simple as that."

"I will not let that happen. He is a friend who got involved in this to help me out. Now you want to waste him? No fucking way."

Tony's father looked at him for a long time then turned to leave the room. At the doorway, he turned back and simply said "We'll see" as he left.

Tony left him a message the next morning that his requested fee was agreed to on his end but that they needed to have a conversation about future fees when this was over. As far as Bruce was concerned, there would be no future fees. Now there was nothing left but to get the job done.

Bruce's CIA training had included a number of ways to kill a person without using a weapon. He had been trained in ways to end someone's life while making it look like death by natural causes. The use of drugs that would induce a heart attack and not be detected in an autopsy. He decided that a death by natural causes would be less suspicious than a staged accident. Once again, his CIA training and his access to the necessary materials to make this all happen made him worth the money he was demanding.

He told his supervisor that he was taking a few days off to visit family. He then headed up to New York to meet with Tony again. They met as prearranged in the Park Plaza bar. Bruce arrived first, taking a table in the corner with his back to the wall. Tony arrived a few minutes later and sat across the table from Bruce. The two exchanged greetings but in a cooler, more businesslike manner than usual.

"I need some details about Michael Veno. First, how old is he, and what kind of shape is he in?"

"That's easy enough—he's in his fifties and he's fat. The last time he had any exercise was in high school."

"How fat?"

"He's about five feet, nine inches tall, and he must weigh two hundred fifty pounds to two hundred seventy. He's very fat."

"Okay, that's fat. Where does he live, and does he live alone?"

Tony gave him the address of Veno's New York City condo. His wife had left him years ago, and he had been living alone ever since she left. Except for an occasional hooker, he spent every evening alone.

Bruce nodded, thanked Tony for his information, and told Tony that Veno would be dead within the week. He wanted one hundred fifty thousand wired to his bank account in Switzerland within twenty-four hours. The other one hundred thousand would be wired when Veno was dead. This job would be pushing his account up over eight hundred thousand dollars. A very nice retirement fund.

Two nights later, when Michael Veno came back to his condo, Bruce King was waiting for him. As he walked in, looking over his mail, King came up, behind him wrapping his right arm around his neck, applying pressure to cut off oxygen to his brain until he passed out. Bruce then let him drop to the floor so that he landed in the position he would be in had he dropped from a heart attack. He bent down, undid Veno's belt, and pulled down his pants. He took out a syringe, placing the needle between the cheeks of his ass. He injected him with enough potassium chloride to induce a heart attack. The injection site would not be detected, hidden between his ass cheeks, and the heart attack would seem natural.

He dressed Veno back up, leaving him on the hallway floor with his mail scattered around him. A totally normal-looking scene of a middle-aged, overweight man dying of a heart attack. He was discovered the next morning by his cleaning lady. The FBI agents who had been dealing with him were at the condo as well as the autopsy, examined the body, finding nothing that discredited the heart attack finding. Mission accomplished, and two hundred fifty thousand dollars had been transferred to Bruce King's offshore account.

A few days later, in the same New York City FBI office where the agents had struggled with the loss of their potential informant, a new revelation came up. The man with Tony Fignoni in the picture taken in the Baltimore Hotel had been identified as Bruce King, a CIA agent. What was he doing meeting with a known mobster? What was the connection between them? The answer to that question became a priority in the Fignoni investigation. Bruce King became a person of interest in their investigation.

Chapter XXV

WHEN JACK GOT BACK TO his office, he had three messages from Catherine Merrill, fifteen minutes apart from each other. Obviously, something had happened that had her very upset. He immediately called her back. When she answered, she was in a state of panic.

"Jack, Stanton Merrill sent his driver for my two children. When my brother objected, he was threatened with the police and told he would end up in jail with me if he tried to resist. The driver was accompanied by two Cumberland Count Sherriff's Department officers."

She was speaking rapidly in a high state of agitation and panic. Jack could barely understand her. She was obviously crying, so Jack asked her to take a deep breath and calm down. She did as suggested, and when it seemed she had regained her composure, Jack spoke.

"Obviously, your bail has been posted and you are out, but where are you?"

She took a couple of deep breaths and sounded calmer when she answered, "I'm at my brother's house in Scarborough. I can't go back to my own house. It's a crime scene roped off with yellow tape."

"Have you called your father-in-law to try and pick up your children or try to work something out with him?"

"I don't dare to call him because I would not be able to hold myself together. We do not have a good relationship even in the best of times. He had always treated me like a second-class person of low intelligence."

"How old are your children?"

"Danny is nine, and Lisa is eleven."

"Okay, by virtue of the fact that two deputies showed up with the driver, your father-in-law has filed something with the court in order to take the children. Was there any mention of a court order?"

"No, I don't think so. I've not been thinking straight. I'm so upset I don't know what to do."

"Okay, let me look into it and get back to you. Don't do anything until you hear from me, and, Catherine, please stay calm, I will take care of it."

They hung up, and Jack immediately checked the court filings of the day. He found exactly what he expected to find, Stanton Merrill's attorney, Willard Hancock, had filed a petition for protection from abuse order. Hancock was a high-powered attorney in Portland's largest law firm, Price Adams and Barrett. The client he represented here was intent on taking the two children away from Catherine Merrill. It was a cheap shot, but with all he had heard about the Merrills, it was not a surprise.

Jack called Catherine back to give her the bad news. "Oh no," she said, starting to cry again. "He wants to take my children. No." She was in utter despair.

"Don't panic, Catherine. We will fight the order immediately. It's too late today, but I will file our response first thing in the morning."

Still crying, Catherine said, "You don't know what you are up against, Mr. Roach. You're going head to head with Stanton Merrill and all his money. He will hire the best lawyers money can buy. This will be an uphill battle. This is a nightmare, an unending nightmare."

"I understand, Catherine, but don't underestimate me. I'm not afraid of Stanton Merrill. Try to get some rest. I will call you in the morning with an update."

The last thing Jack heard as they hung up was a pained cry from Catherine. He had a call to return to Elaine Watkens. She had called to see if they could get together that night. Jack had to decline, saying he would be working very late preparing a motion that would need to be filed first thing in the morning. Elaine protested that they were not seeing much of each other. She understood he was tied up in a major case, but she missed seeing him. Jack promised dinner for the next night. Try as he might to control his affections for this lady, he was missing her as much or more than she was missing him. It pained him to be stuck in the office unable to see her, but he had to have his motion ready to file first thing in the morning. He talked Elaine into settling for dinner the next night. Having settled that, he began drafting a motion to dismiss Stanton Merrill's petition.

He did not get back to his home until after ten, when he had a Knob Creek on the rocks before retiring. In the morning, the Portland paper ran a front-page story about the murder and pending trial. The story was full of blushing praise of the Merrill family and a fair amount of history about their contributions to the Portland community. The specifics about the deceased made him sound like a pillar of the community that would be sorely missed. Catherine was included in the article but in much less glowing terms. She was basically described as a poor kid from Waterville who got a chance to mingle with a higher class of people by attending Dartmouth College and was rewarded by being able to marry into the Merrill family. Jack was disgusted by the article and realized fully that it was probably just the beginning of local press praising the rich and powerful Merrills.

When the courthouse opened for business, Jack filed a motion to dismiss the protection order. He also requested an expedited hearing, given the situation with two children caught in the balance. Willard Hancock was also served with the motion so that he could propose his defense against the dismissal.

In the meantime, Jack had Catherine in his office to discuss their defense. She came in at 10:00 a.m. as planned. She sat in Jack's office while he served coffee and offered some light banter to try to get her to relax. She was obviously highly stressed. She constantly folded and unfolded her hands while looking down at her lap. A stately, attractive lady, she now looked very haggard and beaten. Jack had to somehow build her confidence, instill some optimism, and basically bring her back from the depths she seemed to have reached. He needed her to appear humble but self-assured that what she had done was what she had to do. During the trial, he could not have her looking like she felt guilty. He knew the issue with the children was adding insult to injury, but she had to pull herself together.

"Look, Catherine," he started, "I understand the depths of your troubles, but believe me when I say we are going to win."

She started to respond, and he held up a hand to stop her. "Just hold on. You were skeptical about getting bail—we got it. We will win the trial. I need you to believe that because I need you to look cool, calm, and confident in the courtroom at trial. As a lawyer, you know that's true." Jack spoke as he sat on the corner of his desk with her in front of him in a chair. He looked at her waiting for an answer.

She slowly nodded while looking up at Jack. "I will do my best, but I have to tell you, I need my children with me. If that overbearing arrogant ass succeeds in taking them, I will be crushed."

Jack noticed the tears in her eyes as she spoke. "Okay, I have filed a motion to dismiss his petition and we will win that battle this week. Right now, we need to start working on the biggest issue, which is the murder charge against you. So can we start?"

She nodded in response. Jack told her she needed to focus because everything she said to him now was important to building her case. "Some things that may seem insignificant to you may end up being extremely important. So focus your attention on our discussion."

"I understand, and I'm ready."

"Okay, I will be getting the hospital records for your four visits, but are those the only times he physically abused you?"

She went into a very detailed account of thirteen years of mental and physical abuse. She was constantly told by her husband that he had brought her up from the gutter, that without him she was nothing. He often said, in front of the children, that he hoped they inherited qualities from his family and nothing from the "white trash" that their mother came from. She was kept from visiting her parents with or without the children. If she wanted to call them, she would have to do it from a phone booth or from her office because if he saw a long-distance call to them on the phone bill, she would be punished.

Physically, the four hospital visits were only for the worst beatings. On three other occasions, Chadwick had his cousin, Dr. Charles Merrill, examine her at their home. On numerous other occasions, she suffered with bruises, cracked, and/or broken ribs plus internal discomforts. He would beat her if she ever even looked at another man or if she questioned his opinions or judgements. It usually, but not always, happened when he drank. He had a real drinking problem and was drunk often. The drunker he would be, the worse the beating would be.

"Is there anyone, a friend, relative, that could verify these beatings?"

"Well, as I told you, I never admitted them to my brother because I was afraid what he would do, but he suspected it. I do have two friends, Cary Winters and Elizabeth Lane, that I have talked to about it. I swore them to secrecy, but I'm sure they will talk to you now."

Jack spoke as he was writing down the names. "I will need their contact information. What about former girlfriends?"

"I'm his second wife. He was divorced two years before we married."

This answer was a surprise to Jack. He stopped writing and looked up at Catherine. This would open the door to the possibility that there may have been other beatings with other women. This was a whole new avenue of possibilities to help his defense.

"I thought you met in college?"

"We did and we dated then, but I went on to law school while he came back to Portland. He was married to a local girl when I came here to practice law."

This was extremely important, and Jack knew he would need to speak with this ex-wife.

"Where is the ex-wife?"

"She moved to Providence, Rhode Island, after the divorce. She works there as a professor at Providence College."

"I need a name and any contact information you have."

"Her name is Sharon Tate. I only met her a couple of times. They were married for about three years. I think you can reach her at the college."

A very short marriage, Jack was anxious to find out why. Obviously, the possibility of physical abuse was there.

"Okay, tell me, with all of this abuse, why did you stay?" This was a question that was bound to be asked at trial and Catherine's response could be critical.

"He made it very clear that if I left him, I would never see the kids again. I could not live without them, and he knew it. He used that against me at every opportunity."

"He couldn't do that. In a divorce, you would get the children, most likely, and visiting rights at a minimum. Come on, Catherine, you're a lawyer, you know that's true."

She looked at him and shook her head, saying, "Jack, you don't yet know what it's like to go up against the Merrills, but you are soon going to find out. What you say about my rights in a divorce are true in ninety-nine percent of divorces, but not necessarily in mine."

Jack wrapped up the meeting telling Catherine that he planned to go to Providence to interview the ex-wife, talk to her friends that she had confided in, find any ex-girlfriends, and check into his college social activities. Hopefully, he could find an ex-girlfriend or two from college. He would also talk with Dr. Merrill. He again restated his confidence that they would win this case, telling her to have confidence and not to worry.

Just as she was leaving his office, he was informed by his secretary that his motion to dismiss would be heard the next afternoon in front of Judge Collins. Jack looked at Catherine as she heard the news and gave her a confident wink. She, in turn, told him that Judge Collins came from a similar old Yankee family as the Merrills and the two families were best of friends. She said it was the worst possible draw for a judge. Thus, his confidence may be misplaced.

* * * * *

As Jack arrived at the chambers of Judge Norris Collins to consider his petition to dismiss, he had the distinct honor of meeting Attorney Willard Hancock from the firm of Pierce, Adams, and Barret. As they greeted one another with handshakes Hancock's expression seemed to indicate he was smelling something foul. They barely had time to exchange names before being called into the judge's chambers. Attorney Hancock requested that before beginning, they wait for his client, Mr. Stanton Merrill. Obviously, Hancock felt that Merrill's presence would provide a positive influence on His Honor. To Jack's amazement, Judge Collins agreed. Jack began to object, but the judge held his hand up indicating an objection would do no good, then went back to reading the papers on his desk without saying a word. Jack sat in stunned silence.

After ten minutes of awkward silence, in walked the great man himself, Stanton Merrill. At 6'2" with broad shoulders, a full head of white hair combed straight back and piercing blue eyes, he cut an impressive figure. Without a word, he pulled a chair up next to his attorney who said, "We can begin now, Judge Collins."

This amazing start to the proceeding set the tone for what would follow.

His Honor looked up from his paperwork and began by greeting the great man. "How have you been, Stanton?"

Merrill didn't answer, simply shrugged in a way that said he was undecided.

The judge nodded then turned his attention to Jack. At this point, Jack felt as out of place as a skunk at a lawn party. The judge's expression seemed to say that he was annoyed by Jack's filing and maybe even more annoyed by Jack's presence in his chamber.

"You have filed your motion for dismissal of the petition for protection from abuse. I have read your motion, Mr. Roach, do you have anything to add?"

Jack cleared his throat before saying, "Your Honor, the petition from abuse gives no evidence of abuse. These two children have lived with their mother all their lives with no evidence or even suggestion of abuse. The idea that they now need to be removed from their abuse-free home because of some notion that abuse is now in the offing is ludicrous on its face."

Judge Collins turned to Attorney Hancock, who responded, "Quite simply put, Your Honor, this woman has admitted to murdering her husband, the father of these children. That type of mental abuse on these children cannot be overstated. They need protection from the violence they have been subjected to by this woman. Her presence in their lives on a day-to-day basis will certainly serve as a reminder to them of what happened to their father."

"Ms. Merrill has not been tried yet," Jack responded. "You are still innocent until proven guilty in this country. Taking the children away from their mother would constitute punishment in advance of conviction." Jack made the obvious point.

"Your Honor, she has admitted killing her husband. I'm sure Mr. Roach will concoct some story of extenuating circumstances to try to justify the act, but a confession is a confession."

"Your Honor," an outraged Jack began, but he was cut off by the raised hand of Judge Collins. "I've heard enough gentlemen. Mr. Roach, I'm ruling against your motion to dismiss. There is more than enough here to justify a hearing on the original petition for protection. I will have my clerk schedule a hearing date. In the meantime, the children will stay with Mr. Merrill."

Jack started again, "Your Honor."

"Save it for the hearing, Mr. Roach."

He had been warned about the influence of the Merrill family; he was now seeing it in action.

Jack sat looking across the desk at Judge Collins. Finally shaking his head, he muttered half to himself, "I can see now how the hearing will go."

Judge Collins heard the mutter and his head snapped around to look at Jack. "What was that, Mr. Roach?" he snapped.

Jack was reloading his briefcase. He looked at the judge, "Nothing, Your Honor."

Judge Collins narrowed his eyes and pointed at Jack. "Be very careful, Mr. Roach. Being found in contempt would be a tough way to start your career in Cumberland County."

Jack said nothing as he closed his briefcase and stood to leave. On his way to the door, he threw a "Thank you, Your Honor" over his shoulder, trying not to load it with too much of a sarcastic tone.

Attorney Hancock and Stanton Merrill walked out ahead of Jack. Once in the hall, they shook hands as Jack walked by. Before he could exit the building, Stanton Merrill hurried to catch up with him and from behind asked Jack if he could have a minute. Having just seen firsthand this man's influence in the Cumberland County Court system, Jack was not anxious for a discussion. He turned to face him as he approached. "We really should not be talking, Mr. Merrill, without your attorney being present."

"This is not a matter that concerns him." He was now standing two feet in front of Jack. "You're new here in Portland, aren't you, Mr. Roach?"

"I don't know why that would be of any interest to you, Mr. Merrill."

"It isn't really. It's just that you should understand you're no longer in a trashy little mill town like the one you grew up in, Mr. Roach, and if you want to make anything of yourself here, you need to be careful whose toes you step on in your pitiful little practice."

Jack couldn't remember ever being insulted so many times in one sentence. He was somewhat impressed.

"So I'm being threatened by the high and mighty Mr. Merrill."

"No threat, Mr. Roach. More a word of advice to which you should pay attention if you wish to survive in Cumberland County."

Merrill stood looking Jack in the eye as he finished his warning. Jack gave it a moment before he replied, "Fine, let me give you some advice, Mr. Merrill. Keep both hands on your ass because when I'm done with that sniveling coward son of yours, it will be far more than your toes you will have to worry about."

With that, Jack abruptly turned and walked away. Merrill made a comment that Jack made a conscious point not to hear. He went back to his office and called Catherine with the bad news. As expected, it devastated her. He spent forty-five minutes trying to calm her down and give her some confidence that they could still win her case. They hung up, with Jack feeling he had accomplished neither.

That night at dinner, Jack told Elaine about the entire encounter. "The judge ruled against my motion to dismiss, so we will have a hearing in front of the same judge. You can guess how that will go. Then I was threatened by the great man himself, Stanton Merrill."

"You better watch your back. The Merrills are a family with a lot of influence."

"I thought you were watching my back?"

"I would, Jack, but I don't see enough of you lately." Elaine said this with a smile, but Jack knew there was some real concern and this was not all lighthearted. Prior to the Merrill case, they had been spending a lot of time together; now it had become more difficult. He thought deep down that she understood why, but it may be that he was wrong.

"Listen, Elaine, I'm sorry we are not seeing as much of each other, and unfortunately, it is going to be this way until I finish this case. I feel as bad about it as you, and I will try to get together as often as I can, but a murder trial is very time consuming."

"I understand that, Jack, and I'm really not complaining. It's just that I miss you when I don't see you enough."

"I miss you too. I will make this up to you when the dust settles."

He raised his wine glass for a toast on the subject, and they clinked glasses. Jack knew he was really falling for this girl. He worried that he would get in too deep and wind up getting emotionally crushed again, but when he looked at her, his thought was that it would be worth the risk.

Chapter XXVI

BRUCE RECEIVED A REQUEST TO be in the office of Agent Flanagan, his direct supervisor, at nine hundred hours on Wednesday morning, October 23. This was not an unusual request. He would often be called in either to be given his next assignment or to give details of a mission already completed. What turned out to be unusual was the purpose of the meeting. Upon his arrival, Flanagan informed him that there were two FBI agents in the adjoining conference room who wanted to talk with him. This unexpected news caught him completely by surprise. He flashed back to Tony's conversation informing him of FBI scrutiny on the Fignoni family. He did not know how, or if, they had made a connection to him.

"Why would they want to speak to me? Is it something to do with a CIA mission?"

"I don't know why they are looking to talk with you, but it's not CIA connected. I asked that question and told them that if it was CIA related, they could talk with me. They claim it has nothing to do with the agency."

Bruce took this in with a perplexed look on his face. "Well, I have no idea what they want."

"The way to find out is to drag your ass in there and ask them."

Bruce nodded at this and moved toward the conference room door.

"By the way," Flanagan said as Bruce turned to see what he wanted, "I want a full briefing when you're done."

"Yes, sir."

Bruce walked into the conference room to find the two agents standing at the table awaiting his arrival. They were dressed in the normal drab FBI attire of dark suits, white shirts, dark ties, and black wing tips. They both looked to be in their early thirties, and they sported that traditional FBI buzzcut, a hairstyle the Bruce always found annoying. Very serious, almost ominous, expressions on both their faces. They were either intending to convey the very serious nature of their visit or they were trying to intimidate Bruce.

"Agent King, I'm FBI agent Daryl Stone, and this is Agent James Harris. We have a few questions we would like to go over with you." Stone stood over six feet, blond hair, blue eyes. Harris was a bit shorter with dark hair. Both were obviously in great physical condition.

"So I've been told. What is this all about?"

"Please sit down, Agent King, and we will get into that with you." Stone again was doing the talking.

Bruce stood for a moment, a bit troubled by the prospect of being questioned by FBI agents. Finally, he took a seat at the head of the conference table while the two agents sat down on his right. The table would handle a group of twelve in the oak-paneled room off Flanagan's office. The three currently seated at the table appeared a bit diminished by the size of the table.

"Okay, so what is this all about?" Bruce asked again to begin the conversation.

"Let me start by saying that everything we discuss here needs to stay between the people in this room. Do you understand, Agent King?" This opening statement immediately set Bruce on edge.

"Look, Agent Stone, I have been a CIA agent for a long time. I know more about top-secret assignments and discussions than two baby FBI agents. So let's get down to business, and tell me why I'm wasting my morning talking to two guys who would be carded in any bar in DC." They had angered Bruce by showing up to question him then treating him like some bush league suspect. He figured he might as well come right at them. His comments did not sit well with the two FBI agents either.

Agents Stone and Harris were both staring menacingly at Bruce, obviously not liking his comments. This time, it was Harris who spoke up. "Your flippant attitude is not impressive, Agent King. We are here because we are charged with investigating an organized crime family that we have reason to believe you are overly friendly with."

Ah, so this was it, Bruce thought. They have made some connection with me and the Fignonis. Not knowing what they had, the best course of action for him was to listen and find out how much they knew and how they knew it.

"Okay, so what does that have to do with me? My family back in Maine was not organized in criminal activity or anything else." His reaction gave no indication that he was at all shaken by the prospect of the FBI inquiry.

Stone said this time, "We are looking into the activities of the Fignoni family in New York and New Jersey. It seems you have some familiarity with them."

"What would make you think I know anything about a Fignoni family?"

"Cut the crap, Agent King." Harris was the bad cop. "You met with Tony Fignoni in Baltimore, and you've been to his home in Secaucus, New Jersey."

That was easy enough. They have had eyes on the estate for a while, and they have been keeping an eye on Tony. *So they have seen me with him*, Bruce thought. *That's easy to explain*. Hopefully that was all they had.

"Tony Fignoni and I were in Vietnam together. We served in the same unit and became friends. We fought in a war together, an experience you two pups have probably not had. We are still friends, so yeah, I have been to his place and when he's in town, we will get together for a drink. Is that all you guys want to know?"

"Agent King, you're a very world-wise man." Stone was the good cop, this time. "Surely you have not been blind to the fact that the entire Fignoni family is involved in drugs, prostitution, and extortion. We aren't concerned with your wartime friendships. What we are concerned with is your knowledge of the family's crime activities and your involvement, if any, in those activities."

"Are you accusing me of criminal activity, Agent Stone?" The two agents looked at Bruce without responding. "If you are, you better have some goddamn good proof." Bruce raised his voice, showing his displeasure with this line of questioning. His intent was to put his inquisitor on the defensive.

"Nobody is accusing you of anything at this stage." Harris was talking now as the two continued to pass it back and forth. "However, we want to know what you have picked up about the Fignoni family business over the many years you've known Tony Fignoni."

Bruce let that statement settle for a bit before standing, putting his two hands on the table and leaning into the two agents. "Look, boys, Tony Fignoni is a friend of mine. I don't know anything about his business. I have never asked because I have never cared what he did. I expected the family business involved things I was better off not knowing about so I left it alone. That's all I have to say on the matter and this conversation is over. My attorney is Jack Roach in Portland, Maine. If you two want to talk to me again, call him first. Good day."

With that, Bruce walked out of the room. He knew he would have to go over the entire thing with Flanagan, but he did not want to do it just then, so he exited into the hall instead of the door to Flanagan's office. He knew one thing for certain, he needed to talk to a good lawyer. Fortunately, he grew up with a friend who had become a very good lawyer. He determined to call Jack at his first opportunity.

Back in the conference room, the two agents tried to digest the meeting that just ended. They had been manhandled by a CIA agent that they knew going in was a tough customer. They also knew from their research that Bruce had been involved in tipping off the DEA as well as the FBI about the Columbian drug ring that had been broken up a few years ago. They also knew that the Columbians had been competing with the Fignonis. They had no proof that Bruce had been acting on behalf of the Fignonis, but it was a fairly logical conclusion.

"Do you believe that line of bullshit?" Harris asked.

"No, he certainly knew full well what his little buddy was up to," Stone answered. "Just knowing you are associated with a known criminal is not a crime in itself. So he's right about one thing: if we are going to pursue anything with him, we better have the goods on him before we make a move."

"True, but acting on their behalf can certainly qualify."

Harris thought about that and said, "You know as I have thought about the connection with him and the Fignonis, the death of our stooley, Veno, becomes more suspect."

"How exactly do you mean? Veno had a heart attack."

"I know, that was the coroner's report. I also know that any CIA agent that has spent a career in black ops would know how to induce a heart attack and how to do it in a manner that was undetectable."

Stone listened to this and looked at his partner for a long time without a response. No response was really necessary, they both knew that Harris was right.

Chapter XXVII

AFTER HIS ENCOUNTER WITH STANTON Merrill, Jack was absolutely determined to not only win the case for his client, but to expose the Merrill family, particularly Chadwick Merrill, for what they are in the process. He went back to his office and laid out a plan to compile the evidence that would demonstrate what a monster Chadwick Merrill was to his wife and children. He had the names of the two friends Catherine had confided in, plus the ex-wife. He planned to meet with them face to face. He was particularly anxious to hear what the ex-wife would have to say.

The hospital records for Catherine's four visits were the first order of business. They painted a horrific picture, much like the medical report from the night of the incident, of broken ribs, internal injuries, and bruises covering three quarters of her body. He interviewed the two of her friends to whom she had confided over the years of her married life. Their testimony indicated that the four hospital visits were the tip of the iceberg. In fact, they said she had received a number of lesser beatings that did not require hospital attention, as well as good number that required treatment from Chadwick's doctor cousin. They further confirmed the systematic mental abuse of a domineering bully, who controlled every aspect of Catherine's life as well as the children they shared. Catherine's best friend, Elizabeth Lane, summed up Chadwick Merrill appropriately. "He was a conceited, spoiled, bully who made life miserable for everyone around him, but especially for his wife Catherine." The two friends were both very credible witnesses, and Jack felt good about their value at trial.

The next step was a trip to Rhode Island to interview his ex-wife and a stop in New Hampshire to take a look at Merrill's activities at

Dartmouth. Before he could do that, however, he would have to argue against the petition for protection from abuse filed by attorneys for Stanton Merrill. The hearing was in front of the very same Judge Collins who had ruled on Jack's motion to dismiss the petition. That being the case, the hearing held few surprises. Jack argued that Catherine Merrill stood convicted of no offenses and that the petitioners have given no evidence of abuse by her and that the children belonged with their mother. Judge Collins's body language, as well as expressions of impatience and inattentiveness, as Jack spoke signaled a bad outcome. Attorney Hancock reiterated his case, that while not yet convicted, Catherine Merrill had admitted killing her husband in a "very violent manner" and that the children need not be continually reminded of this by virtue of their living with the person who perpetrated the act.

Judge Collins heard the arguments with very little comment. He did not immediately issue his ruling. Catherine was not confident of the outcome. "Mr. Roach, I don't see any way that he will rule in our favor," was her feeling immediately following the hearing. Jack shared her pessimism but tried to act confident for her benefit. He had made up his mind that if Judge Collins was assigned to the murder trial, he would move to have him recuse himself. The way he handled this matter made Jack think he might as well have had Stanton Merrill presiding.

"Don't give up hope, Catherine. We gave the judge a very good case to send the children back to you. He may well surprise us." He didn't really believe it himself.

They went back to Jack's office as he went over his plans to travel to Rhode Island and New Hampshire. "I'm building a very strong case of spousal abuse that the court will find very difficult to ignore. I aim to show that it did not start with you but rather has been a pattern of behavior for years. Normally, in a murder trial the defense attorney will ask for as much time as he can get in order to prepare his case. Our case is so strong I intend to request a speedy trial."

Catherine allowed that she could see and appreciate this as a solid strategy, but she remained pessimistic about the possibility of beating the Merrills. Two days later, her pessimism was justified when the court ruled in favor of the petition for protection so that Catherine did not get her children back. The only concession to Catherine in the judgement was that she could have supervised visitation rights for one hour a day. She was devastated by the decision, and Jack was left with a client in a murder trial who had all but given up completely before the trial began. He did his best to convince her that winning the trial would not only set her free but would also result in her winning back her children. She remained inconsolable in spite of Jack's efforts. One more reason to set a trial date as soon as possible.

He made an appointment with Sharon Tate, the first wife of Chadwick Merrill, and headed for Rhode Island to interview her. Jack had researched her history with Chad Merrill. They were married only for three years and had been divorced for fifteen. She was a professor of English literature at Providence College. They were to meet in her office. Jack found her seated at her desk going over some papers. She was a strikingly attractive woman of around forty with brown hair and eyes. She stood about five ten with a trim athletic body. She rose to meet Jack as he entered the office.

"Mr. Roach, it's a pleasure to meet you," she said as she offered a hand.

"I appreciate you seeing me, Ms. Tate. I will try not to take up too much of your time."

"You can take as much time as you like, Mr. Roach. I read about what happened to Chadwick, and I want to be helpful."

Jack was not sure what that meant, so he went right to the heart of the matter to see where she stood. "Catherine Merrill killed your ex-husband in self-defense. He was in the process of administering a particularly brutal beating, not for the first time, and she was in fear of her life. I want to ask you some questions about your own relationship with Mr. Merrill. I need to know if spousal abuse was a characterization of your own marriage."

She looked at him with a rather cynical smile and replied, "I'm not surprised to hear that. The Portland papers account spoke of the late Chadwick Merrill in rather glowing terms, but I knew better. He was an overbearing bully, and I was lucky to survive our marriage. It is my undying shame that I did not recognize what he was long before I married him. I consider myself an intelligent woman. How I misread him enough to marry him is both puzzling and embarrassing."

With that response, Jack knew he had the potential for a very strong witness to support Catherine's defense. He pressed on. "So were there incidents of physical abuse in your own marriage, Ms. Tate?"

Sharon Tate sat back down as she contemplated her response to that question. She offered Jack the chair at the side of her desk and looked him right in the eye as she responded, "Things were fine for the first year of our marriage. As we passed our first anniversary, he became gradually more domineering. I'm not a woman who takes well to that type of treatment. I was then, and still am, very independent. So we argued. One night, after returning from an event at the Chamber of Commerce we were in a disagreement, and he pushed me rather violently. I looked at him with a rather shocked expression, and I was stunned at the rage in his face. I turned and went to the bedroom. He followed after me, but I made it to the bedroom and locked him out."

"Was that the end of it?"

"No, he pounded on the door, threatened me if I didn't let him in. I told him I was calling the police from the bedroom phone, and that calmed him down."

"Did you let him in?"

"No, I came out the next morning, and of course, he was all apologizing. Said it would never happen again, the usual lines for the morning after from every abusive spouse. I should have left him then, but I wanted to believe that it was an isolated incident that would never happen again."

"Did it happen again? Were there other incidents?"

"A month and a half later, in the middle of another fight, he hit me across the face. When I looked back at him, he grabbed me by the hair, angrily telling me I would not be escaping to the bedroom. He pulled my head back as he spoke, then punched me with a closed fist in the ribs. He cracked two ribs. I really don't know why he stopped with that. He was much stronger than I, so he could have kept on, but I suppose in his mind, I had learned my lesson."

"Is there a hospital record of this?"

"No. I wanted to go to the emergency room, but he wouldn't hear of it. He had his cousin who's a doctor check me out in the morning. While he was there, I told Chad I was leaving him. I walked out with his cousin. I would have walked out the night before, but I knew how he would react, so I waited until there was a witness so he would not dare to try to stop me."

"He let you go?"

"I went directly to my parents' home in Saco, where I stayed until the divorce was final. Oh, the family hounded me to move back. The old man offered money. Chad pleaded, threatened, all of the above, but I filed for divorce, and that was it. I took this job and moved down here after the divorce was final. I was very happy to leave Portland and the Merrills behind."

"Would you be willing to testify at Catherine's trial?"

She looked at Jack and broke into a broad smile. "I would love to testify at her trial. They offered me a lot of money during the divorce if I would not talk about what happened, but I told them to keep their money. My own family may not be in the same income area as the Merrills, but we are far from destitute. That family needs to own up to the fact that Chad Merrill was a wife-beating terror of a man. Anything I can do to help deliver that message I am prepared to do."

Jack had not yet pulled the divorce filing, waiting to see what kind of attitude Sharon Tate would have about it. He now determined to make that a priority upon his return to Portland. If it read as he hoped, he would submit it as an exhibit at trial.

"I thank you for all this, Ms. Tate. Did you know Mr. Merrill when he was a student at Dartmouth?"

"I did, but at a distance. He was a very heavy drinker. I know he had some disciplinary problems, but I never got the details. He was dating a girl whose name escapes me, but mostly I knew him as a frat boy who drank too much."

"I'm headed there next, to see what I can find out."

"Good luck, but don't get your hopes up. The Merrill family have been big contributors to the college for years. Chad was a third-generation student from the Merrills. I doubt anyone will be willing to talk to you. They are a family of old money and privilege. Like most people in that category, they have a history of getting away with whatever they do because they buy their way out of things."

Jack spent another hour or so talking with Sharon Tate. She was a delightful person to talk to. Upon leaving, he headed for New Hampshire and Dartmouth College. Upon arrival, he quickly found out Ms. Tate had been correct about his potential access to information at the Ivy League school. He quickly hit a wall that barred any access to undergraduate records or disciplinary actions that might involve Chadwick Merrill. After a constant flow of no comment or no access, delivered in very rude terms, he asked point-blank if anyone speaking for the Merrill family had given the school any advance warning of his coming to ask questions. This query was also met with a stony look accompanied by no answer. He had obviously made no friends on the campus. That was all right with him; he thought the place was a snob factory anyway. He left Dartmouth College with nothing to show for his trip.

When he got back to his office, he had a number of messages waiting for him, two of which got his primary attention. The first was from Bruce King requesting a call back. The note stated the priority was urgent. The use of the word *urgent* was not like the Bruce King he knew.

The second message was a long one from none other than Susan Frazier. He knew she was working as a field reporter for the nightly news on a major network out of New York. The note said she was working on a special news report on domestic violence and she wanted to feature the Catherine Merrill case. The note closed, saying, "I know you hate me but we are on the same side here. I can help you and your client by airing a report that documents the abuse she had been through. Please call me."

Jack sat at his desk digesting this note and the possibilities it presented. He knew she was right that a well-done report aired on national television could be a tremendous benefit to his case. That is if he could trust her. Did he want to see her again, even in a capacity in which they both worked the same side of the street? A difficult decision that he planned to take some time to consider. He would, however, return Bruce King's call without delay.

Chapter XXVIII

BRUCE KING FELT HE WAS under siege from two directions. On the one hand, the Iran Contra scandal had resulted in dramatically increased scrutiny from the Congress, as well as the press, and the American public in general. He had been operating under the radar performing functions that were in clear violation of directives from the Congress and executive branch of government. The agency had basically worked around President Ford's executive order 11905, prohibiting political assassinations. Bruce had been the number one CIA agent called on to engage in that as well as other activity frowned on by the elected officials. He was a respected and trusted field agent within the agency, called on to perform very dangerous tasks. He had never been called to testify in front of Congress because he was so far down the CIA food chain that his name was basically unknown to those who felt the agency needed more oversight. He was purposely kept out of any lime light in order to carry on assignments deemed necessary but not popular.

On a second front, the visit from the FBI agents was a wakeup call that came out of nowhere. He had no idea the Fignoni family was under such scrutiny from the FBI. He had no idea they had made a connection with him and the Fignonis. He mentally kicked himself for not seeing this coming. Tony Fignoni was a friend, but he was also a criminal. His family was involved in criminal activity. Bruce had known this for a long time, yet he allowed himself to be brought into this criminal enterprise as an assassin. His own conscience had told him it was wrong. His activities on behalf of the government were haunting him enough. This step into criminal work had totally stretched what little moral fiber he had left.

He was more and more troubled by what he had become. He could justify the killings as a soldier telling himself that what he did, he did for God and country. That process became more strained as he worked on black ops for the CIA. There was no rationale for his activities for the Fignoni family. What he had done, torture, murder, he had done for money. He had more money in an offshore bank account than he ever thought he would see in his life. Yet his activities made him feel less and less humane. He was not the man he wanted to be, he was far from what he expected of himself. He needed advice. He needed counseling from someone who was more than just a lawyer. He needed counseling from Jack Roach.

In spite of his workload and his troubling call from Sue Frazier, Jack returned Bruce's call the very next morning. "Bruce, my man, what's going on in your life that can require an urgent note?"

"Hello, Jack. I appreciate your getting right back to me."

Bruce's tone was far more serious than normal. "You sound troubled, Bruce, what's going on?"

"Well, I'm in kind of a bind from a couple of different directions, and I think I need some help from a good lawyer and good friend. You're the only guy I know that fills both roles."

"Hey, you know I will be here for you. Tell me what's going on."

Bruce went into an explanation of the troubles within the CIA. He expected to be under a great deal of scrutiny from the Congress. He also expected to be made a scapegoat by his supervisors, who were also under a lot of pressure. All in all, a very bad situation that was putting him personally in peril. In government, there was no truer statement than "shit rolls downhill" and he was near the bottom of the hill. As congressional oversight of CIA activity got more intense, the brass would be looking to divert the heat, and Bruce King, along with a couple of other field agents, would be the perfect scapegoats. Bruce could see it all coming.

"Apart from the CIA problems, I have other legal issues that I need your lawyerly expertise to resolve."

"What exactly are we talking about?"

Bruce was not sure his phone line was not tapped. "I do not feel comfortable talking about these issues over the phone. We need to meet. Can you meet me in New York?"

Jack wanted to be there to help his friend, but given his workload, at the present time, there was no way he could break away. "I'm up to my ears right now in a murder trial. There's no way I can get away right now. Can you come up to Portland?"

Bruce did not answer right away, obviously trying to think of a way to get up to Portland. Jack gave him a moment then pushed on. "This sounds very serious, Bruce, and I hate to make you come up here, but I really can't get away. Plan on staying with me, and we can go over everything as soon as you get here."

Bruce finally answered, "Okay, I will have to tell my supervisors that I need some personal time for a family issue. I will get away as soon as I can."

Bruce had met with Agent Flanagan to explain that the FBI deal was much ado about nothing. He had a friend from the military who was under investigation for mob activity, and they knew he was a friend of Bruce's, so they were trying to make a connection. He was not sure Flanagan was buying it, but he could not prove otherwise.

After his call with Jack, he went back and requested some personal time for a family issue back in Maine. Flanagan gave a long pause before saying, "How much does this have to do with the FBI visit?"

"It has nothing to do with it," Bruce lied. "The FBI visit was nothing but a fishing expedition. I told you Tony Fignoni is nothing more to me than an old army buddy. My mother is very sick. That's the emergency, nothing else."

"I hope so, Bruce, for your sake, but I have to tell you I'm waiting for the other shoe to drop. If it does, we are going to have a lot to talk about."

Having thrown that warning out, he okayed the personal time off. Bruce immediately began making arrangements for his trip to Maine. He made plane reservations for the following evening. He was very anxious to see his old friend and begin working on a plan to deal with what he felt had become a very serious situation. The vice was closing on him; he could feel it.

Even as he made his arrangements for Portland, the wheels were in motion at CIA headquarters to further complicate his life. FBI agents Stone and Harris were in meetings with Bruce's immediate supervisor, Flanagan. Flanagan had granted their request for a meeting, but he was no fan of the FBI in general and these two guys in particular.

"Agent Bruce King is under investigation for activities involving organized crime. We need the complete history of his activities with the agency." Agent Stone came right to the point.

Agent Flanagan considered the request before answering. Relations between the two law enforcement agencies were generally strained, with neither trusting the other. Personnel information was not typically shared. He wondered if these two agents had cleared their visit with anyone higher up the food chain or if they just took it upon themselves.

"It's not customary to share personnel files with the FBI or anyone else. What's more, details of his activities would involve many cases of top-secret information. Did you really think I would just turn it over to you?"

"I understand your resistance, and normally I would agree. Normally we would not even ask. But we have reason to believe that Agent King has been working off and on for a crime family we have under investigation. It's imperative that we get some answers from the agency about his activities so that we can be informed of his experience to judge if his expertise in certain things would lend itself to some of the crimes committed on behalf of the family."

Flanagan nodded in understanding of their situation, but there was no way he was going to turn over a personnel file. King may well have put himself in a position to be under scrutiny. He may well be headed for major trouble, but Flanagan was going to do his best to keep the CIA out of the whole thing.

"I could not do as you ask even if I wanted to, but I'll tell you what I will do. Write down a series of questions spelling out exactly what you are looking to find, as well as what you want from us, and I will consider responses to the questions I can address."

Agent Stone looked at his fellow agent. "I guess for the time being, this will have to do." Agent Harris allowed that he agreed. They both stood to leave, and Agent Stone said, "We will be back to you with our questions within a few days."

They shook hands, and the two FBI agents took their leave. Flanagan stood, considering the visit as they left. He would have to bring in Agent King to get to the bottom of this before he answered any FBI questions. He would also have to speak with his own supervisors to clue them in on what was happening with his field agent. There were storm clouds gathering around Bruce King. Flanagan would have to see to it that the CIA brass did not get caught by surprise.

Chapter XXIX

JACK CONSIDERED THE NOTE FROM Susan Frazier for a full twenty-four hours before he acted on it. He was not sure he could trust her—he was not even sure he wanted to talk to her—but on the other hand, the national exposure could be great for his client. He decided he owed it to Catherine Merrill to at least explore the possibilities. He made the call.

"This is Susan Frazier."

The sound of her voice raised the hairs on the back of his neck. "This is Jack. I got your note and wanted to discuss your interest in my case."

Her tone changed as she realized she was talking to Jack, from all business to a more pleasant, friendly approach.

"Thank you for calling, Jack. How have you been?"

Jack noticed the change in tone but wanted none of it.

"I really don't want to get into a lot of small talk, Ms. Frazier. This is purely a business discussion. I can help you with your planned television special, and you can help me with a very difficult case. So, let's discuss business. He knew he was being incredibly cold, but he wanted no misunderstanding. He was calling for the sake of his client, not to renew an old acquaintance."

After a short hesitation, she went back to the all-business voice she started with.

"Okay, Jack, I'm about halfway through filming a special report on domestic abuse. I saw the write up in the Portland paper about the Merrill case. It fits right into the theme of what will be a one-hour special. Depending upon what I find, I could give a full ten or fifteen minutes to your case on a national broadcast on network television."

"Are any of the other examples of domestic violence that you intend to feature involved in murder trials?"

"No, which is one reason I really want to feature this case. If this is a situation where a woman defended herself, as I think it is, then it is exactly what I'm looking to feature."

Jack knew before she said this that Catherine's case would be exactly what she was looking to feature. Letting her in the door would be a finishing piece to her documentary.

"I have given this a lot of thought, and what I would suggest is that we have a written agreement that I approve the final product. I can assure you that this case will give you everything you're looking to present. I will let you have access to my client as well as the witnesses involved. I will be accused of trying a case in the press, but in order to limit that criticism, I will give you only a brief statement from my office with a brief interview. Does that work for you?"

"That works fine. I know you don't trust me, Jack, but we are on the same side here. Whatever you may think of me, I talked the network into this special because domestic violence, spousal abuse, is a cause I'm passionate about, and I would never do anything to jeopardize the case of any abused woman. That's true, Jack, no matter what I feel about you."

The final remark was a message to Jack that he was not the only one with some bitterness. "All right then, we are in agreement. When do you plan to be in Portland so I can have Catherine available?"

They ironed out the details, with Jack providing a list of his witnesses, including Chad Merrill's ex-wife in Rhode Island. Susan gave him the dates that she would be in Portland so he could make Catherine, as well as himself, available. After he hung up from Susan Frazier, he called Catherine to tell her about the conversation and to make sure she was in agreement with him that it was a good idea. Catherine was in total agreement and more than willing to tell her story. She knew as well as Jack did that this type of exposure could be very beneficial to her case.

This was the first time he had spoken with Catherine since he returned from Rhode Island and New Hampshire. He relayed his discussion with Chadwick's ex-wife as well as the stone wall he ran into at Dartmouth. Catherine gave him a pleasant surprise when he talked about Dartmouth.

"Jack, I was at Dartmouth College with Chad. I did not know him that well, but it's a small college, so I knew who he was and heard all the gossip. He was dating a girl named Sara Brennan, and I remember there was an incident involving her that got Chad in trouble. I don't recall all the details, but it was a big deal at the time and he was in real serious trouble. I would have mentioned it earlier but it actually just came back to me."

This was exactly the kind of thing Jack was hoping to find at Dartmouth.

"Really, what were the specifics?"

"I don't recall all the details, just that there was a lot of scuttle-butt around the incident, and Chad was in a bit of trouble. It didn't involve me or any of my friends, so I only paid passive attention to it. As I said, I didn't know him that well back then."

"I will never get any details from the college about incidents involving Chadwick Merrill. Do you know what happened to Sara Brennan?"

"Not offhand, but I can check with some of my old college friends to see if I can find out."

"That would be good. I would really like to talk with her and maybe get something to use from his college days."

That night, at dinner with Elaine, Jack told her about Sue Frazier, his relationship with her from years past right up to the offer to feature Catherine's case on her documentary. He was looking for her opinion of his decision to trust Susan. After hearing him out, Elaine asked with a cute little smile, "Should I be jealous here, Jack?"

Jack had downplayed his earlier relationship with Sue, saying only that she was an old girlfriend. He did not tell her how serious it became. He did not tell her how Susan broke his heart.

"Don't be silly, Elaine. It was an ugly breakup with hard feelings on both sides. My only concern here is if she can help my case for Catherine. I only called her back for Catherine's benefit, otherwise I would have ignored the call."

Elaine laughed, saying, "Well, I've seen her on network television. She's beautiful, so I'm glad there were hard feelings." With that, she put forward her wine glass for a toast. Jack clinked her glass, smiling.

"Anyway, in answer to your question, exposure on national television can only help Catherine's case." Elaine offered.

"That's my sense as well. Should I trust her?"

"I can't see why not. You get to approve the final product."

This time, Jack offered his glass for a toast. It was nice to have Elaine in agreement with his decision.

Susan Frazier wasted no time coming to Portland three days after her conversation with Jack. Her first interview was with Catherine in Jack's office. His first impression as Sue walked in was that she had not lost a thing. If anything, she was even more stunning. Prior to the sit-down with Catherine, Jack provided her with the medical record from the night of the incident showing two broken ribs, facial bruising, and dark-red marks around her neck from her husband's attempts to choke her. Susan asked great questions, giving Jack a preview of how Catherine would look on the witness stand. He was very impressed as she went through an account of the attack by Chadwick Merrill.

"You say that he had physically abused you before, and I've seen the hospital records. What was different this time to make you think your life was in danger?" This was the exact question Jack knew he would ask during the trial.

"When he banged my head up against the cabinets and began choking me, the look in his eyes was the likes of which I had never before seen. The rage in those eyes was horrifying. He had lost all control. I could not breathe, and he showed no sign of easing up."

That statement concluded the interview. Jack felt it could not have ended any better. She appeared completely sincere and completely believable. He pictured a jury seeing that same performance, they could not help but be impressed with the sincerity. Her legal background, the training she had received, would make her a great witness in her own defense.

Next, she interviewed Jack. By his insistence, it was a brief interview in which Jack answered her direct questions by saying, "It's a clear case of self-defense following years of physical abuse, pure and simple."

Interviews over, they discussed the next steps. "I plan to interview the ex-wife, Catherine's two friends, and finally, the DA."

Jack smiled at the thought of her interviewing the DA. She would take his smugness and turn him inside out; she was that good at what she did.

"I can't imagine DA Rideout will be very happy about the interview."

"I'm hoping he's not. I want him to look like the whole thing is just an irritation to him."

"Look, Jack, I won't bore you with any small talk about old times, but I will just say I appreciate this, and I hope it helps, and I really mean that."

"For Catherine, I appreciate you doing this. I share your hope that it helps. I also hope you have an award-winning documentary when it's done." After a long look between them, Susan left.

The next morning, Jack was greeted first thing with a call from DA Rideout.

"Mr. Roach, I got a call yesterday afternoon from a reporter that I think you know, requesting to interview me on the Merrill case. We don't try cases in the press here in Portland, but I guess this must be a Boston thing." He was obviously agitated, a situation that made Jack smile. He had expected Susan would get under his skin.

"I appreciate you giving me credit, but I think it's much more a case of a reporter sniffing out a bad case that should not even be brought to trial," he responded, hoping to fan the flames.

"It might just be that a judge would find a reporter like this prejudicial to a jury pool."

This statement got under Jack's skin. "That may be the stupidest statement I've heard this week. Did you think this case would draw no press, or did you think that only the press that favored your case would be fair or nonprejudicial? Certainly, the two puff pieces in the Portland Press that painted the deceased as ready for sainthood were not objectionable to you."

"Very well, Mr. Roach, we will see you at the pretrial conference."

"I'm looking forward to it."

With that, DA Rideout hung up his phone. Jack chuckled as he did the same.

Apparently, he was not the only person Susan Frazier could aggravate. He planned to put a lot more heat on the DA. This was only the beginning.

Two days later, Susan met with Jack to lay out the sequence of interviews, as well as the overall message of the program. "It will be a full twelve minutes out of a one-hour show. The case will take up the greatest amount of time of any single case on the documentary."

Jack looked over the written agenda and interviews of the program segment. It was laid out perfectly with statements from the ex-wife that would be very damaging to the image of Chadwick Merrill.

"You asked Rideout point-blank if he felt comfortable bringing this to trial?"

This Jack found amusing and was probably what really aggravated Rideout.

"I did indeed. His response was a short curt yes." She said this with a smile. The same smile that could still bring Jack to his knees. She was obviously proud of her report.

He looked her in the eye for a long moment, finally breaking the spell by standing up to extend his hand. "Thank you, Susan. I think this will help a very nice woman in a very difficult position."

"My pleasure, Jack," she said as she shook his hand. "Good work, I hope you win this case. She seems like a woman who deserves to be acquitted, and you are just the lawyer that could make that happen."

They held a look between them for a moment, then she turned to walk out. Jack watched her go, noticing that she still had that fabulous build that he remembered. He tried not to think about what could have been, but it was not easy. She was still the intelligent, witty, beautiful woman he lost. He still regretted the loss. He still wondered if she was the only woman he would ever love. He wondered if his memory of her would ever allow him to let his guard down and totally give himself to Elaine. Half of him wanted to call her back, but he resisted the urge, sat back down, and called Elaine Watkens.

Sue Frazier's work had not gone unnoticed Stanton Merrill heard about the reporter running around Portland interviewing people. He heard about the planned television show. He was not happy. He called Attorney Hancock, requesting him to stop the broadcast from airing.

Hancock knew the request was an impossible one.

"This is a major network carrying a show on national television. It's not something that can be easily discouraged."

"Goddamn you, this will serve to smear the good name of my son as well as the rest of my family. I pay you a lot of money to keep things like this from happening, so you better do something or you will pay a price."

"Very well, Stanton, I will send a letter threatening a lawsuit."

The receiver was slammed down so hard it hurt Hancock's ear. He would send the letter, but he knew full well that the attorneys for the network would laugh at it. Part of the price you pay for representing the Merrills. Sometimes you had to look like a fool just to keep them happy.

Chapter XXX

EVEN AS JACK DEALT WITH Sue Frazier's interviews, he was simultaneously dealing with an old friend who was his current houseguest. Bruce had arrived the same day as Sue Frazier, and with all that he had on his plate, Jack had no time for socializing. He got right down to business the first night Bruce joined him.

"So tell me, what could be going on in your life that you would need the services of a lawyer?" The two had not been together for some time. Bruce looked a bit different to Jack, a bit harder, a bit colder.

They were sitting in Jack's living room, drinking beer together for the first time in quite a while. "Okay, Jack, we are getting right down to the subject at hand. It's good that you're all business these days." Bruce sounded a bit touchy, so Jack backed off a bit.

"I don't mean to be rude or unfriendly, but your use of the word *urgent* in your message is a bit alarming, so that's why I'm all business. I'm concerned about what's going on with you."

Bruce took a long haul off his beer, paused a moment, then went into a long explanation of his activities in the CIA. He didn't get into details of top-secret assignments he had been on, but he made it clear that many of his black-ops assignments were in violation of what elected officials expected the agency to be doing. His feeling was that with increased congressional scrutiny, including direct investigations, that he might well end up a scapegoat rolled on by his superiors. He would be presented as a rogue agent who was very difficult to control, who went on his own initiatives to do things beyond his assignments. This would be done to get his superiors off the hook, making Bruce the bad guy.

"Okay, that sounds like trouble in the workplace that a lawyer may or may not be able to help with. If I'm going to help, I will need to know the specifics of your activities. When I have that, I will do what I can. But there must be something else going on with you. What else is going on that brings you to the conclusion that you need legal counsel?"

Bruce again took a haul off his beer, looked Jack in the eye, and got into his answer.

"As always, you are very perceptive, Jack. I do have another issue hanging over my head. I know we are longtime friends and I would trust you with my life. But if I'm going to get into top-secret CIA activities plus give you the details of my other problems, I need to be sure you are my lawyer."

"Okay, give me a dollar," Jack said, reaching his hand out to collect the dollar.

"Why would I give you a dollar?"

"Just hand it over." Jack continued to hold his hand out, waiting as Bruce dug in his pocket, pulling out a one-dollar bill and handing it to Jack.

"Okay, you just hired me as your attorney. Anything we say now is protected by attorney client privilege. I will not be able to repeat it even if I want to, so give me the complete story and don't hold anything back."

For the next hour and a half, Bruce King told his longtime friend about the Fignoni crime family and all the details of his criminal acts committed on behalf of the Fignoni family. The tortures, the murders, basically all that he had done as well as the money he was paid. He told about the FBI agents who were investigating the Fignoni family and of their questioning of his connection to them. He further went into specific details about all his activities for the CIA including assassinations he committed. Jack took notes, asking only a few questions. Mostly he sat in shocked silence as he listened to what his friend had become. He knew he was in the CIA but was stunned to listen to the details of the acts he had committed on behalf of the CIA. He also knew Bruce had become friends with Tony Fignoni in the service but was unaware of the Fignoni family's criminal activities. Most of all, he was shocked to hear of Bruce's direct involvement in those criminal activities. When Bruce had finished, Jack took a moment to digest everything he had heard from his friend. Obviously, Bruce was in serious trouble on two fronts. He stood up and began pacting the room. Finally, he said, "Okay, Bruce, first, if you are contacted again by the FBI, you refer them to me. If they place you under arrest or want you in front of a grand jury, contact me, and do not, I repeat, do not answer any questions or make any comments until I'm with you. As concerns your problems at the agency, you need to keep me informed. If you are called on the carpet, request permission to have a lawyer present. If they refuse that request, you should say as little as possible. If you are called to testify before Congress, let me know so I can be there with you. Are we clear?"

Bruce nodded his understanding, saying, "I understand all that, Jack, but what's the strategy?"

A good question that Jack was only ready to answer if Bruce was looking to change.

"That depends on you." Jack sat back down and thought a bit before continuing. He turned back to Bruce. "Look what you've become, Bruce. You are a killer for hire, are you happy with this? Do you want this for the rest of your life?" Jack raised his voice with emotion. "You've become a monster, my friend. You've just told me a list of things you have done that I would never have thought you capable of doing. So what's your strategy? Where do you go from here? Because if you're happy doing what you're doing, happy with what you've become, my strategy will be a lot different than it will be if you want a new direction. I will defend you either way, but the defense will look a lot different."

Brue raised his own voice in responding with emotions that matched Jack's. "I want it over, Jack," he hollered. "I want to be out of the CIA. I want to be away from the Fignonis. I want to be able to sleep at night. I want a normal life. Do you think for a minute that I like what I see when I look in the mirror?"

Bruce's face was flushed, and there were tears in his eyes. He was literally shaking with emotion. Jack asked in a calmer voice, "How did it happen, Bruce, this transformation?"

Bruce took a moment to calm himself then went through the history of his time in the service, his time in the Tiger Force, in the CIA, his training in the CIA camp for fourteen months, up to his involvement with the Fignonis. He talked about how proud he was to be selected for Tiger Force. He told Jack what a mistake it turned out to be joining the Tiger Force. He told of the atrocities he saw and took part in as part of that force. He told Jack about the CIA training to make him a killer, the assignments he was sent on as an assassin. In the end, he realized that the pride he felt in being recruited to the Tiger Force as well as the CIA was misplaced pride. The only reason he was recruited was his ability to kill, to kill without any apparent remorse. But there was remorse. He held it in while it built up to the point that he now could no longer live with the remorse. He just wanted it all to end.

Jack listened intently to the emotional outpouring. He was convinced of Bruce's sincerity. Nobody knew Bruce King as well as he knew him. He was convinced Bruce wanted a total change in his life, not just to settle the two problems he faced presently. He wanted to get away, far enough away that he wouldn't be reminded of all this. Far away enough that he could begin to forget, to have a new life.

"Okay, Bruce, we are going to work together to set your life back on track. We will resolve the current problems, but more than that, we are going to get you back to a good place."

"Nice words, Jack, but what's the plan? How are we proceeding here?"

"I have to work it all out, but work it out I will. I want all the details of the atrocities you spoke of with Tiger Force. I want full information on CIA activities that were in conflict with congressional expectations. I want all the ugly details of any CIA activity that would be embarrassing to the agency if made public. For now, just follow the instructions I just gave you about not sating anything while I work out a plan to make it all happen. Bruce, you have to have faith in me here. I will make things right, but I will need all the information I just requested."

Bruce stood up, walked over to Jack, and embraced him, a move he had never done before. As close as the two of them had been for years, this type of display of emotion had never happened. After getting over his initial surprise, Jack embraced him back. "Bruce, stay here for a couple of days away from Washington. I'm busy as hell with not much time for socializing, but you need time away from that bullshit."

"I agree, Jack, and I appreciate your hospitality. I do have faith in you to help me make this all right again."

The next day in Washington, the two FBI agents delivered a list of nineteen questions to CIA Agent Flanagan. Looking the list over, he knew he would not be answering most of these questions. He also knew that he had initiated an internal discussion on what to do about Agent King. The wheels were in motion at the highest levels of the agency to deal with the situation. It would be dealt with, but not with any cooperation with or from the FBI. The CIA took care of its own problems. Flanagan's discussions with his superiors had laid out the strategy to deal with Agent King. As congressional heat continued to build, they would keep King around, protected from the FBI. They would keep him until the proper moment when making him the key part of their defensive posture would relieve some of the congressional pressure. Once scapegoated, they would let him go. Then the FBI could do whatever they wanted to do with him.

Chapter XXXI

THROUGH A COLLEGE FRIEND, CATHERINE Merrill was able to track down Sara Brennan, who was now Sara Kemp, living in New Haven, Connecticut. She got a phone number and gave it to Jack so that he could place the call. As soon as he had the number, Jack made the call from his office. When he got her on the line, Jack explained that he was an attorney representing the former Catherine Shaw in a murder trial. Thinking that she would probably not be inclined to talk to him, he spoke fast in hopes that she wouldn't hang up on him, but she surprised him by interrupting his rapid explanation to say she had heard about the case.

"How did you hear about it in Connecticut? Was it covered in the press down there?"

"Word of mouth. Our graduating class from Dartmouth was not that big. All my friends knew I dated Chad. That, of course, made sense. His death would be significant news to those who knew him in college, and it would be passed around quickly.

"That's what I want to talk to you about, your dating Chadwick Merrill. Catherine acted in self-defense after years of abuse and a final attack in which she feared for her life. I plan to defend her by making the case for self-defense. I have been told that you had your own incident with Mr. Merrill, in college."

There was a long pause, so long Jack thought he might have lost her. He was about to ask if she was still there when she finally spoke.

"Mr. Roach, I did date Chad Merrill in college, but how can my experience possibly be of any relevance to your client's situation?"

"Ms. Kemp, I intend to show that the attack on Catherine was far from an isolated incident. That Chadwick Merrill had a long history of physical abuse against women. His first wife is planning to testify about her own experiences. I'm not sure what happened between the two of you, but I would like to hear your account to see if it's just more of the same behavior on his part. If it is, that would certainly be relevant to Catherine's defense."

There was another long pause on the other end of the line. Jack waited for a response for as long as he could, finally saying, "Ms. Kemp, are you still there?"

"Yes, I'm here, and I would like to be of help, but I don't think I can be."

A disappointing response, but Jack pressed on. "Please tell me what happened so I can make the determination on whether or not it's helpful."

Yet another pause on the other end. She was obviously wrestling with what to do in this whole situation.

"I can't tell you," she blurted out. "I took money from the Merrills and signed an agreement that I would never discuss the details."

Jack's first thought was that this should not be a surprise. He should have known he would run into Merrill family money as an obstacle. He also knew that if Stanton Merrill paid her for her silence, then what happened would be valuable to his defense. It must have been an incident that had the old bastard worried for him to shell out a pack of dough to keep her quiet.

Thinking quickly, Jack pressed for a way to overcome the agreement with the Merrills.

"Let me ask you this, Ms. Kemp, how much money are we talking about?"

"It was only ten thousand dollars, but this was a long time ago. Ten thousand dollars was a lot of money to me then. I was a poor college student trying to make ends meet. So I signed an agreement that would prevent me from telling you or anyone else anything about the incident. Why don't you go to the college? They have a record of the incident."

"I have been there already, and any questions about Chadwick Merrill's activities are off-limits as far as the college is concerned."

"That's not a surprise," she offered. "The Merrills paid off the college as well."

Jack was thinking hard to try to figure a way around this obstacle.

With only ten thousand dollars involved, Jack felt confident he could get Catherine's family to offer to make that amount part of his legal fees. So he offered a solution. "Ms. Kemp, agreements of that type are very difficult to enforce. If you would agree to testify, I would defend you pro bono against a claim from the Merrill family. What's more, if we lose, I will pay the ten thousand dollars back to the Merrills myself."

There was a long silence again, so Jack continued. "I would be glad to put that in writing in legal form to verify my commitment."

"Let me talk to my husband about this, Mr. Roach. Give me your number so I can get back to you."

Jack gave her his office number as well as his home number. "Ms. Kemp, please consider this because I really need your participation. Call me anytime, and include your husband in on the call if that would be helpful."

With that, they hung up. Jack felt that he had made progress with her but was unsure of her support. Depending on the details of what happened between them, he felt sure that her testimony could be a huge benefit. He spoke with Catherine about the offer he had made to Ms. Kemp. "There is a slight possibility that it may end up costing you ten thousand dollars, but I think it will be worth it."

Catherine agreed.

The next morning, Jack had a call in his office from Peter Kemp. He was more than happy to encourage his wife to be helpful in the case against Catherine Merrill. "I would insist on a written agreement that memorializes the arrangement you described to Sara. As soon as we get it and my attorney approves it, she will tell you the whole story. I have seen the aftereffects of that bastard's attack on her all the years we have been together. She has never fully recovered. I know the complete story, and believe me, I have often considered driving to Portland to confront him. She still wakes up some nights screaming then crying." Peter Kemp spoke with rage in his voice, the result of watching his wife live with the drama of her attack by Chadwick Merrill.

The agreement was faxed to Peter and Sara Kemp's attorney. The following day, Jack heard the full story of a horrific attack by Chadwick Merrill on Sara Brennan. It happened at a fraternity party when a drunken Chad Merrill accused her of flirting with a fellow frat brother. He then struck Sara in the face with a closed fist, knocking her down. He landed on top of her, striking her again in the face, then he choked her until she lost consciousness. Several frat brothers had to pull him off or he might have killed her. She was brought to the campus infirmary for treatment after she regained consciousness. She reported everything to the dean of student affairs the next morning. Pictures were taken of her black eye, swollen face, and choke marks around her neck. Fortunately, she still had the pictures. Chadwick was about to be expelled, but Stanton made a huge contribution to the college and paid off Sara so the whole thing was swept under the rug. It was exactly what Jack was looking for and he got Sara's commitment to testify.

The week following his interaction with the Kemps, he met in Judge Murray's office with Attorney Kenneth Coleman of the DA's office for a pretrial conference. Jack submitted his witness list at the conference, and Coleman immediately raised objections.

"Your Honor, this list, Mr. Merrill's ex-wife, friends of Ms. Merrill, some girl from college. Obviously, Mr. Roach's entire defense will be to besmirch the good name of Chadwick Merrill. This is outrageous and should not be allowed."

"Your Honor, I intend to show that the attack on Ms. Merrill was not an isolated incident. I will produce hospital records as well as sworn testimony of a pattern of physical abuse that culminated in this final attack. It is critical to the defense that I'm allowed to demonstrate the history of brutal attacks against women that goes back twenty years." Despite further objections from Attorney Coleman about the good name of the Merrills, Judge Murray's decision was swift.

"Self-defense is a legitimate defense and a pattern of behavior is a proper approach to substantiate that defense," Judge Murray stated.

"I see no problem with the witness list, Mr. Coleman." Obviously, Judge Murry was not as easily swayed by the Merrill name as Judge Collins. This was the first indication that he would not be carrying the same open bias as Collins.

Coleman continued to make arguments against the defense strategy, but Judge Murray was not buying it. Jack was glad to be dealing with Murray rather than Judge Collins. Coleman's witness list included the responding police officer, the medical examiner, plus a list of character witnesses. No surprises for Jack. The meeting broke up with Jack feeling very good about his defense. A trial date had been set with jury selection to begin in three weeks.

Two days later, Stanton Merrill walked into a meeting that he had requested with DA Rideout and Attorney Coleman. He looked at the witness list Jack had submitted and exploded with the same reaction as Coleman.

"This son of a bitch is just looking to make Catherine look the victim at my son's expense."

"He's pleading self-defense," DA Rideout said. "That's no surprise."

Mr. Merrill continued to look at the witness list. "Sara Brennan Kemp, I paid that bitch good money for her silence. He's got Chad's ex-wife on here. She hated Chad. She will say anything. And my nephew, Dr. Merrill. What the fuck is he doing testifying against his cousin?" He was red-faced, shaking with rage.

"I'm not sure why these witnesses are on here, Mr. Merrill. I can only tell you that Roach is expecting their testimony to support his claim of self-defense."

Stanton Merrill threw the discovery papers across the desk at Rideout as he rose from his chair. He bellowed with rage at Rideout. "This is an outrage, first a television show, now this, all intended to smear my son's good name. You sit on your fat ass letting this all happen. I swear you will pay." With that, he turned and stormed out of the office. Rideout started after him for a moment, then turned to his assistant Coleman in obvious exasperation. "I think Roach is correct that we have a weak case. I also think that we are prosecuting it to please that old son of a bitch. I also think the whole thing is making me sick to my stomach." He sat back in his chair, swiveling it around to look out the window from his office. "If this was anyone else, I would not even be prosecuting this dog of a case."

As Jack returned to his office, he was joined by the firm's senior partner, Jared McCarthy. He walked into Jack's office, closing the door behind him. "Jack, I want you to know that because of Stanton Merrill's influence, I have lost two of the firm's corporate clients. I'm not telling you this so that you will change in any way what you are doing in Catherine Merrill's defense, I'm telling you so you will know what a bastard Stanton Merrill is."

Jack sat quiet for a moment, looking at this senior partner, finally saying, "How can I make his up to you, Jared?"

"You can win the case and rub it in that bastard's face." With that, he turned and left Jack's office.

One week later, two weeks prior to jury selection beginning, Sue Frazier's documentary on domestic violence aired on national television. Twelve minutes of the hour-long telecast was dedicated to the Catherine Merrill case. The effect of the broadcast was DA Rideout's worst nightmare. It sparked an outrage among women across the country, but especially in Maine. As the trial date approached, all hell broke out.

Chapter XXXII

THE REACTION TO THE AIRING of Sue Frazier's program was immediate. She did an impressive job of detailing the history of Chad Merrill's relationships with women and the interview with Catherine was devastating. It all led to a public outcry featuring op-ed pieces and letters to the editor of Portland area newspapers, dozens of calls to the DA's office strongly suggesting he drop the case as well as a press conference featuring several Maine women's groups decrying domestic violence and the prosecution of a woman who defended herself against the violence.

All this led up to the opening of the trial. Not surprisingly, the first day featured a protest with a good-sized crowd of women outside the courthouse picketing and carrying signs. Jack and Catherine walked through the crowd of protesters and news reporters to get into the courthouse. The protesters applauded and cheered for Catherine as she walked by them. There was little point in discussing a change of venue as the strong emotions and outrage from the national broadcast spread well beyond Maine.

Jury selection commenced on that first day, with the prosecution asking every potential juror if they had seen the broadcast. If they had seen it, the next question was if they could be impartial given what they saw. Attorney Coleman did all he could to get an all-male jury while Jack was working to seat as many women as possible preferably young women. Given the uproar about the trial, the protests and overall reaction to the broadcast, many potential jurors were dismissed. By the time twelve jurors and two alternates were finally seated, the process had pretty well depleted the jury pool. Jack ended up with five women on the jury and one woman as an alternate. Better still, three of the five women jurors were under forty so presumably apt to be sympathetic to women's rights. Altogether, Jack felt good about where he ended up after the two-day process. After all, he only needed one vote in order to hang the jury.

During the entire jury selection process, Stanton Merrill sat in the front row directly behind the prosecution table. The first two rows of seats were held down by Merrill family members. Stanton sat on the aisle seat, no more than twenty feet from Jack. He spent the entire two days staring at Jack in an attempt to intimidate him.

For his part, Jack had to stifle a laugh on a couple of occasions as he observed the ham-handed attempt to cower him.

At one point, Catherine made mention of Mr. Merrill's unbroken stares.

"Jack, I don't know if you have noticed, but my father-in-law has not taken his eyes off of you."

"Oh, I've noticed. Believe me, Catherine, I have had a lot tougher guys than him try to intimidate me over the years. He doesn't scare me. In fact, I find the whole attempt amusing."

"Don't underestimate him, Jack."

Jack just gave her a confident wink as he went back to his notes. He was not afraid of the Merrill Family's influence. This trial would make his reputation one way or the other in Maine as a defense attorney. He had no expectations of ever doing legal work for the Merrills or any of their friends. The firm had lost corporate clients, but thankfully, corporate law was not a big part of the firm's business. If he wins this case, the defense attorneys in his firm would all reap the benefits. He was very confident that he would win. When he did, there would be very little Stanton Merrill and company could do to dampen his reputation.

On the third day of the trial, the protests continued outside the courtroom. News coverage of the protests was extensive to the point that Judge Murray sequestered the jury. Never a popular move with jurors. The entire third day was taken up with opening arguments. The prosecution's case was quite simple and laid out in their opening statement. Attorney Coleman pointed out that Catherine Merrill had stabbed Chadwick Merrill to death. It was a violent crime of passion. She admitted doing it and it was murder, pure and simple.

What's more, it was murder committed by an attacker who stood to benefit financially if the deceased was no longer alive.

"The defense will try to sell you on its theory of mitigating circumstances that add up to self-defense. Do not buy it. Catherine Merrill stabbed Chadwick Merrill several times in a fit of rage so that she could dispose of her husband and inherit his wealth, pure and simple."

This was the motive the prosecution had settled on presenting. Catherine was in it for the money. The argument they had that night was brought on by her, and it presented her with the opportunity to take the action that would get her out of the relationship a wealthy woman.

Jack's opening arguments were obviously quite different. He said he agreed with one point made by Attorney Coleman; it is a quite simple case because it is quite simply self-defense. He went on to explain the defense.

"We will show that Catherine Merrill was beaten that night to a point where she feared for her life. We will show that Chadwick Merrill has a long history of violent behavior with women, going back to his time in college. We will show that Catherine Merrill has sustained a number of beatings over the years and that this last one was so severe that she feared she would not live through it. In the end, we will prove beyond a shadow of a doubt that Catherine Merrill acted in self-defense."

It being a Friday, Judge Murray adjourned the court until Monday after Jack finished. Jack filled his briefcase with his papers and escorted Catherine out of the courtroom for a planned meeting in his office. As they got to the aisle, they were met by Stanton Merrill who stood at the end of the row of seats to deliver an icy stare to the two of them. Jack couldn't help himself as on his way past him he said, "Good afternoon, Mr. Merrill. Isn't it a lovely day?" The look of pure rage on his face kept Jack in a good mood the rest of the day.

Attorney Coleman went back to his office, where he was greeted by District Attorney Rideout. "Well, how was the first day?"

Coleman settled into his chair with a sigh, rubbed his face with both hands, and answered, "What can I tell you? This case is a fucking loser. You know it and I know it, and those women out front carrying signs know it. My chances of getting a conviction are under ten percent."

Rideout took a seat across the desk from Coleman. "It's a tough case, Dan, I will give you that. But it's winnable, and we have no choice but to go balls to the wall, given who the victim is here."

"Really, you will be running for reelection next year. Do you think for a minute this is helpful? The great majority of people, especially women, don't seem to support us on this. Most men who knew Chad Merrill thought he was an asshole. So tell me how this is helpful."

Rideout knew Coleman was right about the current public attitude. He also knew he needed money to get reelected and enough money can change public attitude.

"You know the Merrills are my biggest campaign contributors. I need their support. You know that's true."

"Yeah, well, I also know this is true: When this trial is over and all of Chad Merrill's warts have been exposed to the public and we lose the case, Stanton Merrill, as well as every other Merrill will be contributing nothing to you. We will be to blame for it all in his eyes, but you and I will know that if he hadn't pushed us to take it to trial, we probably would not have tried the case."

District Attorney Rideout heard this rather dire assessment of the situation and was quite sure Coleman was correct. He had been put in this no-win situation by Stanton Merrill's insistence that Catherine be charged with murder. He had no idea that this new attorney in town, this Jack Roach, would put together such an in-depth case involving the years of abuse with a number of different women. He thought because of the Merrill family influence that any attempt at using Chad Merrill's history at trial would be blocked by the judge. Judge Murray had surprised him by supporting Attorney Roach at the pretrial conference. Of course, he had no forewarning of a network television show featuring the case would be broadcast nationwide a mere two weeks before the trial. Altogether, he felt the deck had been stacked against him. There was nothing he could do now but try the damn case and hope for a miracle outcome in his favor. The reality was that he knew Coleman was right.

Chapter XXXIII

CIA DIRECTOR OF OPERATIONS, DAVID Stark, and Bruce's immediate supervisor, John Flanagan, had called Bruce King to come into the office for a meeting. The two sat in Deputy Director Russ Campbell's office discussing their plans for King in advance of his arrival. Congressional hearings into CIA activities were set to begin in three weeks immediately after the congressional recess. A tremendous amount of data had already been given to the Senate oversight committee in response to the committee's request. They had not yet received the list of CIA personnel that would be asked to testify after the director, but it was expected any day. As the three sat discussing their future, they knew they would all be called to testify. They had no intention of accepting any responsibility for operations and activities the committee might find objectionable. That's where people like Bruce King would become useful. He had operated from the beginning below the radar screen performing missions, carrying nothing that would identify him as a United States operative. That being the case, many of his actions did not necessarily have CIA fingerprints and may be able to be denied all together. He worked in David Stark's Special Activities Division said to be the most secretive special operations force within the agency, performing covert missions, or "black-ops."

"King has operated in both paramilitary operations as well as covert political missions," said his immediate supervisor Flanagan. "He is the perfect foil to demonstrate how field operators can sometimes go rogue."

"That may be true, John," Russ Campbell agreed. "But we can use him to explain a few hiccups over the years, but we are going to have to limit the missteps that are brought to light. Even this guy can't be used to explain everything. We need to be careful what we give them, careful what we say. In the end, we deny responsibility for anything that can't be proven."

"True enough, Russ," David Stark said. "Still, we need to keep him under control for now. The purpose of today's meeting is to scare him with the prospect of this FBI investigation, then soften the blow by letting him know we have his back."

"Okay, David, as deputy director, I will let him know we are backing him and you open things by stressing the potential problem with the FBI."

As they spoke of his future, Bruce sat outside the deputy director's office, waiting to be called into the meeting. In all his years with the agency, he had never been called to a meeting with the Deputy Director. David Stark was as high up the food chain as he had ever gone. He expected this was all about the FBI investigation, and as he was called in, finally, he was not disappointed.

The three inquisitors sat at a round conference table facing Bruce as he walked in the room. Nobody stood to greet him; the deputy director motioned for him to take a chair. Once he was seated, the conversation was opened by David Stark as planned.

"Good morning, Agent King. As you know we have been approached by FBI agents Stone and Harris concerning your activities with us. This inquiry is prompted, apparently, by your relationship with a member of a New York crime family they have under investigation. I don't have to tell you that we consider this a very serious matter. We do not have a history of working closely with the FBI, especially when the subject of their investigation is one of our agents. This whole thing has the potential to prove to be very embarrassing to the CIA. So we would like to hear you explain why we should not be concerned about this."

Bruce looked at the three upper echelon agents, one at a time, expecting the other two to have their say. After concluding that they would not, he spoke, "I have already explained to Agent Flanagan that the two agents are trying to make a case out of whole cloth. When I met with them, I explained that Tony Fignoni and I have been friends since we served together in Vietnam. We occasionally get together when we are in the same area. There is no more to it than that."

"Obviously, Stone and Harris are not buying that explanation," Stark responded. "Since they met with you, they have been back in touch with Agent Flanagan requesting information about your CIA activities. They seem to be somehow attempting to tie your experience here to events involving the Fignonis. It's bad enough that you are being investigated for your connection to a crime family. Trying to connect that to your CIA duties is most troubling."

"Obviously, it's a fishing expedition by two FBI agents that need to have more to do."

Stark looked over at Deputy Director Campbell, signaling he was out of questions, so Campbell picked up the conversation.

"Agent King, I hope that you are correct in your assessment and that you are being truthful with us about your relationship with this Fignoni chap. In three weeks, a congressional committee will begin hearings delving into CIA activities, so we have enough on our plates right now without this turning into something."

"I assure you, Deputy Director, that nothing can come of this."

The deputy director went on, "I hope that's true. I want you to know that we take you at your word and the agency will stand behind you. My staff will be writing a response to the list of questions the two agents gave to Agent Flanagan, and the response will address few of the questions, basically sending the message that we are not in the habit of sharing top secret details with anyone, even the FBI."

"I appreciate that, sir."

"We will protect your interests, Agent King, as well as ours, but for the foreseeable future, I think it best if you stay away from Mr. Fignoni."

"Understood, sir."

With that said, the three inquisitors looked at each other as Campbell asked if there was anything else. Concluding there was not, he informed Bruce he was dismissed. He left the office thankful the meeting was over. He intended to find a pay phone later in the day to call Jack. All things considered, he was not sure that his own phone was not tapped. He would also make sure he was not being followed before he stopped at a pay phone. He was well schooled in clandestine work; he just never expected to have to use those skills to protect himself from his own agency.

After he left Director Stark told Agent Flanagan to be sure to place a number of back dated reprimands in King's file so they would have proof of the rogue nature of his service. So began the plans to use him as a scapegoat.

Chapter XXXIV

As court was brought back into session the next Monday, a crowd of thirty to forty protesters continued their vigil in front of the courthouse. They were covered by more press than the Cumberland County Courthouse had ever seen. Television, radio, and print media were all represented, both from local outlets as well as regional and national press. Print media was allowed inside the courthouse but not television or radio. Outside, the courthouse was like a circus. Getting through the press was like running a gauntlet. Questions were fired at Jack and Catherine as they walked through, even as the protesters cheered their arrival. Jack had instructed her in advance to say nothing while he repeated "No comment" to all requests.

Once inside, Jack and Catherine settled in to the defense table. Catherine being a lawyer, Jack did not have to explain anything about the trial. It was refreshing to be defending somebody whom you did not have to educate about court procedure before you went to trial with them.

Attorney Coleman came in, accompanied for the first time by a second attorney who came right over to introduce himself. "Mr. Roach, my name is Adam Chapman, and I will be assisting Mr. Coleman during the trial."

Jack rose to shake his hand. "Pleased to meet you, Mr. Chapman," he said, doing his best to be professional.

All this happened under the watchful eye of Stanton Merrill as well as the rest of the Merrills in the front row directly behind the prosecution desk. Jack looked past Chapman to stare into the eyes of Stanton Merrill, who looked at Jack and Catherine with a scowl. He and Jack locked eyes for a long moment before Jack smiled and nodded at him before looking away.

Judge Murray called the court to order asking Attorney Coleman if he was ready to present his case. Coleman answered in the affirmative as he stood to address the court. As expected, his first witness was county medical examiner, Dr. Nolan Emery. Emery had held his position for almost twenty years and was seen as a straight shooter, well respected by the legal fraternity and law enforcement officials.

He took the stand, answering Coleman's questions concerning the cause of death, time of death, and identifying the murder weapon. Everything in his testimony was to be expected, so Jack offered no objections. At the end of his questioning, Coleman started dancing close to motive.

"In your opinion, Dr. Emery, were the stab wounds indicative of being delivered by someone in a rage, someone who had lost control?"

"Yes, one could conclude that from the number of wounds as well as the type of wounds."

With that, Coleman, looking right a the jury concluded his questions. Walking back to his desk, the witness was turned over to the defense. Jack rose slowly from his chair with his right hand, rubbing his forehead as if he were deep in thought. He approached the witness stand and asked, "Dr. Emery, you just testified that the stab wounds on Mr. Merrill indicated that they were delivered by someone in a rage. I think that was the term you used."

"Yes, that's what I said."

"From the same wounds, could you just as easily conclude that the perpetrator was acting out of fear rather than rage?"

Emery did not hesitate with his answer. "One can conclude that the perpetrator acted with extreme emotion. That emotion could be driven by fear just as well as rage."

"Thank you, Dr. Emery." Jack looked at the jury as the doctor answered.

Jack returned to his seat next to Catherine, who gave him a thumbs-up sign under the table to let him know she felt he had scored some points. Next witness for the prosecution was Officer Daniel Donovan of the Falmouth Police Department. He was the first responding officer to the scene and the author of the official police report. Coleman walked him through his recollection of the scene he found, specifically that Chad Merrill lay dead on the floor and Catherine Merrill was the only other person in the house. He also testified that she admitted to stabbing her husband as Coleman made sure to get the confession on record. When it was Jack's turn, he rose quickly, walking right at the witness. He wanted to give the jury the impression that he couldn't wait to question him because cross-examination would help Catherine, not the state's case. Confidence in presenting the defense position was important.

"Officer Donovan, who made the 911 call to which you responded?"

"Catherine Merrill."

Typical of an experienced officer to give short answers and addressed only what has been asked. "Are you familiar with the content of that call?"

"Yes, I have listened to the whole call."

"Did Ms. Merrill also request an ambulance?"

"Yes, she did."

"In your experience, is it customary for someone who had intentionally, violently committed a premeditated murder to request an ambulance?"

Donovan thought for a moment before answering in the negative.

"In fact, Officer, in cases of violent premeditated murder, it's even rare in such circumstances for the perpetrator to make a call at all, is it not?"

"It would not be a normal thing to do." Next, Jack asked the officer to describe his impression of Catherine Merrill's condition when he arrived. The officer stated that she was crying, obviously very distraught, almost to the point of being in shock.

"Would you describe her as remorseful?"

Donovan again hesitated before answering this question. He looked a bit lost in thought before finally answering, "Yes, she seemed sorry and remorseful for what had happened."

"In fact, Officer, didn't you ask the paramedics when they arrived to check on her to make sure she was okay?"

"Yes, I did."

"Not something you would do for a hardened murderer, is it, Officer?"

"No, it would not be."

"Thank you, Officer Donovan."

Again, Jack returned to his seat greeted by a signal from fellow attorney, Catherine Merrill, that he had scored points with his cross.

The next three witnesses were character witnesses, friends of Chad who testified to what a great man he was. Jack made a point of offering no cross to the first two character witnesses. He did it with a bit of flair for two reasons. First, he knew these close friends would say nothing bad about their deceased friend. Second, the third character-reference-type witness on the list of witnesses was a former fraternity brother of Chad's at Dartmouth. Jack had different plans for him. His name was Tom Johnson, and Jack had checked with Sara Kemp to make sure Mr. Johnson was present at the frat party to witness "the incident." In fact, Sara was quite sure Johnson was one of the guys who pulled Chad off her. By making a bit of a display of having no questions for the first two, Jack wanted to put Johnson at ease. When Coleman had finished throwing Johnson his soft balls, he walked back to his seat, saying, "Your witness," to Jack.

"Your Honor," Jack said, rising, "my cross-examination for this witness could be quite lengthy. Where it is already a bit past four, may I suggest we adjourn for today and I can begin my cross in the morning." Jack said this while looking Johnson directly in the eye. Johnson looked absolutely panicked as he tried to figure out why the first two character witnesses got nothing but he was going to get a lengthy cross.

This, of course, was exactly what Jack wanted. The judge agreed with the request, banged his gavel, and court was adjourned for the day. Now Mr. Johnson would have all night to wonder what Jack had in mind for him. Jack returned to his office with Catherine and they spent an hour going over that day's testimony as well as what to expect on Tuesday. Following that, Jack had dinner with Elaine as they discussed a plan to deal with Bruce King's problems. Elaine had met Bruce while he stayed in Portland and wanted to help Jack figure out a path forward.

The following morning, there were even more protesters in front of the courthouse. National women's groups had teamed with Maine groups to swell the crowd, which was now over sixty active protesters. As Jack approached the courthouse with Catherine, the protesters broke into applause as well as shouts of support, all of which made for good fodder for the news agencies. The phone calls to DA Rideout's office encouraging him to drop the prosecution had increased daily.

Back in the courtroom, Judge Murray entered, calling the court to order. Tom Johnson was called back to the witness chair, reminded that he was still under oath. Judge Murray called on Jack to begin his cross-examination. Jack rose, picked up the notes from his interview with Sara Kemp, and slowly approached the witness as he appeared to be reviewing the papers he held in his hands.

"Mr. Johnson, you were a fraternity brother of Chadwick Merrill. Is that correct?"

"Yes, we were both in Phi Eta Fraternity."

"Did you both live at the fraternity house?"

Johnson looked both thoughtful and perplexed. He was clearly trying to figure out where Jack was headed. "Yeah, we both lived there." He looked at the judge as he answered, raising his arms in a motion that said, "What's this got to do with anything?" Coleman read the cue from Johnson and stood to object.

"Your Honor, is there a purpose to this line of questioning?"

"Your Honor, the purpose will soon be made clear to Mr. Coleman and the court," answered Jack.

"Continue, Councillor," Judge Murray ruled, "but get to the point."

"Yes, Your Honor."

"Mr. Johnson, when there were functions at the house, were you pretty faithful in your attendance?"

Johnson hesitated to answer, trying to figure out if he was falling into a trap.

"Well, yeah, we were brothers in the house, so where would I be?" This was spoken with a grin.

"Yes, where would you be? This would include attendance at fraternity parties."

"Why would I miss one?"

Jack made a point of referring to his notes. "Do you recall attending a fraternity party of November 10, 1969?"

Johnson's face dropped. He had suddenly realized where this was going. He looked at Attorney Coleman, then at the judge, and finally, back at Jack. "I, ah, don't recall a particular party."

"Well, let me try to refresh your memory. There was a particular incident at this party involving Mr. Merrill. Do you remember the incident?"

"I, ah, don't know what you are referring to." But his body language and facial expression said otherwise. He knew he would be perjuring himself if he flatly denied the assault by his frat brother.

"Come now, Mr. Johnson, we have established that you would be in attendance for a fraternity party, but you're telling this court now, under oath, that you have no recollection of this particular party and the incident that happened at it, that nearly resulted in Chadwick Merrill being expelled from the college."

Coleman rose again to object but only got the "Your Honor" out before Jack cut him off. "Your Honor, I would like to end my questioning of Mr. Johnson but reserve the right to recall him at a later time."

Judge Murray nodded his consent, and a clearly nervous Tom Johnson was told he could step down. Coleman's next witness was the family's attorney who testified as to the amount of money Chadwick Merrill had and how much Catherine would stand to inherit upon the death of her husband. This was a rather ham-handed attempt to provide a motive that surprised Jack only because it was so easy for the defense to deal with in cross. When the witness was turned over to him, he again rose quickly and walked right at the witness chair to give the same impression to the jury that he did with Officer Donovan.

"Just two questions. First, did the couple have a prenuptial agreement?"

"No, they did not."

"So in divorce, Catherine Merrill would stand to receive a fair amount of the estate you just described, would that be a fair statement?"

"Presumably, that would be the case."

Jack started walking back then turned to ask, "Wouldn't that be a lot easier for her than this?"

Coleman again stood to object, but Jack withdrew the question. There were two other witnesses on the list from the prosecution. One of them was Stanton Merrill himself. Jack was looking forward to cross-examining the great man, but to his surprise, Attorney Coleman stood to say, "The prosecution rests."

Judge Murray looked at Jack and asked, "Will the defense be prepared to present their case tomorrow morning?"

"Yes, Your Honor."

"Court will stand adjourned until nine o'clock tomorrow morning." He banged his gavel as he rose to leave.

They all stood until Murray left, then Jack sat back down with Catherine. "Their case as presented is even weaker than I expected. Coleman knows he has a loser. Stanton Merrill must know it too, that's why he is not testifying. I think Coleman just wants to get it over with. Tomorrow, I will be first calling Dr. Adams, who examined you the day after the incident while you were in jail. I will present as defense exhibits his report, as well as the records from your previous hospital visits and the photos we took at the jail. Then your two friends who you have confided in over the years, and if I have enough time, his ex-wife. I'm saving Sara Kemp for last because when she finishes, I'm bringing Johnson back. It's only four o'clock, so I'm going to meet with tomorrow's witnesses in my office this afternoon."

"Jack, I know you feel confident, but it's my neck on the line, so you will excuse me if I continue to feel scared."

"I would be worried about you if you weren't." He smiled at her, patting her outstretched arm.

As they got up to leave, pretty much everyone had filed out, but Stanton Merrill who was standing alone in front of his chair glaring at the two of them menacingly. Jack smiled as he passed him. "Have a nice day," was his parting comment.

Chapter XXXV

WHEN JACK RETURNED TO HIS office, he had a call from Bruce with a message that he call a certain number at nine that evening. Jack assumed the number was to a pay phone and that Bruce was afraid his line was tapped. A good precaution on Bruce's part, and not surprising, given his CIA training.

He met with his witnesses for tomorrow's session in order to run through their testimony one more time. He assured them that the prosecution would be asking difficult questions, but all they needed to do was tell the truth. He would be there to object if Coleman got out of line, so they should relax and get a good night's sleep. He was anxious to present the case for the defense.

He finished up at six thirty and met Elaine at seven for dinner at DiMillo's. She, of course, was full of questions about the trial, so he brought her up to speed on where things stood. Then he told her about the nine o'clock call he was going to have with Bruce.

"What do you suppose has happened with Bruce to make him call?" Elaine asked.

"Well, I would guess that he is receiving more heat either from the FBI or his superiors in the CIA."

"Do you have a plan in mind to help him, Jack?"

"I'm pretty close. I've been giving it a lot of thought trying to settle on an approach that is sound for everyone involved."

"Well, you're pretty smart, almost smart enough to be a teacher, so you'll come up with something. I'll just be happy when this trial and Brue's problems are all settled so that our lives can get back to normal."

"I know, it's been difficult, but when the dust settles, I will make it up to you."

"You bet your ass you will," she responded with a smile.

Jack went back to his office to place the call at nine. He was correct in his assumption that the number was for a pay phone. Bruce picked up on the third ring, going right into a full explanation of his meeting in the deputy director's office. He told Jack how he was assured that they would "protect his interest."

"Do you think they were being honest, Bruce?"

"Fuck, no. They will turn on me, blame me for everything, including the Lindburg kidnapping and hang me out to dry. They won't cooperate with the FBI—that part is true—but when the congressional hearings start, they will use me as well as a few other field agents to take the heat off the brass. Their strategy is as transparent as glass."

"When do the congressional hearings begin?"

"In three weeks. The director is first on the list, then the director of operations. They have requested a list of field agents who have been involved in special operations, also known as 'black ops' over the past ten years, but the list has not yet been provided."

"I assume when it is, your name will be on it."

"You are correct, sir," in Bruce's best Ed Mahon impersonation.

"Okay, so it's at least three weeks before you would be required to give any testimony before Congress."

"Yes, that's if they call on me at all."

"Right. Okay, listen I know how I plan to approach this. I will get on it as soon as I wrap up this murder trial."

"How long will that be, Jack? Crunch time is upon me."

"I start with defense witnesses tomorrow. That should go two or three days. Then closing arguments and we hand it to the jury. It should be wrapped up by the first of next week. The jury is sequestered, so they shouldn't take too much time reaching a decision, they want their freedom. In the meantime, if you hear any more from the two FBI agents, refer them to me. Don't meet with them unless I'm there."

With that, they ended the call. Jack assured his friend that it would all turn out all right. He just had to trust Jack to bring it all together. As they ended the call, Bruce felt extremely nervous about where things were headed. Jack, on the other hand, was absolutely sure he knew how to put it all to rest.

Chapter XXXVI

THE MORNING JACK WAS TO begin the defense of Catherine Merrill, the crowd outside the courthouse had grown even larger. They had also become louder as they chanted for Catherine's release. They again cheered and applauded her and Jack as they arrived. Jack could not wait to get started.

Jack's defense exhibits included the medical reports from Catherine's hospital visits as well as the report from the night of her arrest. His first witness for the defense was Dr. Hall, who examined her in the jail the following morning. Jack walked him through the various bruises, as well as the broken ribs caused from the punches and kicks. The doctor acknowledged them all, as well as his own opinion on how they were caused. When they got to the neck bruises, Jack's questioning got more specific.

"Doctor, in your opinion, how were the bruises around her neck caused?"

"They were caused by an attempt to choke her with two hands around her neck." He demonstrated with his own hands how Chad Merrill would have held his hands.

"Can you determine from the bruising the amount of pressure being applied?"

"Absolutely, there was tremendous pressure being applied. It would take a great deal of pressure over a period to cause the type of bruising I saw on Ms. Merrill."

"Would that type of pressure be enough to completely cut off her ability to breathe?"

"It certainly could, yes."

"So in your opinion, Doctor, would it be a reasonable conclusion by Ms. Merrill that she would have been in fear for her life?"

"She would not have been able to breathe, which would have made it a reasonable conclusion that she was in fear for her life."

"Thank you, Doctor. I have no further questions, Your Honor, for this witness, and at this time I would offer the pictures taken of Ms. Merrill the morning after her arrest as Defense Exhibit E."

Coleman's cross-examination of the doctor was rather weak as there was really not much for him to grab. He asked if there were alternative ways by which the bruising might have been caused. He stayed away from the neck bruises, basically gaining nothing in his cross. Given the pictures to go along with the doctor's testimony, there was not much Coleman could do with his cross.

Next, Jack brought in Cary Winters and Elizabeth Lane in succession, the two friends Catherine had confided in about her beatings. Coleman objected to the question Jack asked Cary Winters on the basis of relevance. This would be his attempt to lay a precedent for keeping out any testimony about prior acts.

Jack responded to the objection. "Your Honor, the long pattern of abuse that we will establish goes to the defense's position that the deceased had a long history of physical abuse and the defendant had reason to fear for her life and acted in self-defense."

Judge Murray had already stated in the pretrial conference that he would allow such testimony, and here he again agreed so Jack went into questions concerning Ms. Winter's knowledge of abuses over the years. She described the bruising she witnessed herself while relaying her own impressions of the effects of abuse. Coleman objected a number of times either claiming the testimony was hearsay or that the witness lacked the expertise to make the judgment being asked for by Jack. He won several objections, but overall, the two witnesses were able to provide the historical reference Jack was looking to establish. On cross, Coleman tried to cast doubt on their testimony by questioning the accuracy of their memory, as well as questioning why the police were never brought into the situation. Altogether, Jack was reasonably happy with the effect of their testimony.

Next, Jack called Sharon Tate, the first wife of Chad Merrill. In answer to Jack's questions, she went into details about the same two incidents she had described to Jack at their meeting in Rhode

Island. She was a compelling witness, Jack's best so far. She addressed her answers to the jury, appeared calm and professional. He found himself wishing he could keep her on the stand longer. Jack wanted especially to impress on the jury how she left.

Did you go to the hospital to have your ribs examined, Ms. Tate?"

"No, I did not. The next morning, my husband had his cousin, Dr. Merrill, examine me at our home after I had said I should see a doctor."

"So we have heard in previous testimony from Ms. Lane and Ms. Winters that your ex-husband sometimes used his cousin in this fashion rather than have his victims go to a hospital. But you would have preferred to go to the hospital."

"Of course."

"What did you do after the exam?"

"I told Chadwick I was leaving him, and I walked out with Dr. Merrill."

"Why did you pick this moment to leave?"

"Because I had the protection of a witness. If we had been alone, he would not have let me leave."

"You mean he would have physically detained you?"

"Yes."

"Did you file for divorce?"

"That same day, I contacted a lawyer and filed divorce papers as well as a protection order against Chadwick."

"Why did you feel you needed a protection order?"

"Because I did not know what he would do. I did not want any interaction with him unless my attorney was present. He was dangerous."

"Objection, Your Honor, that's pure speculation by the witness," Coleman maintained, jumping to his feet."

"Your Honor, given her history with the deceased I think she was well qualified to feel that she was at risk."

Judge Murray thought for a moment before ruling in Jack's favor. "Objection overruled."

Jack couldn't resist a shot at Stanton. "Did you have any inter-action with members of Chadwick Merrill's family?"

"Yes, Stanton Merrill offered me money to, as he put it, go away quietly without saying anything about physical abuse."

"How did you react to that offer?"

"I told him I was not interested."

Jack had concluded his questioning, so Judge Murray adjourned the court for the day before Coleman's cross. The testimony of Catherine's two friends had been solid and effective. The testimony of Sharon Tate was devastating, both in terms of content and of delivery. The day ended on a very high note for the defense. Even the ever-pessimistic Catherine was starting to feel positive. The picture of Chadwick Merrill being painted for the jury was not pretty. By the time Jack was finished, he intended to keep his word to Stanton Merrill that he would expose his son for what he really was. He was not even halfway finished with him.

Chapter XXXVII

THAT EVENING, AS JACK RETURNED to his office, he worked late taking the first steps to address Bruce King's issues. He dictated a letter to be typed and mailed the following day. The letter was to CIA Deputy Director Russell Campbell. In the letter, he requested a time in the following week when he could either meet with or have a telephone conversation concerning Agent Bruce King.

He introduced himself as King's attorney. He made it very clear that in that capacity, he intended to take actions that could well affect the CIA. His language made it very clear that his intention was to protect his client even if it would be at the expense of the agency. He finished the letter, saying, "It is in the interest of both Agent King as well as the CIA that we talk before either of us takes any action." He left his own "actions to be taken" to the imagination of the deputy director. He did, however, point out that Bruce King had been in the agency long enough to know where the bodies were buried. While subtle, the letter in general was threatening in tone enough that it should catch the attention of the director.

It was the first step in addressing Bruce's problem with the CIA. Jack had a course of action in mind that in the end would address both the CIA as well as the FBI investigation.

Chapter XXXVIII

COLEMAN'S CROSS-EXAMINATION OF SHARON TATE began the fifth day of the trial. He attempted to cast doubt on her testimony of having experienced physical abuse by pointing to the lack of a police report or medical record of either incident she testified to in direct. She answered the lack of medical record by again pointing out that Dr. Merrill had treated her the following morning. Jack had listed the good doctor as a potential witness so Coleman's line of questioning confirmed that he would call him next. After Coleman finished his questions, Jack rose to announce he would ask redirect questions.

"Ms. Tate, as regards to the lack of police record of the incidents of abuse, did you ever file any record of the incidents with law enforcement or the court system?" Jack had anticipated Coleman's tactic on the lack of a police report and prepped Ms. Tate for the question he had just asked.

"Yes, the incidents are documented in my divorce filing."

"Which I would point out has been submitted as Defense Exhibit C. Before you made that filing, was it discussed with any member of the Merrill family?"

"Yes, Mr. Stanton Merrill offered me money to not include the account in my divorce filing."

"In spite of that offer, I point out to the court that the incident on the night Ms. Tate left is documented in the divorce filing."

Jack's next witness was Dr. Charles Merrill, whose testimony was best described as bizarre. He had to be subpoenaed to testify so he was not a willing witness.

Jack wasted no time in going right after him.

"Dr. Merrill, have you ever treated a patient for injuries suffered during a domestic abuse incident?"

"Yes, I have on a number of occasions."

"We just heard testimony from Ms. Tate concerning one particular incident where you treated her after a domestic violence incident. Can you tell us how many other times you treated victims of your cousin's attacks?"

Dr. Merrill scowled at Jack then looked at the judge, saying, "At this time, I would like to exercise my rights under the Fifth Amendment."

Judge Murray was about to respond to this when Jack jumped in, saying, "Your Honor, permission to treat Dr. Merrill as a hostile witness."

"Permission granted." Apparently, Judge Murray found the doctor's claim of Fifth Amendment protection as bizarre as Jack found it.

Jack went on. "Dr. Merrill, a doctor treating a patient is not a crime. In cases of domestic abuse, there is no legal requirement for an attending physician to report the abuse unless a minor is involved. You have no legal liability for the action in question. Therefore, there is no Fifth Amendment rights. Answer the question."

Dr. Merrill looked at Judge Murray for help, but the judge instructed him to answer. "I cannot recall the incident in question."

Jack went back to his desk, picked up his notes, and asked the doctor one more time if he recalled treating Catherine Merrill on the dates that Jack knew he did. Taking the dates one at a time, the doctor answered each time that he did not recall.

Jack put down his notepad and asked, "Doctor, are you familiar with the punishment in Maine for perjury?"

Coleman rose and objected. Jack turned to Judge Murray, saying, "Hostile witness, Your Honor." The judge overruled the objection.

"Do you know the penalty, Doctor?"

"Not completely."

"The penalty for lying under oath can result in up to five years in prison. There are witnesses to each of the dates of treatment that I just went through with you. So reminding you that you are under oath, I will ask again, do you recall the times you treated Ms. Tate and Catherine Merrill for injuries sustained while being physically abused by your cousin Chadwick Merrill?"

The doctor looked at Attorney Coleman then to the judge before looking down at the floor. Jack pushed on, "We are waiting for an answer."

Without raising his head, he answered, "Yes, I recall some of those treatments."

"How many times did you treat Catherine Merrill after beatings from your cousin?" Jack repeated the relationship in order to drive it home to the jury. The fact that another member of the Merrill family was complicit in covering for Chadwick Merrill's abuse not only helped his case that he had gotten away with these actions for years, but it also drove another dagger into the reputation of the Merrill family.

"I'm not sure…three, maybe four."

"And Sharon Tate once?"

"Yes."

"And these treatments were for substantial bruising as well as cracked and broken ribs?"

"Yes."

"Would you normally advise a patient who had these types of injuries to go to a hospital for x-rays to determine the degree of internal injury?"

The good doctor looked a bit strained as he struggled to hedge his answer. "That's difficult to say."

"Come now, Doctor. Broken ribs—is that not an automatic recommendation for a trip to the x-ray technician, if not a CT scan?"

Dr. Merrill continued to look at the floor, not answering. Jack pressed on, "I would imagine, Doctor, that a trip through your files would show very few, if any, incidents of patients coming in with broken ribs not being sent for x-rays. Isn't that true?"

"Normally, yes, we would require x-rays."

"Why did you not require them here?"

The doctor paused, looking at the floor, obviously not wanting to answer. So Jack pushed on again. "Wasn't it because your cousin asked you not to so he could avoid the hospital record?"

The doctor finally looked up at Jack with absolute contempt on his face. Jack stared back at him. "Doctor, we are waiting."

"Yes." An emphatic reply given by an angry man who obviously loathed his inquisitor. Jack smiled at him, saying, "Thank you, Doctor." He had enjoyed grilling the doctor who he considered to be just one more arrogant, privileged Merrill. As he turned the witness over to Attorney Coleman, he looked past the prosecution table at Stanton Merrill, taking satisfaction that he was obviously seething. Jack discreetly, away from the sight of the judge and jury, gave Stanton a wink.

Coleman's cross of the doctor was brief, asking if he knew for certain how the injuries were sustained and if any explanation was given. The doctor said he recalled at least on one occasion Chadwick had said his wife had fallen down the stairs. Jack could have gone back at him on redirect, but he did not think the jury bought it anyway. He saw it more as a feeble attempt to gain points that failed miserably.

Jack had saved the best for last, calling Sara Kemp as his last witness before Catherine herself. Sara Kemp calmly testified to the entire incident where Chadwick Merrill went into a jealous rage because he thought she was flirting with one of his fraternity brothers. He punched her twice in the face then choked her until she lost consciousness.

"Were you in fear for your life, Ms. Kemp?"

"I certainly was. There were several of his fraternity brothers trying to pull him off of me, but I lost consciousness before they were able to break his hold. If they had not pulled him off, I know he would have killed me."

Jack nodded in response as he looked at the jury.

"Did you receive medical assistance?"

"Yes, at the campus infirmary. Two of the boys who pulled him off of me brought me there."

"Your Honor, I submit as defense exhibits G and H the record from the infirmary as well as the pictures of Ms. Kemp showing the black eye, facial bruises, and neck bruises received that night. Now do you remember the names of the two fraternity brothers who helped pull Mr. Merrill off of you and then took you to the infirmary?"

Coleman rose. "Objection, Your Honor, relevance."

Jack expected the objection because Coleman would know where he was going with the question.

"It goes to the credibility of one of the prosecution's witnesses."

"I'll allow it." Judge Murray was taking Jack's side again.

"Do you remember Ms. Kemp?"

"Yes, it was Ray Cobb and Tom Johnson."

Jack looked at the jury, saying, "The same Tom Johnson who earlier testified that he had no recollection of this incident." He made it as a statement rather than a question, then quickly moved to his next question.

"Ms. Kemp, did you file any charges against Mr. Merrill for this vicious attack?"

"I was planning to file charges the following day after I reported it to campus officials. But I did not file them."

Jack faked a puzzled look for the jurors' benefit as if he were hearing this for the first time.

"Why, after such a brutal attack, would you not file charges with police?"

"Because while I was in the office of the dean of student affairs, I was told Stanton Merrill was waiting to see me in an adjacent conference room."

"Oh, really? Tell us about that meeting."

"Mr. Merrill offered me ten thousand dollars if I would sign an agreement not to discuss the incident with anyone or to file charges."

Jack had his back to her as she said this. He spun around as if shocked. The theatrics may not have been necessary, but he felt they added to the drama.

"And you took the money and signed?"

"I did. I was a poor college student who needed the money."

Jack walked to the bench, offering the agreement to Judge Murray. "Your Honor, I submit the agreement as Defense Exhibit I."

"Ms. Kemp, do you know if any disciplinary action was taken by the college against Chadwick Merrill?"

"When I met with the dean, he told me Chad would be expelled. However, when Stanton Merrill left his meeting with me, he went into the dean's office. Eventually, no action was taken by the college."

"Presumably the college was paid off as well."

Coleman jumped to his feet. "Objection, Your Honor, speculation."

"Withdrawn. I have no further questions of this witness."

Her testimony was pure gold to Jack. She could not have handled herself any better on the witness stand. Coleman cross-examined her, trying to cast doubt on her memory, suggesting that perhaps it had been someone else who administered the beating. It had been many years since it happened, perhaps her memory was not accurate. She responded that she could not forget the incident; it haunted her daily. It was the cause of a hundred nightmares. When Coleman pressed on, she pointed out that it would strain credibility to think Stanton Merrill paid ten thousand dollars to protect someone other than his son. He then switched tactics asking if she came to hate Chad Merrill, trying to imply that now she was just trying to destroy his memory. She responded by suggesting Mr. Coleman should look at the pictures of what he did to her and ask himself how he would feel about someone who did that to him. All in all, a stellar performance by a star witness. Jack was even beginning to feel sorry for Coleman and the pathetically weak case he was stuck with presenting.

After Coleman's cross, Judge Murray asked Jack how many more witnesses he intended to call. Jack responded that his only witness left was Catherine Merrill herself. He was not even sure her testimony was necessary, but he knew with her legal training, she would be a great witness. Coleman allowed that he did not anticipate calling any rebuttal witnesses. So the judge wrapped things up for the day.

"Tomorrow is Friday, our sixth day of trial. We will hear from Ms. Merrill then go to closing arguments so we can hand this case off to the jury. I hereby instruct both attorneys to have their closing arguments prepared for tomorrow as I intend to send this to the jury tomorrow even if we have to run late. They have been sequestered now for over a week. I want to hand this to them tomorrow."

With that, he banged the gavel, leaving the room. Jack sat back down with Catherine, who asked, "That was a bit unusual, wasn't it, Jack?"

"Yes, it was. It tells me two things. First, Judge Murray can see that the prosecution's case is extremely weak and should never have been brought to trial. Second, he has a jury that has been sequestered long enough and he wants to set them free as soon as possible. Now you and I are going to my office, and as much as you hate the idea, we are going over your testimony one more time."

Catherine winced at the thought of reviewing her testimony for what must be the second dozenth time, but she knew it was necessary. As they got up to leave, they both were surprised to notice that Stanton Merrill was not standing in his usual spot. For the first time, he had left with the rest of the crowd. Catherine looked at Jack for his reaction. "Catherine, I take this as yet another good sign. Maybe even that asshole is throwing in the towel."

Chapter XXXIX

CIA Deputy Director Russell Campbell reread the letter from Jack Roach for the third time, shaking his head. This hick lawyer from Maine requesting a meeting to discuss issues around Agent Bruce King. His first reaction to the letter was that King was becoming a lot more trouble than he was worth. Still they were in a bit of a sticky situation what with congressional hearing just over a week away and two FBI agents nosing around. Perhaps he shouldn't be too quick to dismiss this Roach fellow. He decided to send for Director of Operations Stark to get his input. Upon his arrival, Campbell handed him the letter and sat quietly while he read it.

"Well, tell me your impression," Campbell asked as Stark finish reading.

"It seems our friend Mr. King has lawyered up. He is not going to be as easy to deal with, as we thought he might be."

"That's one way to look at it, and frankly, it was also my impression. But look at it this way: this guy knows King is in a squeeze. He is planning to meet with me to help King out of a tough situation. What he may not know is we are in a squeeze as well. Perhaps whatever he has in mind can be adjusted somehow to help us as well as, or instead of, King."

Stark considered this angle for a moment then said, "That is a possibility. My thought has been that King can be used as protection for us along with a couple of field agents."

"Yes," Campbell said. "We have been over this. We blame him and others for going rogue on us during missions, doing things they were not authorized to do. We have already placed back dated letters of reprimand in his files just to cover our ass. But maybe this lawyer has an idea that can help us improve the story."

Again, Stark considered the idea. "I suppose we could meet with him. Hear him out without divulging what our plans are for King."

"My thinking exactly. He gave me his office number. I will call to set up a meeting for next week. Give me a day you will be free. I want you at the meeting."

It was agreed to set up the meeting for the following Thursday morning at nine in Deputy Director Campbell's office. Director of Operations Stark would also attend. Campbell had his assistant call Jack's office to leave the message with the time and date. The meeting would be only days before the first congressional hearings were due to begin.

The same night that Jack sent the letter requesting the meeting, he explained his plan to Bruce. The ultimate goal was to get him the new life he wanted. A quiet life without the danger, without the killing. Bruce loved the approach. After receiving the call to confirm the meeting, they were both anxious for the meeting.

Jack was certain he could pull off a positive result. Bruce was hopeful.

Chapter XXXX

On Friday morning, Jack and Catherine were greeted on the courthouse steps by the largest group of protesters yet. The crowd had grown every day since the first day of the trial. The news coverage included print media, both local and national. All three local news channels were there, along with two field reporters from the national news teams. One of the reporters was none other than Sue Frazier, who stepped up with her microphone to ask Jack a question. This, of course, brought the entire news contingent over to join in the fun.

"Attorney Roach, this is the final day of testimony. Do you feel confident of an outcome in your favor?" As she asked this question, a bevy of microphones were thrust in his face.

"No comment." Jack had Catherine by the elbow, leading her through the crowd of reporters. The protesters were shouting their well wishes in the background.

Sue pressed for an answer. "Come now, Mr. Roach, this trial has seemed to be going your way since day one. You must have a feel for what to expect for an outcome?"

Jack stopped walking to respond. "I will simply say this: Catherine Merrill and I both have confidence in the judicial system to find the truth and properly administer justice. Now please excuse us as we have a lot of work to do."

He actually felt a little bad about being so cold in his response to Susan after the national coverage she gave the trial, but he pushed forward with Catherine ignoring all the follow-up questions, making his way to the courthouse. The courtroom was packed with an overflow crowd for the sixth straight day. Attorney Coleman and his assistant were already seated at their table. Notably absent was Stanton

Merrill. Entering the courtroom, Jack noticed he was not in his usual seat. In fact, none of the Merrills were there.

"Catherine, did you notice who is not here?"

"Oh my god, I'm stunned."

"Another good sign."

As they took their seats, Jack looked over at the prosecution table. He and Coleman locked eyes for a moment, and to Jack's surprise, Coleman shrugged his shoulders then nodded at Jack in a manner that almost seemed congratulatory. He nodded back at him just as the bailiff announced the entrance of Judge Murray, who called the room to order while telling Jack to call his witness.

Catherine Merrill took the stand, looking like the stately, dignified woman Jack knew her to be. She no longer gave the appearance of a person beaten down by the system. She looked exactly the way Jack had hoped she would look, confident and calm.

Jack walked her through the years of abuse, touching on the physical abuse that resulted in hospital visits and/or treatments from Dr. Merrill. He then shifted to the mental abuse, giving examples of the domineering bullying she had to endure in the relationship. He went through all that for the first hour before turning to that fateful night that resulted in her arrest. Here he started at the social event at the golf club, pointing out that Chadwick had drunk too much, so she had to drive home. He had her describe the rage he exhibited during the ride home then the attack as they entered their kitchen.

"He hit me with a closed fist, knocking me to the floor. Then he kicked me two, maybe three times, breaking two ribs, then he pulled me part way off the floor by the hair of my head and punched me in the face again." Jack listened intently while never taking his eyes off the jury.

"He stopped that beating at the point?"

"Yes, he walked over to the portable bar we had in our kitchen and poured himself a scotch."

"What did you do, Ms. Merrill?"

"I picked myself up off the floor. I was in a great deal of pain, so I leaned against the counter and tried to stop my nose from bleeding."

"Was that the end?"

"No, I told him I was leaving him. Before I could move toward the door to leave, he dashed across the kitchen, grabbing me by the throat, choking me while he beat my head against the cupboard doors."

"Did he say anything?"

"He said I have always told you that I would kill you before I let you leave. The rage in his face was like nothing I had ever seen before. He squeezed my neck harder and harder. I could not breathe. I was about to lose consciousness."

"Did you feel that he would stop at this point, or were you convinced he would just keep choking you?"

"I felt he was going to kill me. In desperation, I was feeling around behind me for something to hit him with, something to defend myself. I felt the rack of carving knives and pulled one out. I stabbed him first in the hip, thinking it would make him stop but not kill him."

"You just wanted to wound him?"

"Yes, so he would stop."

"Did he stop?"

"No, he looked shocked, and his grip loosened a bit for a moment. Then he shouted, 'I will kill you, bitch,' and he began choking me with more force."

She appeared at this point to choke up a bit, so Jack suggested she take a break. She put her hand up, and after a moment to gather herself, she said, "No, I'm all right."

"Can you continue as to what happened next?"

After a pause, she said, "I could see he was not going to stop, that he was intending to kill me. I stabbed him again, two or three times until his grip around my throat eased up enough that I could breathe. His eyes rolled back, and he fell to the floor."

"What did you do then?"

"I called 911, requesting the police as well as an ambulance."

"You requested an ambulance. Were you hoping they could save him?" Jack said this as he looked at the jury. Catherine looked down before answering. When she looked up, she had tears in her eyes.

She answered, "Yes." Jack paused for effect while still looking at the jurors. "After all that, you still wanted to save him?"

"Yes."

After a moment, he walked back to his seat.

"Thank you, Ms. Merrill, your witness."

Her testimony took two hours and fifteen minutes. It was perfectly delivered by a very intelligent lady. It was so emotional that before Coleman's cross, Judge Murray, called for a fifteen-minute break.

When court resumed, the prosecution began their cross-examination of Ms. Merrill. It started off by trying to make a case that she was a constant flirt. Coleman questioned her on the various claims of physical abuse and whether they all followed on the heels of her "throwing herself at other men."

"I never throw myself at anyone. All I had to do for Chad to accuse me of flirting was to say hello or look in the direction of another man."

"Come now, Ms. Merrill, you never found another man attractive?"

"I was married to Chad. I took those vows seriously."

"You never had an affair?"

"Absolutely not!"

Coleman went back to the table to check his notes. Jack was momentarily afraid the he might have something to contradict her statement. But after a pause to check his notes, he moved on. The pause Jack thought was a weak attempt to leave the jury, thinking that there was something in his notes to prove her wrong that might be brought out later.

He then went into the night of the final attack. Coleman got very aggressive to the surprise of Jack. He stood, leaning on the witness stand, right in Catherine's face, trying to rattle her.

"You viciously stabbed your husband four times. Isn't that true, Ms. Merrill?"

"I have so testified."

"Was it truly necessary to thrust that knife into him that many times?"

"I was in fear of my life. I wasn't counting the numbers."

Jack objected that Coleman was badgering the witness. Judge Murray told the prosecutor to give the witness her space. So he backed away a couple of steps but continued.

"We have heard testimony that the wounds appeared to have been made in anger. Was that the case, Ms. Merrill? Was it just a vicious, angry attack on a man you hated?"

"No, I was acting out of fear." In spite of his badgering attempts to make her lose her cool, she remained under control as she answered.

"Fear that he might leave you and you would not gain his fortune like you would if he was dead?"

Again, Jack objected that the witness was being badgered, but Murray overruled him this time, telling the witness to respond. Catherine took a deep breath then calmly responded.

"The question really needs no response. I was not thinking of anything other than saving my life." Coleman tried to interrupt with another question, but she continued, "He said he was going to kill me, and by the rage on his face, I believed he would."

Her response cut Coleman off. He looked confused as he searched for his next question. He walked back to the prosecution table, picked up a yellow pad, and looked at it, finally saying, "I have no further questions."

His cross had been far more aggressive than anything else he had done to that point. It caught both Jack and Catherine by surprise. However, Catherine had handled it well, remaining calm while making her points. She stepped down after almost three hours on the witness stand with Jack feeling she could not have handled herself any better. Jack felt, that if anything, Coleman's badgering only made Catherine look more sympathetic to the jury. Judge Murray broke for lunch with closing arguments to be given that afternoon.

Jack and Catherine went into a small room in the courthouse used for attorney client meetings. He had some sandwiches brought over from the office by Gerry Conley, who helped him go over his closing. He rehearsed the points he planned to make as Gerry critiqued his presentation. As they prepared to go back in, Catherine took Jack's hand and, looking him in the eye, said, "Whatever happens in there, I could not have had any better council than you have provided. I wanted you to know that."

"Thank you, Catherine. We are going to win this."

Conley chimed in, "I believe you will. What's more, you will be establishing new ground for all women who suffer through abusive relationships. You will be giving them new recognition and new standing. One hell of a job." Jack's closing statement started with Chadwick Merrill's history of abuse. His college incident, his first wife, then the years of abuse of Catherine. He encouraged the jurors to review the defense exhibits of hospital records and pictures. To look at the attempts by the Merrill family to cover it up by using their cousin, the doctor, and paying off victims to keep them quiet. Finally, he asked the jurors to close their eyes and put themselves in the position of Catherine Merrill having the life choked out of her while her abusive husband screamed in her face that he was going to kill her. He took great pains to emotionally describe the situation where he had her by the throat, banging her head against the cupboard, hollering that he would kill her as she was unable to breathe, fighting for her life.

"The question you then need to ask yourselves is, does an abused woman in total fear of her life have a right to defend herself from the abusive man who would kill her?"

After asking that question, he sat down. On his way back to his seat, he noticed Elaine standing in the back of the courtroom. She blew him a kiss. To his surprise, it brought tears to his eyes.

Coleman's close included no surprises. He raised the question of why this woman did not go to the police, why she did not leave, two questions that were covered in her testimony. He talked about Chadwick Merrill's standing in the community. His history in business and community involvement. He ended with a question of his own.

"The defense attorney, Mr. Roach, is correct that you have a question to ask yourselves, but his is the wrong question. The real question is, was this an act of self-defense, or is it the act of an angry woman seizing the opportunity to kill the man she hates so she can inherit his wealth?"

Coleman sat down with Jack, thinking his cross of Catherine and his closing statement were his best efforts of the trial. It gave him just a bit of doubt as to the outcome. Judge Murray gave his instructions and turned the case over to the jury at ten minutes to four. Jack and Catherine went back to his office to wait, in case the sequestered jurors reached a quick verdict. They were joined by Elaine Watkens. By six thirty, with no call having come in to announce a verdict had been reached, they ordered Chinese food. Nerves were on edge as their doubts about the outcome grew with every passing minute. They did not get a chance to finish all the Chinese food. They were called back to the courthouse at seven ten.

The crowd of protesters, eighty or ninety strong, were still outside along with the press contingent. Jack looked for Sue Frazier, but she had apparently gone back to New York. They got inside without answering any questions from the press and took their seats at the defense table. They waited for what seemed an eternity but was really less than ten minutes for the judge to come in and call the room to order. The jury filed in observed by a packed courtroom, but a crowd that did not include the Merrill family. They were conspicuous by their absence.

"Has the jury reached a verdict?" Judge Murray's voice boomed over the very quiet courtroom.

"Yes, Your Honor."

"The defendant will please rise." Jack and Catherine stood.

You could hear a pin drop in the courtroom as the judge asked, "As to the charge of murder in the second degree, how does the jury find the defendant?"

The response was delivered only moments after the question, but to Jack and Catherine, it seemed much longer. "Your Honor, the jury finds the defendant not guilty."

The courtroom erupted into applause and chatter, followed closely by the eruption from outside as the protesters heard the news. The judge banged his gavel, calling for order. Catherine embraced Jack, as well as her parents and brother, who were in the row right behind her. When order was restored, the judge dismissed the jury, told Catherine she was free to go, then gaveled the trial closed.

As they walked out of the building, Jack was stopped by the press. He finally decided to give them a statement, with Catherine on one side and Elaine on the other. He held up his hands to stop the questions coming from all directions before he spoke.

"This verdict is a victory, not just for Catherine Merrill but for all people who suffer in an abusive situation. Catherine acted to defend her life, which she had every right to do. Justice has been served here today, and a wrongly accused woman can go on with her life. Thank you, all."

They continued to throw questions at him, but the three of them moved through the crowd, headed for Jack's office. Upon their arrival, he told Catherine that Monday morning, they would file the necessary papers to get her children back to her. They received a congratulatory call from Susan Frazier, who spoke with both Jack and Catherine. He thanked her for what she did, assuring her it was very helpful. Catherine again thanked him for all he had done for her. Before she left, Jack put his hands on Catherine's shoulders to say, "Catherine, I want you to think about joining this firm. I know your specialty is family law, and it's an area in which we plan to expand our presence. Having you on board would be a great boost for us."

"Don't answer me right now, but give it some thought. We would love to have you join us."

With tears in her eyes, she thanked him for the offer, promising to think about it. She left while Jack was looking over the messages he had received. The most important one was from his secretary, reminding him to make arrangements to go to Washington, DC, next week to meet with Deputy Director Russell Campbell of the CIA.

"Elaine, can you take a couple of days off next week?"

"I can if it's for a good reason. Why?"

"When's the last time you were in Washington, DC?"

"It's been years."

"Well, I would like you to take three days off next week and travel down there with me. I have a very important meeting at the CIA that I can explain to you, but the rest of the time will be Jack and Elaine fun time."

"Sounds delightful. I will put in for Tuesday through Thursday, for personal days."

"Great, for now, let's go home to crack open a bottle of champagne and have some Jack and Elaine time right here in Portland."

Chapter XXXXI

JACK AND ELAINE ARRIVED IN Washington late on Tuesday afternoon. They checked into a Marriot and had dinner at the Dubliner, where they stayed late listening to Irish music. The next day, they did some sightseeing around Capitol Park until three o'clock, when Jack left her at the Smithsonian while he went back to prepare for his meeting the next morning. He had his presentation set in his mind, but he wanted to rehearse it and jot down a few notes that would keep him on track.

At nine on Thursday morning, Jack walked into the office of CIA Deputy Director Russell Campbell, where he was greeted by Campbell, as well as Director of Operations Stark. Introductions were made with handshakes all around, but there was no small talk; Campbell got right down to business.

"This meeting is highly unusual, Mr. Roach. It is not our policy to discuss personnel matters with anyone outside the agency. I'm unsure as to your angle here, but I would suggest you state your business and be very direct."

Jack took their direction and went right to the point.

"Very well. I have met with Agent King, who is convinced you mean to make him the scapegoat for your own litany of misdeeds. If that is to be your tactic, I think it only fair to warn you that I will hang it around your nuts. I also mean to tell you that I have a better plan of action that can address yours, as well as Agent King's issues. I would be glad to give you that proposal if you can listen for half an hour. If not, I will go back to Maine to plan my moves against you."

There was only a brief hesitation before an angry Campbell gave a response. "You have a lot of nerve to come in here threatening us, Mr. Roach. Do you have any conception of whom you are dealing with? I've half a mind to throw you out of here on your ass"

Jack leaned forward in his chair and pressed on with a very intense look about him. "I know exactly who I'm dealing with, Mr. Campbell, so let's not bullshit one another. I have read a full copy of the so-called 'family jewels' folder. I have listened to recordings made by Agent King as he was instructed to take actions in direct conflict with presidential executive orders, instructing this agency to not do the exact thing King was being instructed to do, and I have those recordings. (The recordings were a bluff, but he hoped they would buy it.) Bruce King has enough inside information on the contra deal to embarrass the CIA and possibly bring down an administration. If it is your intention to scapegoat him then feed him to the FBI, we plan to have a press conference to release the family jewels folder, play the tapes, and give other verbal accounts of your misdeeds that were not authorized by the congress or the executive."

Stark spoke. "You know about the FBI?"

"Yes, I do, and one more thing. At that press conference, we will also discuss the atrocities committed by the Tiger Force when Agent King was a member, so you may want to talk with Colonel David Hargrove before you dismiss me and reject my proposal and throw me out of here on my ass."

"So your purpose in the press conference is to smear the CIA as well as the United States military, for what purpose?"

"These facts will make up Agent King's defense against any charges from you, the FBI, or anyone else. If we go to court, I will have him on the witness stand for hours telling all."

The two CIA men were silent for a long moment, so Jack pressed on. "There is a better way by which everyone gets what they want. You should hear me out."

Jack had obviously grabbed their attention.

After a bit of silence during which the two CIA agents looked at Jack a bit menacingly, Campbell spoke, "Give us a few minutes, Mr. Roach. You can wait in the outer office." Jack got up and walked to the outer office, where he sat waiting to be summoned. He was not sure if all his bravado had worked but figured he would soon know. Fifteen minutes later, he was asked to step back into the main office.

"All right, Mr. Roach, you have your thirty minutes." The directive was from Campbell.

Jack started off by going through the double-sided attack that he knew the CIA was under. The congressional hearings that were coming plus the FBI investigation of Agent King. Then he shifted to what he knew was being considered by the CIA brass as an explanation to all the ways the agency had ignored congressional and administrative directives.

"You are, no doubt, planning on assessing any blame on a number of rogue agents who acted on their own to bring disgrace to the agency by their actions. That's a good strategy that we can agree to use."

This statement of agreement caught the brass a bit by surprise. "The question is, will it be enough to blame him as a rogue agent, or do we need more?"

"What do you mean by *more?*" questioned Agent Stark.

"What I mean is, do you still want him testifying after you have nailed him to a cross? Do you want him to have the opportunity to defend himself of your charges? You can discredit his denials and feed him to the FBI, but wouldn't it be better if he was not even here to give those denials?"

Again, a silent moment of contemplation from the brass. "What would be the alternative?"

"Now we are getting down to brass tacks," Jack said. "My proposal is this: to the world you have assigned Bruce King to a dangerous mission in wherever. Wherever would be a dangerous assignment today. He did not come back, and from all the information you have, he is not going to come back. He is dead.

"At the same time, you do what you do best. You create a new identity for him, complete with passport history, social security, the whole works. He disappears from the face of the earth just like a person put in the witness protection program. The FBI lets it go because to them he is dead. You scapegoat him all you want because we no longer care. He's no longer here to argue about it because he is dead.

You get what you want, the FBI gets to chase their tails, and Bruce King moves on to a new life. The alternative is the press coverage plus court coverage I previously described, which would be ugly all round. What's your choice?"

Jack stopped there and went silent. The two CIA agents silently reflected on the exchange as they looked at one another. Finally, Campbell again asked Jack to step in the outer room while he and Stark discussed things. Jack left and waited. Their looks, their body language all seemed to tell him that he had made progress with them. But these were tough guys. He was just not sure.

This time, it took more than a half hour before Jack was called back into the main office. The two CIA agents were seated in their original places as Jack walked back in and took his seat. He said nothing, waiting to hear from Campbell, who eventually spoke.

"Here is our counter proposal. We want a sworn statement from you as well as Agent King that you and he will never speak to the press or anyone else about any of what has been discussed here. That includes, as will be listed in a formal agreement, the family jewels, the Tiger Force, or any other matters connected to the CIA or the Tiger Force. In addition, Agent King will disappear from the press, as well as any other scrutiny with a new identity that we will provide. His attorney, you, will also agree to confirm, whenever asked, that the agent in question, Bruce King, has apparently died in action. Furthermore, neither you nor Agent King will object to nor disagree with any statements or presentations delivered to the congressional inquiry that involve Agent King. This would include anything presented that paints Agent King in a negative light or specifically accuses him of wrong doing. In exchange for this, the agency will provide a new identification for Agent King, complete with passports, social security numbers, credit cards, as well a complete history of his existence. We will agree to present and defend an explanation of his demise by supporting the story that he was sent on an assignment in a dangerous place from which he never returned and we assume him as dead. Is that satisfactory to you, Mr. Roach?"

"It sounds acceptable. Put it all in writing, send it to me in Maine, and if it's exactly as you say, I will send you my agreement as well as Agent King's agreement. In addition, I will take Agent King out of Washington, keep him well hidden until you send his new identity. At that time, he will disappear completely."

Jack stood and extended his hand to the two CIA men who took it and shook his hand. He walked out, satisfied that he had appropriately defended his longtime friend.

He went from CIA headquarters back to the Marriot, where he met Elaine and Bruce for lunch. It was exactly the result he had hoped for when he explained his approach to Bruce a week earlier.

"Jack, that's amazing that you pulled this off. When will I know what my new identity is and where I'm going to live?"

"Everything will be sent to my office in Portland. That includes the formal deal for our signature, the details on your new identity, including the history, passports, social security number, credit cards, the whole deal."

"Holy shit, it's going to happen. What do I do in the meantime?"

"You need to disappear now. Get in your car, drive up to Maine, and stay with me until we hear from them. Get some cash, but don't close out your bank accounts. If you clean them out completely it will look suspicious. Cut up your credit cards. You can't use them anymore they leave a trail. We need it to appear to any inquiring eyes that you are dead. Don't be leaving a trail. When you get to Maine, I will take care of getting rid of the car. I have arranged for a new identity that will get you dual citizenship in another country. The CIA will arrange for the dual citizenship, and you will be in another country presumed dead by all who knew you here except Elaine and me."

With that, they finished lunch and checked out of the hotel. Jack and Elaine headed to the airport to return to Maine. Bruce would be following by car.

Chapter XXXXII

THE CATHERINE MERRILL TRIAL MADE Jack the most well-known as well as sought after defense lawyer in Greater Portland if not all of Maine. The case was among the first high-profile cases to end in an acquittal for an abused woman who took the life of her husband. Thanks in part to Sue Frazier, it gained national attention. The small firm in Portland that he joined for a quieter practice was now one of the busiest defense teams in Maine.

Catherine Merrill did join the firm, practicing family law. Her first case was to represent herself in getting her children back. In addition to Catherine, the firm added two new associates within six months of the trial in order to handle the increased workload. Business was booming in spite of Stanton Merrill's efforts to the contrary.

The deal with the CIA was finalized, and Bruce had his new identity. Only Jack knew where he was located in his new life, and he told nobody, not even Elaine. The official word from the CIA was that he never came back from his last mission to South America and he was presumed dead. This also ended any FBI inquiries. During the congressional hearings, he, along with two other field agents, was described as an agent that was difficult to manage and often went off the rails, resulting in reprimands.

As Jack approached forty, his life was well settled. He was in his home state of Maine, which he loved. He was a partner in a growing, successful law firm. He was very popular and well respected by his peers. He got to see plenty of his family on weekends and holidays up in Old Town. His parents and siblings were all still healthy, and he had eight nieces and nephews. There was only one piece of the puzzle missing. He knew it was time to fill that last piece.

He took Elaine Watkens out to dinner at DiMillo's restaurant one Saturday night. They often went out accompanied by one or two other couples, but on this night, Jack made it just the two of them. After the wine was served, Jack reached across the table with an open jewelry box that held a two-and-a-half-karat diamond with an emerald on either side of the diamond. Elaine looked at it then at Jack, who said, "You are the most beautiful, engaging lady on this planet. I would like to spend the rest of my life with you. Please accept this engagement ring and say yes to my proposal of marriage."

Elaine stood with tears in her eyes, went around the table, and with everyone watching, embraced and kissed Jack. When she pulled back from the kiss, she answered, "Of course, my answer is yes. I want to be your wife and spend the rest of my life with you."

Their waitress began applauding, followed by the rest of the room, as Jack stood and the two of them embraced. While still standing, he put the ring on her finger, looked at the other diners, and announced, "I am one happy son of a bitch."

Three months later, the wedding was held, followed by a honeymoon in Italy. Elaine picked the place for the honeymoon, but Jack insisted that they stop off in Ireland on the way back home. After ten days in Tuscany, they flew to Ireland, landing in Shannon Airport. They rented a car and drove down to the town of Dingle, checking into the Benners Hotel. Jack explained to Elaine that while she had always wanted to visit Tuscany, he had always wanted to visit the Dingle peninsula. They planned to drive around the peninsula as well as the ring of Kerry and Connor Pass, but first, he told her, "I want to visit a very famous pub, O'Flaherty's, for a pint of Guinness." Elaine was a bit puzzled by his need to have a pint, but she was game for the pub crawl.

As they walked into the pub, Elaine was stunned to see the very familiar face of Bruce King, tending bar.

"Oh my god, Jack, why didn't you warn me?"

Jack laughed and told her he was sworn to secrecy.

Bruce came out from behind the bar and gave Elaine a big bear hug, picking her up while twirling around. Putting her down, he shook Jack's hand. Jack explained that they had just married and were on their honeymoon. Bruce gave his congratulations. He could not contain his euphoria.

"Jackie Boy, I can't thank you enough. Working here is almost as great as working in your father's place twenty-five years ago. Come over here and meet O'Flaherty."

Bruce led them over to meet his boss, the owner of the pub. The pub owner was a typical charming harp with a great wit. "These are two friends of mine from the States who have just married, Jack and Elaine Roach. O'Flaherty here is the best musician in Dingle. If you come tonight, you can hear him play."

O'Flaherty told Bruce to take some time to enjoy a pint or two with his friends. They sat together while Bruce explained his new life. He was no longer Bruce King; his name was Sean Reardon. He grew up in South Boston, graduated from Northeastern, moved over to Ireland a couple of years ago, and got dual citizenship. He moved down to Dingle three months ago and began tending bar at O'Flaherty's.

"Well, you look like you're enjoying your new life," Jack offered.

"Couldn't be happier. Bought a house, about a five-minute walk from the pub. I love this entire area, it's beautiful. Finish these pints, and I will take you up to the top of Connor Pass, which may well be the most beautiful place on earth."

"How are you set financially?" Elaine asked. "I mean, do you make enough money here?"

"Absolutely. Plus I have a nice little nest egg in a Swiss bank." He said this while giving Jack a wink.

The three talked and laughed over a couple of pints. After an hour enjoying catching up, swapping old stories, and just enjoying each other, Jack summed it all up. He raised his pint of Guinness for a toast. "Well, for my new wife and my best friend, all's well that ends well."

About the Author

JACK CASHMAN HAS FOLLOWED UP his highly successful first novel, *An Irish Immigrant's Story,* with his second novel about two young men growing up in a New England mill town in a turbulent period.

Jack lives in Hampden, Maine, with his wife, Betty, near their two sons Derek and Danny, their daughters-in-law, Michelle and Karen and their five granddaughters, Katy, Sarah, Jackie, Caroline and Briana.

CPSIA information can be obtained
at www.ICGtesting.com
Printed in the USA
BVHW080945291219
568055BV00001B/93/P